THE INDECENCIES OF ISABELLE

Portia's beautiful rounded peach of a bottom was duly unveiled. The full pale mounds of her bottom cheeks were quivering slightly in her agitation as she braced herself for punishment. Sarah had kept hold of the slipper throughout Portia's stripping, and now tapped it to the meaty crests of the bare bottom she was about to spank.

I settled back, sipping my tea in comfort as Sarah began, applying the slipper with hard swats. Portia went wild, and I couldn't help but laugh – at the faces she was making, at the way her bottom wobbled, at the way her thighs pumped. When she started to make desperate little scissor motions with her legs it was so funny I had to put my teacup down or risk spilling it, and it was all the better because she could see me laughing and was getting even more furious. She thought I should be among those getting it, and she resented being watched by me almost as much as she did by men.

Why not visit Penny's website at
www.pennybirch.com

By the same author:

By the same author:
THE INDIGNITIES OF ISABELLE
THE INDISCRETIONS OF ISABELLE
(Writing as Cruella)

BARE BEHIND
IN DISGRACE
NURSE'S ORDERS
KNICKERS AND BOOTS
PENNY PIECES
PETTING GIRLS
TEMPET TANTRUMS
TICKLE TORTURE
UNIFORM DOLL
WHEN SHE WAS BAD

THE INDECENCIES
OF ISABELLE

Penny Birch
writing as Cruella

This book is a work of fiction.
In real life, make sure you practise safe, sane and
consensual sex.

First published in 2005 by
Nexus
Thames Wharf Studios
Rainville Road
London W6 9HA

www.nexus-books.co.uk

Typeset by TW Typesetting, Plymouth, Devon

ISBN 0 352 33989 6

Penguin Random House is committed to a sustainable future for
our business, our readers and our planet. This book is made from
Forest Stewardship Council® certified paper.

MIX
Paper | Supporting
responsible forestry
FSC® C018179
www.fsc.org

Printed and bound in Great Britain by Clays Ltd, St Ives plc

You'll notice that we have introduced a set of symbols onto our book jackets, so that you can tell at a glance what fetishes each of our brand new novels contains. Here's the key – enjoy!

cp (traditional)

cp (modern)

spanking

restraint/bondage

rope bondage/hojojutsu

latex/rubber/leather/enclosure

fem dom

willing captivity

medical

period setting

uniforms

sex rituals

Dedicated to all Isabelle fans
and especially BE

One

'Five little bad girls, Lined up by the door, One got caned, And then there were four.'

I laughed, almost spilling my tea, at the sudden reaction of the five girls standing against the wall. They'd been expecting something mild for the first go. Every single one looked around. Jasmine was pouting. Portia wore an angry scowl. Caroline's hands had gone to her meaty bottom cheeks. Katie looked as if she was about to cry. Only Pippa reacted with any bravery, tight-lipped as she gave a tiny nod.

'Fetch the cane,' Laura ordered.

Pippa broke line. With her neatly done brown hair, her soft, shy face, her long dress of printed blue-and-white cotton, she looked as if she might have been attending tea at the vicar's house. Not that there was much difference, as Sarah's sunlit Oxford flat was as respectable as any country vicarage. Except that in addition to tea and cake, Sarah, Laura and I intended to amuse ourselves by making each of the five girls choose a painful or humiliating punishment as part of a little game.

The rules were simple. We three dominant women would take turns to make up a little verse, counting down from five to zero, and each time offering a punishment. One of the girls had to accept and could then join us at tea instead of standing with her nose pressed to the wall in the corner of the room. The punishments might be hard or soft, more or less undignified, but whoever tried to avoid the early ones might find herself in serious trouble.

I sat back to watch, sipping my tea. Pippa knew what to do, well trained by Laura, skipping quickly into the bedroom and returning with Sarah's thin black malacca cane. Falling to her knees, she offered it to Laura, who took it and made a casual gesture to the vacant armchair. Pippa immediately scrambled into it, kneeling, with her back pulled in, to leave her bottom a round tempting ball beneath her dress.

'More tea, Isabelle?' Sarah asked as Laura stood up.

'Yes, thank you.'

I put my cup and saucer down on the table, watching as Sarah prepared tea and Laura prepared her victim's bottom. Sarah's living room looked west, bathing us in warm autumn sunlight that gave a golden tinge to the backs of Pippa's thighs as her dress was lifted. Beneath, she had on big silk camiknickers, pulled taut across her bulging bottom with a puff of lace around her sex and where her cheeks spilled out beneath the hems.

'Sugar?' Sarah asked, as Laura's fingers pinched the catch at Pippa's crotch.

'Just one lump, please,' I answered.

The fastenings came loose and Pippa's soft furry pussy was put on show. She gave a little sob as she was exposed and hung her head in embarrassment. Laura took no notice, but turned up the tail of the camiknickers, baring the full cheeky globe beneath. Everything showed – Pippa's firm, slightly fleshy cheeks wide enough apart to reveal her tightly dimpled anus as well as each tiny fold and wrinkle of her sex.

I picked up my cup as Laura tapped the thin black cane to the crest of Pippa's cheeks. Pippa stiffened, a fresh sob escaped her lips and then a sharp cry of pain as the cane bit into her flesh. Sipping my tea, I watched

2

as six firm, even strokes were laid across the quivering globe of girl flesh, to leave Pippa sobbing and gasping in the chair. She was quite brave and didn't cry or make a big fuss, which was a pity, but the expression of mingled resentment and ecstasy on her face as she got up was a delight. Briefly she kissed Laura's shoes, before taking the cup of tea Sarah had poured for her and sitting rather gingerly in the chair across which she'd just been beaten.

'Your turn, Isabelle dear,' Sarah stated.

'Let me see,' I replied, although I already had my verse worked out. 'I know ... Four little bad girls, Dying for a pee, One wet her panties, And then there were three.'

'Isabelle!' Sarah chided. 'Not on my carpet, girls, or there really will be trouble.'

All four girls were looking around again. Katie was the most embarrassed, but I knew she was far too shy to do it. Portia looked more resentful than ever, but didn't speak. Jasmine and Caroline shared a glance, no doubt weighing the indignity of having to pee in their knickers against the pain of the beatings they would certainly get otherwise. Jasmine spoke first.

'OK, I will.'

'In the kitchen doorway,' Sarah instructed, 'and you're to mop up if you make a mess.'

Jasmine responded with a single miserable nod and broke line. I tried to catch Sarah's eye, but she was deliberately looking the other way. Knowing exactly what would be going through her head, I hid a smile behind my teacup. For all her assertive, dominant poise, she'd be thinking back to her own time as Dr Eliza Abbot's plaything and being trained to wet herself on command.

That knowledge made it even more delicious as Jasmine came to stand in the open doorway to the kitchen, her feet braced a little way apart on the tiles.

3

She was in hipsters, tight around her neat apple-shaped bottom, with the waistband of her bright-red thong just showing. As her hands went to the button of her jeans I gave a low cough. She stopped, turning, her elfin face half-hidden behind a curtain of ash-blonde hair, her face set in uncertainty.

'Mistress?'

'Leave them up,' I instructed.

'But, Mistress . . .'

'Leave them up, I said.'

'But . . . but how am I supposed to get home?'

'You should have thought of that before putting on that silly thong. Now do as you're told.'

'I'll lend you a skirt,' Sarah offered, with real sympathy.

'There we are,' I assured Jasmine. 'Sarah will lend you a skirt. Now come along, we're waiting.'

She swallowed and turned away, her head hung down. Her cheeks tightened in her jeans, she gave a tiny, broken sob and she was doing it – a dark stain growing slowly on the back of her jeans, trickling down her legs and spreading gradually across her bottom. She was shaking as she did it, full of shame and remorse, and I was no longer bothering to hide my smile.

By the time she'd finished the wet patch covered most of her bottom and the pee had begun to soak into her socks and fill her shoes. She looked a fine sight and she knew it, her emotions strong on her face as she carefully peeled her jeans and knickers off her little wet bottom and hobbled across to Sarah's washing machine. I couldn't help chuckling as she performed a clumsy strip, taking off everything below her waist and stuffing jeans, panties and socks into the machine before scampering off to the bathroom.

'You can stay like that until we leave,' I called out to her, ignoring the fact that she was supposed to be allowed her dignity back after taking her punishment.

Nobody contradicted me and when Jasmine came back she was still naked below the waist, her neatly turned bottom bare at front and back, with the little puff of pale down that hid her sex and the little tattoo that marked her as mine on show. Rather than take her own chair, she curled herself up on the carpet beside mine, her head pressed to my leg. I could think of a rhyme that would have had all three of the remaining girls begging to be let off, but it was Sarah's turn.

She didn't speak, sipping tea and admiring them: Caroline, cheeky by nature and by physique, with her voluptuous bottom packed into tight black jeans and her breasts straining the fabric of her top; Portia, immaculate in white slacks and a silk blouse, her dark curls in artless disarray, looking as if butter wouldn't melt in her mouth; Katie, small and soft and pretty, with her blonde bobbed hair and freckles adding to her shyness. At last Sarah put her teacup down and nodded.

'Let's see then . . . Three little bad girls, Feeling rather blue, One went naked, And then there were two.'

Katie went bright pink. Portia and Caroline spoke almost at the same instant.

'Me!'

'I will!'

'Caroline,' Sarah decided. 'And when you're in the nude you can take over serving tea.'

Caroline broke line with her face wreathed in smiles. Going nude in front of other women was nothing to her and she began to strip with enthusiasm, peeling it all off and kicking each garment aside until she was stark naked. If I had her figure – a tiny waist dividing big heavy breasts and a, frankly, fat bottom – I'd have been embarrassed. Not Caroline, who happily took over serving, with her big boobs lolling forwards and her bottom almost in my face as she bent to pick up a plate of biscuits. I smacked her, making her cheeks wobble and drawing out a sound halfway between a squeak and a giggle.

5

'You're a slut, Caroline,' I told her. 'What are you?'

'A slut, Mistress Isabelle,' she answered happily.

I drew a sigh, wishing I'd had a chance to spank her big bottom and wondering if I should do it anyway. She'd have howled, because it would have been unfair, and because she always does, but Laura had put her teacup down and I held back.

'I think you got off very lightly, Caroline,' she remarked, 'but I suppose that's the nature of the game. So let me see, yes ... Two little bad girls, Standing in the sun, One got slippered, And then there was one.'

Katie winced, looking seriously unhappy. Portia opened her mouth to speak, but hesitated. Both knew that whoever was left would have to take whatever I decreed. Both also knew that Sarah's slippers had thick rubber soles that stung like anything. Portia glanced at me, perhaps trying to negotiate, but I ignored her. Katie was biting her lip and didn't seem able to speak at all. Finally Portia spoke, deeply sulky.

'OK, you can slipper me, but not too hard.'

'That,' Sarah answered her, 'is for me to decide. Fetch a slipper.'

Portia made for the bedroom, genuinely reluctant for she knew full well what the punishment would do to her. Sarah moved to middle of the sofa, her face set in a faint smile and, as Portia came back, she patted her lap. Portia made a face, but obeyed, draping herself across Sarah's knees with as much elegance as she could muster.

It was always a joy to see Portia punished, partly because she was so resentful about it, and partly because there was something in her confident, almost arrogant, upper-class English manner that just cried out for her to be put across another woman's knee and absolutely walloped. Now she was going to get it, and she was pouting furiously as Sarah picked up the slipper.

'I think we'd better have these down,' Sarah stated,

patting the taut white seat of Portia's trousers. 'Lift your hips.'

Portia's expression grew sulkier than ever as she raised herself, making her bottom rounder and more tempting still. Sarah burrowed a hand under her girl-friend's tummy to snip open the button and peel down the zip, allowing Portia's bottom to swell out a little from the tight confines of her trousers.

'Down they come,' Sarah said happily, and began to tug on Portia's trousers.

It took four firm heaves to strip Portia's bottom, her tight white trousers peeled down to the top of her thighs to leave her full-cut, blue polka-dot panties far enough down to show the top of her deep bottom cleft. Not that she was allowed even that much dignity for long, Sarah's fingers going straight to them.

'I think we'd better pop these down too,' Sarah announced.

Portia's beautiful rounded peach of a bottom was duly unveiled. Her face was a picture as they were taken down and the full, pale mounds of her bottom cheeks were quivering slightly in her agitation as she braced herself for punishment. Sarah had kept hold of the slipper throughout Portia's stripping, and now tapped it to the meaty crests of the bare bottom she was about to spank.

I settled back, sipping my tea in comfort as Sarah began to spank, applying the slipper with hard swats. Portia's expression of miserable self-pity vanished the instant the slipper made contact with her bottom, breaking to shock and pain, then round-mouthed con-sternation as Sarah took a firm hold and laid in.

Portia went wild, and I couldn't help but laugh – at the faces she was making, at the way her bottom wobbled, at the way her thighs pumped. When she started to make desperate little scissor motions with her legs it was so funny I had to put my teacup down or risk spilling it, and it was made all the better because she could see me laughing and was getting even more furious. Like her Mistress, she thought I should be among those getting it, and she resented being watched by me almost as much as she did by men.

By the time she was done, her bottom was rich pink all over and she was shaking in reaction. Her face was full of shame, but no longer for her bare rosy bottom, but for her own reaction to the spanking, and she made no effort to get up. I knew just what she wanted and was hoping Sarah would provide. Sure enough.

'Like that is it?' Sarah remarked. 'OK. Open your thighs, I'm going to masturbate you.'

Portia's shocked expression grew abruptly stronger, but it was fake. She didn't protest, but spread her thighs as she'd been ordered, to allow Sarah to slip a hand between. It took just moments, the skilled application of Sarah's fingers to Portia's pussy producing a gasping, shivering climax as full of shame as ecstasy. As soon as it was done Sarah popped her fingers into Portia's mouth to have them sucked clean, before wiping them on the polka-dot panties.

As Sarah sent Portia into the bathroom with a final smack to her reddened bottom I was feeling deeply aroused. Sarah followed Portia, and we waited, now with a good deal of tension, as I tried to find a rhyme that would allow me to indulge my needs with Katie. She was always shy, always quiet, always the one who found it most difficult to accept her sexual needs, yet the flush of her cheeks and her eyes as she looked back over her shoulder betrayed her true emotions.

I knew what she wanted – more or less what Portia had just been given – although she'd bawl her eyes out as she was punished. Unfortunately, I needed something different, for the sake of the game, and to outdo Sarah. I could hear Portia giggling in the bathroom, probably as her bottom was creamed, which gave me an idea. By the time Sarah and Portia came back I was ready, but I made Katie wait a couple of minutes while I sipped my tea before addressing her. She was still looking back over her shoulder.

'Put your nose against the wall, Katie,' I ordered. 'You know how you're supposed to stand.'

'Sorry,' she answered, and promptly obeyed, pressing her little snub nose to Sarah's leaf-patterned wallpaper.

'That's better. Was it really wise to go last?'

She shook her head, rubbing her nose on the wall.

'Just think, you could be sitting down like Pippa or Portia, a little warm behind, but quite decent, and knowing it was over and done with.'

She nodded her head, making the tip of her nose turn up against the wallpaper, so that she looked more like a cartoon pig than ever. Her face was flushed pink, which added to the effect, and I took another sip of tea to let her dwell on her fate a bit longer before speaking again.

'But you're not. Instead, you have to accept whatever I suggest.'

'So long as your poem has correct rhyme and meter,' she said stubbornly.

'Of course . . . One little bad girl, Aching to be done, Up went her panties, And then there were none.'

She looked around, puzzled.

'But I haven't had to take my panties down yet.'

'That's not what I meant. Sarah, would you be kind and run to fetch whatever cream you were applying to Portia's cheeks just now?'

Sarah hesitated, no doubt thinking of rebuking me for speaking to her the way I had, before deciding not to make an issue of it. Katie's expression was working between puzzlement and concern as she turned from the wall and came to stand by my chair. I patted my lap.

'Over you go. Bottom well up, please.'

'Am . . . am I to be spanked? With my knickers pulled up tight or something?'

'Something,' I replied. 'Now get over my knee.'

She obeyed, pink faced as she laid herself across the arms of my chair, her bottom lifted beneath her plain black skirt, round and inviting. I took hold of the hem, lifting it up gently to show first her pale shapely thighs and then her panties. They were white and full cut, with a pattern of cherries across the bulging seat, in pairs, but each like a little chubby bottom. Even with so little showing she had begun to sob, her emotions as strong as ever.

I left Katie showing her knickers as Sarah returned from the bathroom with a tube of plain skin cream, ideal for what I had in mind. Thanking Sarah, I took hold of Katie's cherry-patterned panties and pulled them down quickly, making her gasp in shock as her bottom came on show. She had a truly beautiful behind, chubby and firm and smooth, exquisitely feminine. With her panties at half-mast I took a moment to stroke her cheeks, out of sheer admiration, before pulling the little garment off her legs to leave her completely bare behind.

'Pull your cheeks apart,' I ordered.

Her bottom cheeks were quivering, and she was snivelling quite badly, but she did as she was told, reaching back to spread the plump little globe of her bottom and show off the details between, her sweetly turned pussy lips pouting from between her thighs, the tight pink bud of her anus twitching slightly.

Everybody was watching, and Katie knew it, her snivels turning to full-blown tears as she held her bottom open for inspection. I took the tube of cream, placing the nozzle just an inch above the splayed star of her anus and squeezing, to extrude a thick white worm of cream into the little dimple at the very centre. She gasped as she felt it, and her ring tightened, squeezing out a little cream. Her words came broken and urgent as she spoke.

'What ... what are you going to do with me? I thought you were going to spank me.'

'Sh, just keep your cheeks well apart.'

As I spoke I'd pushed my middle finger into the soft thick cotton of her cherry-patterned panties. She went silent, her cheeks still held wide, her bumhole opening and closing to make the creamy centre pout and suck in her apprehension as I applied a second worm of cream to the taut white cotton over my finger.

'And up go your panties,' I announced as I pressed my finger to the slippery ring held so invitingly open between her cheeks.

'No, Isabelle,' she whined as she finally realised what I was going to do.

It was too late. I had already pushed the full length of my finger in up her bottom, taking a good-sized pinch of panty material with it, certainly enough to hold them in place in her hole. As she expelled her breath in a long gasp of shock and outrage I extracted my finger, leaving her panties wedged well in up her bottom.

Portia was giggling and Sarah and Laura were smiling in amusement. Pippa started to clap.

'There we are,' I stated. 'You can let go of your cheeks now, and I think you'd better go back to college like that. After all, it's not far, and nothing will show unless you bend right over.'

'I'm on my bike!'

'That's OK then. Just be careful how you ride.'

'You know what they say about knickerless girls,' Portia said laughing. 'Make her keep her skirt tucked up, Isabelle, I want to see.'

'I'd intended to,' I replied, suiting action to words by tucking Katie's skirt into her waistband. 'Now, do you want to get up, or would you like your botty smacked?'

Her answer was a broken sob, but her bottom came up, pushed high to show off the fleshy tuck of her cheeks where she liked to be smacked, with the cherry-patterned panties hanging down from her bumhole to cover her pussy. I began to smack, firmly, right over the

11

pouted lips of her sex. She'd stopped crying, briefly, but began again as her bottom started to pink up, gulping and snivelling in between little cries of pain. My smacks got harder, slowly, making her panties jump and tug in her bumhole, and harder still as she gave in completely and her thighs came slowly apart.

The odd little gulping noise she always made when she was in tears changed to gasps, her breathing grew deep and heavy, her thighs began to tighten and I spanked harder still. Suddenly she was there, panting and mewling in ecstasy as I brought her to climax, my hand now smacking on the rear of her sex through her dangling panties. She cried out, like Portia, so much shame blended with her ecstasy, a reaction that left me weak with need even as I finished her off with a few deft touches to her soaking pussy. I had to have her, then and there, however undignified Sarah and Laura might think me.

'On your knees!' I snapped as Katie rolled off my lap.

She didn't need telling twice, and was burrowing her face between my legs as I tugged up my skirt. I pulled my French knickers aside to let her in and she was licking, her face buried in my sex, her bare red bottom stuck out with her panties hanging from her bumhole for all to see. Jasmine began to stroke my breasts through my blouse, Caroline came to kiss me, full on my mouth, and I closed my eyes in bliss.

As Katie's tongue worked busily on my sex I was thinking of the sheer joy of having three beautiful girls at my beck and call. All of them were bare, at least from the waist down, made to parade their bottoms and pussies for me, and for my friends. All of them wanted me, needed me, to keep their bottoms warm, to put them on their knees, where they needed to be, as my beautiful Katie was, licking my pussy with her well-spanked bottom thrust out to the room and her panties hanging limp from her penetrated bottom hole.

Caroline had moved to nibbling a nipple through my blouse, and I bit my lip as I came, determined not to scream and risk giving away what we were doing to Sarah's neighbours. My thighs tightened around Katie's head, and I held her in place until I was finished, only then letting my body go limp. She was smiling as she rocked back on her heels, and came up to kiss me, her mouth rich with the taste of my sex.

I couldn't stop grinning as I adjusted myself and went to wash my hands, thoroughly happy with the way our little game had turned out. Not only had it been great fun, and ended in ecstasy, but there was something wonderfully British about it, just the sort of thing an intimate group of Oxford ladies should do over Sunday afternoon tea. Portia had suggested it, and it was typical of her – naughty, elaborate, and designed to ensure that she got what she so badly needed.

After the long summer break I'd been a little worried that we might not be able to pick up where we'd left off. My birthday party had been wonderful, ending with Portia and I tied head to tail while two men did rude things to us, but it had done very little for the dominant image I wanted to cultivate. I'd also had to concentrate on Collections or risk being sent down, making it impossible to reassert myself properly before going back to Scotland.

Fortunately I had passed Collections, while the others had been every bit as keen as I was to bring together a private and highly erotic ladies' society. Now, in noughth week, we'd agreed to meet at Sarah's flat and decide what to do. Having all arrived, there had been a few rather awkward minutes before Portia had suggested the game, which had well and truly broken the ice.

Only the very basics had been agreed, and I was going over what to say in my head as I sat down again, now decent, unlike the three girls clustered around my chair. Sarah had provided brown bread and butter, biscuits and a delicious lemon cake, from which I cut myself a slice before speaking.

'We'd better decide what to do this term then. As I remember it, we'd all agreed that we're called the Rattaners and that we meet once a month and for special occasions, but there are still a couple of points we need to resolve. First, I propose that we accept only female members, and men are invited only by unanimous agreement.'

'Absolutely,' Sarah agreed.

Jasmine made as if to speak and then thought better of it.

'We must be absolutely certain those men we do invite are discreet,' Laura put in, 'so I suggest we give them associate membership. That way know they have a lot to lose if they step out of line.'

'Who then?' Katie asked. 'The three who came to Isabelle's birthday? I like Dr Appledore.'

'Duncan is an obvious choice,' I agreed. 'Mike and Dave I'm not so sure about. They were great at my party, yes, but I can't really believe they haven't been boasting about what happened, probably all summer.'

'They have,' Caroline replied. 'Half the men up at the Red Ox know, even about you and Portia with the cake.'

Portia was blushing pink as she spoke. 'Then they're out. I hate men who can't keep their mouths shut.'

'We should vote on it,' I pointed out. 'Who is against inviting Mike and Big Dave again?'

Laura, Sarah and Portia agreed immediately, the others following after a moment of hesitation, except Caroline.

'We do need some men,' she pointed out. 'Duncan's nice, but –'

'Not particularly virile,' I finished for her. 'But you agree that the men from the Red Ox are likely to be more trouble than they're worth?'

'I suppose so,' she answered.

'Good,' I went on. 'How about Walter Jessop?'

'He's a useful man to know,' Jasmine replied, but not with any great certainty.

'I don't think I could be comfortable in front of him,' Portia put in.

'Who's Walter Jessop?' Katie asked.

'Just some dirty old man,' Sarah replied. 'He runs an antique shop in Whytleigh. He's quite inappropriate.'

'He's OK,' Caroline defended him, 'and he has some great stuff in his shop sometimes, corsets, Victorian drawers . . .'

'We can buy things from him without having to invite him to Rattaners' events,' Sarah pointed out.

'That's true,' Caroline admitted.

'Not Walter then?' I queried.

Nobody objected and I went on.

'If anyone asks, we just say nothing's happening. The official excuse can be . . . can be that we couldn't agree on playing with each other's girlfriends.'

'They will probably believe that,' Sarah agreed.

'They'll have to,' Portia put in.

'That deals with the men then,' I concluded. 'What else do we need to consider?'

'I have a proposal,' Sarah answered. 'We should have a set of rules, with punishments for anybody who breaks them.'

Portia and Caroline both giggled, and I was smiling as I answered. 'Good idea. I'll draw them up.'

'We should all be able to make suggestions,' Sarah responded, with Laura immediately nodding agreement.

'OK,' I agreed. 'Let's set that aside for our first proper meeting. Next, how about premises? Laura's is the obvious choice, but it is rather far away, so –'

'An excellent reason for using it,' Sarah broke in. 'I certainly couldn't risk a full-blown party here. One or two of my neighbours are already being pointed about my relationship with Portia, Mrs Cook downstairs particularly.'

'Interfering old bat,' Portia put in.

'I get the same problem,' Jasmine added, 'not from neighbours so much, but straight friends, and if we're not going to invite the Red Ox mob . . .'

'I agree,' I said. 'College rooms are out, of course. I'm in Cut Mill this year, but with twelve other students.'

'I'd be delighted to host everything,' Laura offered.

'Thank you,' I said.

'How about organisation?' Sarah asked. 'Somebody needs to take charge. I suggest Laura, as we'll be using her premises.'

It took me an instant to realise what she was saying, and I opened my mouth to reply, only to close it again. The Rattaners was my society. I had done all the hard work, over the whole of my first year, carefully seeking out women who shared my tastes for giving or receiving erotic punishment. Unfortunately there was nothing I could say that wouldn't make me look like the presumptuous little brat Sarah thought I was. From her viewpoint, younger girls took it and older ones dished it out, and she'd never really come to terms with the idea of me as a dominant but also the youngest member of the society. Fortunately Katie came to my aid.

'Shouldn't Isabelle organise events? she asked. 'After all, if it wasn't for Isabelle there would not be any events to go to.'

'I'm sure we all appreciate Isabelle's efforts in bringing us together,' Sarah replied patiently, 'but it makes sense to have our hostess organising events. In any case, I propose Laura as society president, or whatever title we choose. Laura?'

'A military title would be more to my taste,' Laura joked, 'but, seriously, it would seem sensible if I choose dates, and there's no harm in a little formality.'

'Far from it,' Sarah agreed.

'We do need somebody to be in charge,' Jasmine said, 'but I propose Isabelle.'

'Then we had better put it to the vote,' Sarah responded. 'Who is in favour of Laura Soames as president of the Rattaners Society?'

She raised her hand as she spoke. So did Portia, then Laura herself and Pippa immediately afterwards. Sarah gave Katie a stern glance, but her arm remained firmly down.

'In favour of Isabelle Colraine?' Jasmine asked.

I raised my hand, as did she, Caroline and Katie.

'It seems we have a dead heat,' Sarah said, 'so I suggest we vote again at our next meeting. When would be convenient for a party, Laura?'

'The weekend after next?' Laura suggested.

As I nodded my agreement I felt every bit as rueful as if I'd been one of those who'd had my bottom smacked, and yet I knew it was silly. They were talking perfect sense, except that Katie was right. The Rattaners was my society.

Two

As I cycled back through the parks towards St George's College I asked myself if my reaction was reasonable, or if I was just being a brat. Sarah clearly thought of me as a brat, and it was hard to see how I could go against her without proving her right.

Perhaps she was right? After all, my instinctive reaction to the idea of somebody other than me organising the Rattaners had been one of frankly childish pique, and I still felt the same. It wasn't fair, however pathetic that might sound, not after I'd gone to so much effort and sacrificed so much to bring the society into existence.

By the time I'd got to the gate into the Fellows' Gardens I decided that I had to make sure it was me who took charge, regardless of whether that made me a brat or not. The question was: how?

We would vote again in two weeks, and it was sure to be a stalemate. Jasmine, Caroline and Katie were first and foremost my friends and would always support me. Among the others, Sarah was evidently determined to put me in what she saw as my place, preferably across her knees. Portia was worse. Not only was she certain to go along with Sarah, but she had always taken a positively wicked delight in my discomfort. Laura was more reasonable, her decision to stand against me based on simple common sense, which was if anything more

annoying than Sarah's attitude. Pippa was less predictable. She liked to be given orders and harsh, unexpected
punishments, but she was married and very much her
own woman, her relationship with Laura more one of
convenience than devotion.

I could work on Pippa in the hope of breaking the
stalemate. As only Laura knew how to get in touch with
her it wouldn't be easy, while at best it would only
provide a stay of execution. The real problem was
Sarah, and her attitude. Unlike the majority of sado-
masochistic women I'd met, she didn't see dominance as
innate, but as something to be developed with time. As
she'd explained when we first met, it was appropriate for
younger women to be disciplined by their seniors.

The fact that Pippa was her own age and more deeply
submissive than any of us except possibly Katie didn't
seem to bother her. She had been trained to think that
way, by Dr Eliza Abbott, and wasn't going to change.
I knew the story from a couple of unguarded conversa-
tions with Portia, who loved to gossip. Sarah had first
come to Oxford to work as a kitchen girl at Erasmus
Darwin, and had met Dr Abbott through the original
university lesbian society.

Dr Abbott had been the harshest of Mistresses, giving
enemas with soapy water before spankings, and, worse,
training the young Sarah to wet herself on command.
The training had stuck and, although Sarah had in turn
used the same technique to give Portia a powerful reflex
to pull her knickers down, she had never managed to
overcome her own conditioning. It was something she
was very sensitive about, a real weak spot, hence her
reaction when I'd had Jasmine wet herself in front of us.

Two possibilities for exploiting the situation had
occurred to me before I reached Cut Mill. First, I could
win Sarah's sympathy by helping her overcome her
conditioning. Second, I could find out where Dr Eliza
Abbot had gone after leaving Oxford and bring her into

the Rattaners. Both schemes had advantages, and both had drawbacks.

I'd been immensely lucky to get a room in the Mill, as just about every single second year student had put their name on the list. It was a genuine converted mill, straddling a leat that led down through the meadows past St Catharine's College, with the high Cotswold stone wall of the deer park on one side and the river on the other. Tall limes and beeches shaded it, creating a tiny rural idyll at the heart of Oxford.

Knowing that I was to live there for a year was so delightful I paused as I reached the little bridge over the leat, just to admire the view. My room was on the first floor, directly above the mill race, which was now a still green pool with the rotting iron carcass of the wheel rusted into place. I could not have asked for more and, after going up, spent a moment gazing out of the window in sheer rapture and thinking how lucky I was.

I'd made a coffee and sat down in my armchair before my mind turned back to Sarah. The first option, helping her overcome her conditioning, would certainly win her gratitude, although she was quite bloody minded enough to still support Laura. Also, Dr Abbott was a zoologist, and a senior one. I was a history student and knew next to nothing about zoology, let alone ethology or psychology. It was still worth exploring, perhaps by asking a few carefully judged questions to some suitable don.

The second option, bringing Dr Abbott into the Rattaners, was far more appealing. Sarah would be horrified, but quite unable to resist. More likely than not, and by her own philosophy, she'd end up back at Dr Abbott's feet, or worse. The thought of watching Sarah given an enema set my mouth into a fixed grin of pure mischief, which stayed as I considered the pros and cons.

The first hurdle was that I had no idea where Dr Abbott was. I knew she was about twenty years Sarah's senior, which meant she would now be in her 50s. That meant she'd still be working, and so could be easily traced. I just had to hope she hadn't accepted a post in the States or somewhere else impractical. Her attitude was also unpredictable, but that was a chance I'd have to take. Lastly was the possibility that she would join but not support me as president, but I was sure I'd be able to come to some suitable agreement.

I'd finished my coffee and was just beginning to let my mind explore the possibilities of what Eliza Abbott might do to Sarah when somebody knocked on my door. Of the twelve other students in the Mill, I'd only met three, with term officially starting on Monday and some of them yet to arrive. Assuming it would be somebody doings the rounds of coffee and chat, I called out a cheerful welcome.

The door swung open, only not to admit a student, but Stan Tierney, my scout from the first year and a major thorn in my side. He looked more shabby and wizened than ever, while the suggestive leer on his face boded no good at all. It was through him I'd met the men at the Red Ox, and he knew far too much.

'What are you doing here?' I demanded.

His bushy grey eyebrows rose a little in mock disapproval before he replied. 'That a way to greet an old mate, that is? What are you doing here indeed! How about a nice kiss, eh, or better still, a nice, slow blow job?'

'Go away, Tierney, you're disgusting.'

'Disgusting is it? Not so disgusting when you needed my help to get it on with your girlie friends, was I?'

'Your help!' I exclaim, stung to instant outrage by the sheer enormity of what he was saying. 'Your help? You didn't help me, Tierney. You lied to me, tricked me and made me look a complete fool . . .'

'Aw, come on, Isa, that was just a laugh, yeah? You got what you wanted in the end, didn't you?'

'No thanks to you.'

I stepped forwards, intending to throw him out bodily, because he was a weedy little runt, a good four inches shorter than me, and I knew I could do it. He knew too, and stepped back in alarm, so that I was about to shut the door in his face when I realised that I had to perfect opportunity to put him off the Rattaners, along with the rest of the men from the Red Ox.

'Besides,' I stated, 'it's not going to work. I've just met up with the other women from my birthday party, and nothing is going to happen.'

He looked surprised.

'No? From what Mike and Dave said you were really going something.'

'Never mind what Mike and Dave said,' I answered, colouring up despite myself. 'We met, and nobody wants other women playing with their girlfriends, so it's not going to happen.'

'Yeah? What about Jas and Carrie, and that gorgeous blonde bit, what's her name . . . Katie?'

'That's none of your business. There aren't going to be any more parties, or anything else, and you can tell them that at the Red Ox. If you don't believe me, just ask Jasmine and Caroline next time they're there.'

'Fucking nice that is,' he said, thoroughly belligerent and obviously not believing me. 'All the help we've given you, and you cut us out.'

'I am not cutting you out. There is nothing to cut you out from. Now go away.'

'Charming!'

'Just go away. I don't want anything more to do with you, and I'd be very happy indeed if I never saw you again.'

'Fucking nice, that is. And you're going to see me again, plenty. I'm your scout.'

'You scout in college.'

'Not this year, I don't. Saw your name down for the Mill, didn't I, and volunteered to change with Mrs

Warrender, on account of her rheumatics. Not popular, the Mill ain't, on account of the extra walk. So you've got me all year.'

'Oh, God. Well, whatever you may have thought, it's not going to happen, so you can put any dirty little ideas right out of your head. As far as I'm concerned you're my scout, a college servant, and that's all.'

He just sneered.

'High and mighty aren't we now, Miss Colraine, but let me tell you this, my girl. Before term's over I'll have you back across my knee with your knickers at half mast, see if I don't, and sucking cock and that, like the little tart you are.'

He'd shouted the last few words because I'd pushed him firmly back into the passage and slammed the door. For one awful moment I imagined my neighbours hearing what he'd said, but I was pretty sure all the rooms on the landing were still empty. It was still acutely embarrassing, and my heart was beating fast as I went back to my chair, now with my mind full of black thoughts.

I had been too upset by Tierney to give much more thought to my plans for Sarah that evening, but my head felt a great deal clearer in the morning. Stan Tierney was nothing more than an irritation. All I needed to do was be firm with him and there was nothing he could do. Certainly he was in no position to make any demands of me, because if his behaviour came out it would undoubtedly mean the loss of his job.

He also knew I had the support of Duncan, Dr Appledore. As my tutor and a member of St George's Senior Common Room, he had considerable influence, while having been at my birthday party, he could be relied on to back me up. He could also be relied upon to cope with my occasional need for submission, and to be discreet about it, allowing me to maintain my dominant role among the Rattaners.

Most of Monday was busy, with all the normal start of term complications to sort out, along with lectures I wanted to attend both in the morning and afternoon. Only after the last lecture, in Keble, did I get a moment to reflect and, as I had to cycle back along South Parks Road anyway, it seemed the ideal opportunity to drop in at the zoology building and see what I could learn about Dr Eliza Abbott.

I was a little bemused at first, as there was just a huge concrete entrance hall with lecture rooms to either side, but no sign of anything in the way of an office. Upstairs looked more promising: a long hall lined with comfy chairs and aquaria set into one wall. Again there was no office, but there was a library, which seemed a good place to try. The woman behind the desk was looking somewhat harassed as she tried to explain something to a student, and I waited patiently until they'd finished before speaking to her.

'Excuse me. I'm hoping to trace a Dr Eliza Abbott. She used to be in the department.'

'Dr Abbott?' she queried. 'I don't recall anyone of that name.'

'No? She was here quite a while ago, maybe as much as fifteen years. Perhaps you can look her up? She studied animal behaviour, if that helps.'

The expression on her face grew a little more impatient than before, but she began to rise, then stopped, looking past me out of the door.

'I could look her up, but it might take some time. You'd be better off asking Dr Treadle, the man over there, with the white beard. He's the Reader in Ethology, and would certainly know.'

'Thank you.'

I'd already turned around, and could see the man she meant. He was perhaps fifty or maybe more, small, dapper, with a neatly trimmed white goatee and spectacles, creating an image of old-fashioned scholarship.

In one hand he held a cup of some hot drink taken from a nearby dispenser, while his gaze was fixed on an aquarium. I crossed over to him, quickly thinking up a story in case he wanted to know the reason for my interest in Eliza Abbott. He didn't turn around, but must have noticed me coming as he spoke before I could introduce myself.

'Fascinating, aren't they? The perfect design.'

He was obviously referring to the fish in the tank he was looking at, two large, dark-grey creatures with curiously bulbous lips, but I had no idea what he was talking about. Given his affable manner, and that I was a student, it seemed safe to ask.

'Why do you say that, Dr Treadle?'

'Why?' he responded. 'Because, my dear, they have remained apparently unchanged since the carboniferous period, three-hundred million years, beside which man's tenure on Earth is a mere flea speck.'

'I didn't know that. I thought there were only sharks and things that long ago.'

He turned to me, looking up with a puzzled expression.

'Not the fish, my dear girl, the snails, *Littorina littorea*, the common winkle.'

'Oh, I see,' I answered, only then realising that there were several winkles crawling on the glass and the rocks at the bottom of the tank. 'I didn't know that either. Only that they're quite nice with a little vinegar.'

The puzzlement in his face deepened.

'Are you one of my students?'

'No. I'm studying history at St George's. Isabelle Colraine.'

'Ah ha. Then to what do I owe the pleasure?'

'I was told you might know Dr Eliza Abbott, by the librarian. She was an old school friend of my mother's, who asked me to say hello.'

'Yes, indeed, I know Eliza, very well. We used to share a lab when I was but a pale young junior lecturer,

25

and I knew her as a postgraduate. Unfortunately you're a little late to catch her, around twelve years late to be precise.'

'Oh ... yes, Mum said they'd lost touch. Do you happen to know where she's working now?'

'Certainly I do. She has the Chair at Portsmouth. A letter to the department should reach her.'

'Perfect. Thank you very much.'

'Not at all, always glad to be of assistance.'

I had what I wanted, but he might very well know the answer to my other question. There was no harm in asking.

'One other thing, just a curious question you might know the answer to. Can a conditioned reflex be removed?'

He paused a moment before answering. 'Can a conditioned reflex be removed? An interesting question ... and one to which there is no clear answer. One paper notes that the excision of the pineal gland in the rat –'

'I was thinking ... more in hypothetical terms.'

'Ah ha. In that case, the answer is yes ... or no. May I enquire the source of your interest?'

'It was just a question that came up the other day, that's all.'

'I see. I suppose you know that Eliza published several papers on the subject?'

'No. I didn't. That's fascinating.'

'Yes, and quite a coincidence. I am a little busy at present, as my tutorial students are supposed to seek me out here, but perhaps if you'd care to drop in at my lab one afternoon we could discuss the matter further?'

'Thank you. I'd be delighted. That's very considerate of you, Dr Treadle.'

'Not at all, my dear. I am only too happy to oblige.'

Two other students had approached and were standing a little way back, but well within earshot. They were evidently his tutees, so I excused myself. Cycling back to St George's, I wondered if there was more to his invitation that met the eye, especially because of his remark about coincidence. Had he been secretly amused? Did he know about Eliza Abbott's sexuality?

It seemed unlikely, and I quickly put it down to the fact that associating with Stan Tierney the previous year had made me instantly suspicious of other people's motives. After all, if Dr Treadle had had dubious intentions he would hardly have invited me to his laboratory, but rather to his private home.

My initial tutorial was on the Tuesday afternoon, although I'd seen Duncan to speak to when I first arrived, dropping in at his rooms for a glass of port. Another don and my fellow historians had been there too, so the conversation had been strictly neutral, despite the tell-tale glitter in his eye and a hand placed negligently on my bottom as I left. Since then, I had only seen him in hall, and there had been no opportunity to discuss the Rattaners.

In the first year my room had been across the quad from his, just a minute's walk away, so I was a trifle late getting there from the Mill. He responded to my knock as ever, with a booming demand to enter. I came in to find him seated in his usual chair, looking more like a Victorian hell-fire preacher than ever, his beard bushier and his belly more expansive. Only his friendly, welcoming smile betrayed his true character: gentle, but distinctly perverse in a very English way.

'Ah, Isabelle,' he greeted me, 'three minutes late, I see. Is it too much to hope that your timing is deliberate?'

He finished with a chuckle and his eyebrows rose into questioning arches.

'Purely accidental,' I replied, trying to keep the smile from my own face. 'I'm in Cut Mill this year and I didn't realise how long it takes to walk around the meadow. Not that my excuse should make any difference.'

'Absolutely not,' he agreed. 'Late is late. However, business before pleasure as the saying goes, although personally I have always thought the expression a sad reflection of the Protestant work ethic. I believe you should have an essay for me on the relationship between eighteenth-century economics and the Highland clearances?'

'I do,' I answered him, handing it across.

'A pity, really,' he answered, taking it from my hand and setting it aside. 'Do sit down. Port?'

'Yes, please.'

He moved ponderously to the sideboard and poured two glasses of deep garnet-red liquid from a decanter, passing one to me before seating himself once more. Quite obviously he was itching to get me across his knee. I knew it would happen. Shortly my skirt would be turned up and my knickers would be taken down to bare my bottom for punishment. Despite my acquiescence, intense feelings of shame were already building within me.

A swallow of the rich, heady port calmed my nerves a little and, as he began to discuss the programme for the year ahead, I managed to pay attention and even make the occasional reasonably intelligent comment. That didn't stop my eyes repeatedly flicking to the clock on his mantelpiece in the sure knowledge that as soon as my official tutorial time was up my knickers would be coming down.

Sure enough, as the first of the six low chimes to mark the hour rang out he stopped talking about eighteenth-century history in mid-sentence. I moved a little in my seat, suddenly uncomfortable. Like Portia, like Katie, I know I like it, but no matter what it does to me, or how often I get it, those awful feelings of embarrassment, indignation and self-pity never go away.

'Six o'clock,' he remarked happily. 'Time, I think, that we went into the little matter of your lateness.'

I couldn't speak, but I managed to nod. He was humming happily to himself and rubbing his hands together as he walked across to lock the door, those big, heavy hands I'd allowed to become so intimately acquainted with my bottom the previous year. I could remember it, every occasion, vividly, how much it stung and how wet it made my pussy, both things that made my agitation worse still. He was also the last man, and the last person, who'd punished me, two months before, and being out of practice was making my feelings worse.

'A hard chair allows me to make the best lap, I think,' he stated, pulling one forwards. 'Come along then, the sooner we're started, the sooner we're finished, eh?'

My response was a wry grimace. He understood my feelings, absolutely, and my fingers were trembling as I swallowed the last of my port. I stood up as he made himself comfortable on the chair, his knees extended to make a lap for me to bend over. My feet felt like lead as I walked across, but I could no more stop myself than fly. Down I went, across his lap, my bottom lifted in that utterly submissive, utterly humiliating position I so enjoy putting other women in. Now it was me, and I could already feel the tears welling up in my eyes as he gave a pleased sigh.

'Beautiful,' he remarked, patting the seat of my skirt, 'beautiful indeed. Is there a finer sight than a woman's bottom offered for pleasure? I doubt it.'

I didn't answer, but closed my eyes, with the first of my tears squeezing gently from beneath the lids. His fingers found the hem of my skirt, a loose, heavily pleated kilt I'd chosen specifically because it allowed me to be laid bare easily. Up it came, lifted to expose the seat of the fresh white panties I'd put on immediately before coming out.

My gusset was already wet, adding to the sharp pang of shame I felt as I was exposed. Duncan gave a knowing chuckle as he turned my skirt onto my back

29

and I wondered if he'd seen, or was simply pleased because I'd put on new panties especially for him. Whichever it was, I was blushing furiously, with my face screwed up and the tears running freely down my cheeks, already crying, and not even spanked, not even bare.

'Ah ha, spanking panties,' he remarked. 'I'm so glad you have the sense to dress for the occasion, but although I do appreciate your choice of underwear, they had better come down all the same, don't you think?'

'Yes,' I mumbled, knowing full well that it was all part of the ritual, and that my bottom would be stripped no matter what I said.

'Absolutely, bare is best,' he said. 'Down they come then . . .'

As he spoke he took hold of my waistband and began to pull. I felt myself exposed, every inch, his knuckles tickling the skin of my bottom as my panties were slowly peeled down. Duncan continued to talk.

'. . . right down, all the way, but not, I think, taken off. No, somehow a girl's bottom is so much prettier with her knickers turned down around her thighs, or even in a tangle around her knees or ankles, than taken right off. Don't you agree?'

I tried to answer, but it came out as a broken sob. He merely chuckled again and adjusted my panties so that they were inverted around my thighs, concealing nothing, but left in place so that it was very clear I'd had them pulled down rather than merely going bare. I tensed, expecting the spanking to start, but I should have known better. He merely tucked one arm around my waist to hold me in place and raised his knee, bringing my bottom up into full prominence.

A fresh sob escaped my lips as I felt my bottom cheeks open. I could see nothing, beyond the frame of my hair where it dangled to the floor, and a little piece of his carpet, but I knew exactly what I was showing

30

behind, and what he could see. Being slim, I show everything when I'm in spanking position: the rude, dark-brown ring of my bumhole on blatant display, my pussy lips pouting out from between my thighs, hairy, naked, wet and deeply shameful.

The tears were running freely down my cheeks as he inspected my open rear view and, when his great heavy hand at last settled on my bottom, I wasn't sure if the spanking was to begin or if he would fondle me a little first. At the thought of being touched up my bumhole started to twitch, making him laugh and my tears run harder still. He didn't, merely giving one cheek a gentle squeeze before he began to spank me.

It was soft, little more than pats to the crests of my cheeks, to make them quiver and bounce, with no more than a tiny bit of sting. That didn't matter. I was in punishment position, my panties had been pulled down and my bare bottom was being spanked. That did, bringing me intense humiliation made worse still because I knew full well I needed it.

As the pats turned to smacks I was already blubbering freely, in pathetic, tear-stained misery as I hung limp across his knees, but I didn't stay that way for long. Soon his smacks had begun to really sting, my pain rising to balance my humiliation. Now it was a proper spanking, firm and purposeful, intended to knock all the bad feelings out of me as well as bring me to ecstasy.

Soon I was gasping, my legs pumping in my panties, my hair flying as I began to toss my head. Duncan merely tightened his grip, spanking harder still, his huge hand enveloping most of my bottom with every smack. I lost control completely, writhing and kicking and squealing like a stuck pig, and it stopped.

'I have neighbours, remember,' Duncan said gently, 'not to mention the fact that the window is open.'

'Sorry,' I managed. 'Perhaps you better put my panties in my mouth?'

'I'm rather enjoying them as they are,' he responded, 'but still . . .'

He changed his grip on my body and reached down under my chest. I'd half expected him to take my breasts out anyway, because he knows having them dangling bare under me adds to my feelings, but I wasn't sure quite what he intended until my blouse was open. My bra was pulled up to leave them showing, my nipples erect and sensitive to the touch of cotton as the cups pulled away, but not left in a tangle as he normally did. Instead he gathered up the material and presented it to my mouth.

'Open wide.'

'But Duncan . . .'

'No nonsense, Isabelle. Open wide.'

I obeyed, despite a fresh pang of consternation as my bra cups were pushed well into my open mouth, leaving me mute, well gagged and feeling more sorry for myself than ever. By the time we'd finished my bra would be soiled with spit and I'd have to walk back to the Mill without it, leaving my nipples showing through my blouse, probably still erect. I kept it in though, knowing he wasn't finished with my bottom and that otherwise I wouldn't be able to hold back my squeals.

Again he adjusted his grip, taking me around my waist as he laid his hand across my now hot rear. His knee came higher, my cheeks spread wide and the spanking began again, maybe even harder than before, to set me pop-eyed and kicking on the instant. It seemed to sting more than ever. I was chewing on my bra and had to be held firmly in place, at first, until the heat began to spread and the moment to make my final surrender came.

I had no choice, unable to stop myself despite the biting humiliation as I began to push my hips up to the spanks. He took no notice, continuing to spank me to a firm, heavy rhythm, my whole bottom now bouncing

32

under his hand, with every smack sending a jolt of ecstasy to my sex. I was still wriggling with pain, even though I felt as if I'd come if he just kept at it, but before I could completely disgrace myself he stopped.

Utterly defeated, I let my legs come apart, stretching my lowered panties taut between my thighs, and went limp, too exhausted to fight my own feelings as he began to touch. I knew what he was going to do, what Sarah had done to Portia, to masturbate me from behind, bringing me up to the orgasm I so desperately needed. For all my need it was bitterly humiliating, just the thought that I could react that way to a spanking, lying there with my bottom stuck up to be touched off.

He'd cupped my sex in his hand, rubbing my pussy lips and between them in a perfunctory manner, designed to bring me off as quickly as possible so that he could have his own needs attended to. His thumb went up my hole and I was being held by my sex, my hot bottom cheeks well splayed as I was masturbated, so rudely, nothing concealed, no modesty left, my tight brown bumhole on full view as it began to pulse.

I was going to come, all my pain and humiliation turning to ecstasy as he manipulated me. My clothes were gone, my dignity gone, and I just didn't care, squirming myself against his hand and groping at my bare, dangling breasts as my feelings rose higher and higher still. His spare hand moved from my waist to my bottom, stroking my hot skin, delving between my cheeks, one finger teasing my anus.

My bra fell out as my mouth opened and I had to quickly stuff it back in, breaking my rising orgasm, but only for an instant, before his finger began to delve in up my bottom. As I felt the little wet mouth of my anus begin to open I was there, my body in violent contraction, my teeth locked hard on my thoroughly soiled bra, my pussy and my bumhole tightening over and over again on his intruding digits.

33

I would have screamed the college down if I hadn't had my bra stuffed in my mouth, and as I came slowly down I was deeply grateful for his ability to keep control. Certainly I hadn't had any, my climax far too strong to let me worry about the consequences. Fortunately he had, and even if I was going to have to walk back to the Mill with my breasts showing through my blouse or a deeply embarrassing wet patch, at least the entire college wasn't going to find out I got spanked after my tutorials.

As I got up I was filled with the delicious sense of absolution that comes only after I've been punished, and properly, on my bare bottom. It goes right to the heart of my beliefs, the way I'd been brought up, to believe that mankind, and woman in particular, is inherently sinful and therefore should be punished. Not that the ministers in the kirk would have approved of the way I responded to my acceptance of the need for punishment, but I wasn't going to be telling them in a hurry.

Duncan was smiling broadly as he rose to pour fresh glasses of port. We both knew what came next, but as always he was unfailing polite, waiting until I'd refreshed myself before putting the question. I'd left my knickers down, on purpose, but my skirt had fallen to cover me, and I turned it up, back and front, to show my smacked cheeks and my pussy fur too.

'Excellent. Very pretty,' he remarked. 'Just how a spanked girl should be. Might I now prevail upon your generosity?'

'Of course. How would you like me?'

'Perhaps not with a glass of port in one hand, it rather spoils the impression of contrition.'

I put my glass down and placed my hands on my head, adopting a pout that was not entirely acting. He deserved his treat, but that didn't make exhibiting myself as a punished girl any less embarrassing. As he sat down once more I turned slowly around, allowing him to admire me from every angle, my red bum, my open blouse, my lowered knickers, all for his delectation.

'Very pretty,' he repeated as he began to unbutton his fly.

He pulled out his cock, his thick shaft already half stiff, his balls too, in obscene contrast to his expensively casual suit and serious, intellectual face. I turned my back to him, sticking my bottom out a little to let him see the rear view of my pussy lips. He began to pull at his cock.

'A little more, please, Isabelle,' he said after a moment, sighing.

I knew what he wanted, a proper view of my bottom hole, and I was blushing hot as I reached back to open my cheeks, deliberately showing off the rude little dimple between. It's really not fair, when my skin's so pale, to have a dark brown bottom hole, and it's long been a source of acute embarrassment to me. Not that Duncan seemed to mind, his eyes feasting on my open cheeks as his cock grew slowly erect in his hand.

Soon he was hard, his erection a thick column of flesh sticking up from his fly, with his big balls lolling beneath. I watched, over my shoulder, keeping my bottom constantly on display, and ready to take him in my hand or go down on my knees to suck him if he asked. He said nothing, his face growing slowly redder with excitement, until I thought he was going to simply come in his hand. When he did speak, his voice was hoarse with passion.

'If . . . if you would sit in my lap, please, Isabelle.'

I nodded and moved back, to seat myself as instructed, first rubbing my bottom against his cock before lifting up to be penetrated. He put it to my sex, rubbing himself in the wet folds of my pussy before placing the firm rounded head to my hole. I settled down, my

35

mouth wide in rapture as I filled with hard cock, all the way in, until I was sitting in his lap and wriggling my bottom against him. He took my cheeks in his hands, squeezing my spanked flesh as he pushed up inside me with short hard thrusts.

'Show me,' he gasped, 'show me everything.'

Even with his cock inside me I felt a flush of chagrin, but I obeyed. Reaching back, I caught up my skirt, making sure he got the best possible view of my bottom, with my pussy hole stretched taut on his shaft and my wrinkled brown bumhole on plain view as I held my cheeks wide. His thrusts grew abruptly faster, he began to grunt and, suddenly, I felt the wet of his come around the mouth of my sex.

He was done, but I wasn't. Making me show myself so rudely had brought me back on heat, and even as he stopped moving inside me I was lying back in his arms, my thighs spread as far as my panties would allow, my pussy open, with his big cock still deep in my hole. I began to masturbate, my eyes shut, my chest heaving. He took hold of me, cupping my breasts in his hands and rubbing his fingers over my nipples.

A moment to get my panties down around my ankles and my legs properly open and I was already approaching orgasm, my fingers busy in the wet crease of my sex, my bottom wriggling in his lap. I thought of how he'd punished me, lifting my skirt, taking down my precious little panties, spanking my bare bottom, making me take my bra in my mouth to shut me up and spanking me some more. It felt perfect, exactly how I should be treated, all my dignity stripped away with my clothes, my breasts exposed, my bare bottom open to show off my pussy and anus, and spanked, and spanked, and spanked . . .

Only Duncan's hand clamped over my mouth at the last possible instant prevented me from screaming aloud as I came for the second time within the space of a few minutes.

Three

Duncan was delighted to learn that the Rattaners now had a formal existence, and that he alone of the men who had attended my birthday party was to be invited to future events. I also told him about Tierney, just so that he knew what was going on. What I didn't tell him about were my plans for Sarah, as I knew he would not merely have disapproved, but shared her opinion that I was being a brat.

I badly wanted to speak to Dr Treadle again, but I didn't want to appear over eager, just in case he did know something, or had guessed something, and was therefore suspicious of my motives. Instead, I looked up Dr Eliza Abbott, or as she now was, Professor Eliza Abbot, in a sort of scientific version of Debrett's. She was listed pretty comprehensively, including her extension number at the department and her email address.

My first thought was to write to her, in carefully neutral language, saying that I was a friend of Sarah Finch and would very much like to meet. She could hardly fail to get the underlying message that I shared her tastes for sapphic indulgence, and would hopefully be keen to see me.

There were two drawbacks, both due to the fact that I had no idea how her relationship with Sarah currently stood, and could hardly ask. If she still got on well with Sarah she was likely to ring and ask about me, with potentially disastrous consequences. If they'd parted on bad terms, then she might not wish to get in touch with me at all, which would bring my wicked scheme to a premature halt.

Phoning was no better, and although I wasn't happy about simply turning up in Portsmouth unannounced, it seemed to be the best option. After all, the worst she could do was tell me to go away, but that had to be considerably less likely to my face. Going down to Portsmouth also meant being prepared to stay at least one night, but again, that was something I could cope with.

As I didn't know her home address I would have to go down on a Friday, preferably in the morning, which meant missing a few lectures. Again I could cope, and I might have gone that Friday, had not a note appeared in my pigeonhole on the Thursday morning from Dr Treadle. He suggested five o'clock on the Friday after-noon as a good time to visit him and discuss condi-tioned reflexes. I'd assumed that he'd have more or less forgotten about me and his eagerness made me suspi-cious again. Yet what could I do?

If I wanted to know, I had to visit him. Even if he did know about Eliza Abbott, it didn't necessarily mean he would use his knowledge against me in any way, and although it would be extremely embarrassing, I'd put up with worse. I accepted.

There was also something from Laura, an envelope containing a gilt-edged card inviting me to dine with her on the Saturday after next. I had to admit it was perfect, absolutely discreet, with no hint of what would actually be going on at the dinner party. For a moment I even considered giving in and withdrawing my candidature for the presidency, but the thought of how unutterably smug Sarah and Portia would be about it changed my mind.

On the Friday morning I had to make a conscious decision not to put on what Duncan had referred to as 'spanking panties'. I felt sure that was how Dr Treadle would like me to dress, and some treacherous element within me was telling me I'd end up showing them to him. It was foolish, in the circumstances, but after the way I'd been handled by Tierney and company I was just too used to men who automatically viewed me as an object for their desires.

I purposely chose an asexual look instead: a big, purple roll-neck jumper that almost entirely concealed my figure, baggy jeans and trainers. It was still a little irritating to think that I was dressing for him, even though nothing whatsoever had been said, but after all, it was, in a sense, Rattaners' business.

By ten to five I was outside the zoology building. Again there was that touch of irritation that I was so keen to oblige him, and I would have hung around on the pavement for a while had I not remembered what had happened the last time I'd been a few minutes late for an appointment. Yet there had been no suggestion whatsoever that Dr Treadle wanted to spank me, or anything else, and as I climbed the stairs I was telling myself not to be so silly.

His lab proved to be directly above the street, in full view of where I'd chained my bicycle, so it was just as well I hadn't lingered. It was also quite large, a long, oblong room lined with windows to one side and specimen cases to the other. There was a slight moment of shock as I realised that those nearest to me contained bird skeletons, each perfectly arranged on an armature of wires in a dozen different postures, before the door at the far end opened and Dr Treadle himself peered out, looking at me over a pair of tiny, semi-circular reading glasses.

'Isabelle, my dear, a pleasure to see you. Are you familiar with Tinbergen's work?'

'No,' I admitted, moving past the skeletons to a collection of stuffed pigeons, again arranged to make some elaborate demonstration.

'A pity,' he replied, 'but no matter. Do come in.'

He waited at the door until I'd reached it, and ushered me inside. I felt myself stiffen instinctively in expectation of a hand placed on my bottom, but he merely gave the lightest of touches to my waist. His room was an extension of the lab and at the corner of the building, brightly lit by large windows with a fine view across the roofs of Oxford, but somewhat sort of shelf space. He seemed to have made up for the lack by piling every available surface with books, documents, loose pieces of paper and even specimens, including a stuffed owl which was not only somewhat moth-eaten but managed to convey a distinctly aggrieved expression with its great glass eyes.

'Do sit down,' he offered, moving a pile of what looked like essays from a chair. 'If you'd like tea or coffee . . .'

'No, thank you, I'm fine.'

'Good, because I was about to say you'd have to go down to the cafeteria. So, your mother is a friend of Eliza Abbott and you want to know if it is possible to remove a conditioned reflex?'

'Yes.'

'I see,' he said, sitting down in front of the computer. 'I think it might help to say, my dear, before we go any further, that I knew Eliza very well indeed.'

I hesitated, although his meaning was clear enough, and backed up by his faint sardonic smile and a distinct glitter in his dark beady eyes. Yet I was determined not to be the first one to say anything too telling. If I did, and he in fact meant something entirely different, the embarrassment would be unendurable. I tried a different angle.

'Do you know Sarah Finch then?'

He looked puzzled and I went on, taking a minor gamble that he would know Eliza was a lesbian.

'Sarah Finch. Eliza's girlfriend a few years ago.'

'Perhaps, yes. Tall, girl, long dark hair, rather timid in her manner?'

'She's fairly tall, yes, and dark haired, but not at all timid.'

'The confidence of maturity, no doubt. That must have been several years ago?'

'Yes. She's still in Oxford though, as head of catering at Erasmus Darwin.'

'Is she indeed? I was dining at Erasmus only the other night. Perhaps I am not as observant as I should be, at least, in visual terms. Mentally, I venture to boast that the years have not robbed me entirely of my acuity. Is Sarah Finch in some way related to your question about conditioned reflexes?'

'Yes,' I admitted.

His eyebrows rose a little but he didn't reply. I hesitated, but my face was going gently pink, leaving me with no choice but to take the plunge.

'Yes,' I repeated, only lying a little. 'Eliza gave Sarah a conditioned reflex, while they were together.'

'And Sarah now wishes to be rid of it, but is perhaps a little embarrassed to come to me directly?'

'Exactly.'

'Good. I'm glad we've got that out of the way. It is always so much more pleasant to be able to speak frankly. And this reflex is of an embarrassing nature?'

'Er . . .'

'Don't worry, I am quite aware of Eliza's somewhat quirky – shall we say – sense of humour.'

'Yes, deeply embarrassing.'

'And you wish me to be of assistance?'

I swallowed hard, expecting the proposition and knowing that unless it was completely outrageous I would comply, or at least negotiate. It never came. Instead he steepled his fingers, peering at me over the top of his glasses as he went on, a trifle amused.

'No doubt you would prefer to keep the exact nature

41

of the reflex to yourself, my dear, but I would esteem it a professional kindness if you were to expand a little. My discretion, needless to say, is absolute.'

I nodded in reply, the blood burning in my cheeks despite the fact that it was not me but Sarah who was involved. He waited patiently until I managed to get my words out.

'She ... that is, Eliza ... Sarah rather, can't hold herself ... or at least she finds it very hard, if a specific command is given ...'

He merely looked puzzled.

'What I mean is,' I went on, trying to pull myself together, 'that when Sarah is given a specific command she ... she feels a powerful urge to ... to urinate ... to wet herself.'

I'd said it, although I was blushing crimson and felt as if I was about to do exactly what Sarah did, only without a command. He looked surprised, shocked also, and I spread my hands in a helpless gesture, keen to disavow any association with Eliza Abbott's behaviour. At last he spoke. 'Goodness gracious! I had guessed that there was an element of the Sadean in their relationship, but nothing like that. Of course I must help her, poor girl. She must come to see me, without delay.'

'No! I mean, that's not possible ... she'd be far too embarrassed.'

'I can imagine, and yet I very much doubt I can achieve anything by proxy, or at all for that matter.'

'Sarah definitely won't see you. I ... we were hoping you could tell me what to do?'

'I suppose I can at least discuss the matter,' he replied, with a shrug. 'You say Sarah has been conditioned in such a way that on a specific command she urinates?'

'Yes.'

'Hmm, interesting, in that it would seem to contradict Skinner's principal theory of operant conditioning.'

'Sorry, that means nothing to me.'

'No?' he said, as if astonished that I could be so ignorant. 'B. F. Skinner postulated that animals, in which group we obviously include humans, would repeat acts that led to favourable outcomes, and suppress those that produced unfavourable results. In this case, the stimulus, the command, would seem to provoke an unfavourable response.'

'No, not really. The thing is that however much she may dislike it at a rational level, wetting herself produces an intensely pleasurable sensation.'

'I see. Yes, that might explain it, especially if the stimulus had also become linked to a release of endorphins. I must say that it also explains a great deal about Eliza Abbott. Presumably this was done by reinforcement?'

'By making her do it until it became instinctive? Yes.'

'So it was entirely voluntary?'

'Yes.'

'Remarkable.'

He shook his head, then once more steepled his fingers, leaning towards me.

'It should be possible, at least in theory. Watson proposed two principal techniques: habituation, by which the reflex dies away through sheer over use, and reconditioning, whereby the stimulus is used to provoke a new reflex. After over a decade, the conditioning is evidently thorough, as I would expect from Eliza, so I suggest the second technique.'

'That seems practical,' I replied cautiously.

'It may be practical,' he admitted, 'or it may not. Even by making the suggestion I feel I have somewhat compromised my ethics, and so I would be grateful for your discretion. Indeed, I rather think this conversation never took place.'

'I understand, absolutely.'

He nodded, a gesture of closure, and I stood up, rather uncertainly. I'd expected him to try to take advantage of me and he hadn't. To my intense irritation I felt less a sense of escape than disappointment. As I stepped hesitantly towards the door he began to speak again.

'Naturally I would be interested to know how you get on . . .'

'Of course.'

'. . . and if you require further advice, please do not hesitate to visit me.'

'Yes. Absolutely.'

I'd reached the door, but hesitated, despite having exactly the information I wanted, and freely given. Suddenly I found myself stammering.

'I feel I should . . . I don't know, treat you to dinner or something, only . . . I'm a student, of course, and . . . well, I could just about run to fish and chips.'

I stopped, laughing, leaving him with every opportunity to make an improper suggestion. He smiled.

'I would be delighted to take you up on your offer, but no doubt a pretty young girl like you has far better things to do with her time than entertain fossilised old dons.'

'No, no, not at all, really, I mean it.'

'How kind of you, but no, I mustn't keep you.'

I smiled to hide the strange mixture of relief and frustration bubbling up within me, and would have left, only he'd also risen. He reached behind the door, where there had been a green coat hanging up, and, instead of walking away, I paused to admire the display of stuffed birds, all the while asking myself what on earth I thought I was doing. When he came out, I fell into step beside him and we took the lift down together, talking of this and that.

He had pressed the button for the car park in the basement, and I knew that if I was going to say anything, now was my last chance. I didn't, unable to get the words out both because I couldn't accept my own needs and for fear of rejection. When the door opened on the ground floor I simply said goodbye, and at the last possible instant, kissed him on the cheek.

As I walked back to my bike I was blushing furiously, feeling extremely foolish and also cross with myself. If he hadn't tried to take advantage of me I should have been grateful for the fact, not disappointed that I hadn't found myself obliged to either back out with a few cold words or do as I was told. Unfortunately it didn't work like that and, as I cycled back to St George's, I couldn't stop thinking about what he might have made me do.

Most people had been leaving and it would have been possible. Perhaps his tastes were straightforward and I'd have been made to go down on my knees to him, to take his cock in my mouth and suck him off. More likely he'd have wanted a little more contact, maybe played dirty with me, making me pull my top up to show him my breasts and letting him feel them as he masturbated. That way, only once he was fully erect would I have been put on my knees to suck him, except with the added humiliation of having my breasts out and my nipples stiff from fondling.

By the time I got back to Cut Mill I was dizzy with arousal, and very nearly fell off while dismounting my bike. I knew what I wanted to do, but I was still fighting it, and told myself I would call in on one of my neighbours for coffee to let my feelings die down. Nobody was in, all twelve having gone to hall for dinner or elsewhere, leaving me prey to my feelings.

I made myself a coffee, still trying to fight it as I stood staring stubbornly out of the window across the meadow. It didn't work. My resistance lasted until the bottom of the coffee cup before I had climbed onto my bed, brought my knees up and closed my eyes. I was still full of chagrin even as I undid my jeans and pushed them down, knickers and all, right down.

With my legs spread wide my top and bra came up, leaving me bare from my neck to my ankles. As I began

45

to tease my pussy and nipples my thoughts went back to Dr Treadle, and what I might have allowed him to do to me had he proved to be a dirty old man. Being made to let him touch me up would have really brought out my sense of humiliation, standing in his room with my top and bra pulled up, my jeans and panties tangled around my ankles, just as they were. Possibly he'd have liked to watch me masturbate, spread open to him, nothing concealed as he enjoyed making me do something so deeply intimate.

That was good, but not enough. He'd have done it, playing with his cock as I brought myself to a shame-filled orgasm in front of him, but he'd have been slow. By the time I'd got over my feelings and come in front of him he'd have barely been stiff. I'd have been made to take him in my mouth, as I was, everything on show as I knelt between his open knees. By the time he was hard in my mouth my jaw would have been aching and I'd have begged to be let off sucking.

He'd have agreed, but on the condition he could fuck me. I'd have given in, too far gone to stop myself, as he told me to stay down but turn around, for rear entry. As I got into position I'd have been burning with embarrassment, red faced and trembling, thinking of how rude I looked with my little breasts dangling naked and my bottom lifted and open, my pussy wide and wet, my knotted brown bumhole on blatant display.

I was close to orgasm, too close to stop myself adding an extra detail to the way I was disgracing myself. Bouncing up on the bed, I quickly turned over, into the position I had been imagining myself in, on all fours, my clothes dishevelled, my bottom lifted to allow myself to be fucked. Once more my hand found my pussy and I was lost, rubbing urgently at my clitoris as my feelings built.

Dr Treadle would have got down behind me, his erect cock in his hand. I'd have hung my head in shame, my eyes blind with tears within the curtain of my hair as he began to play dirty with me. He'd put his cock between my sex lips, rubbing it in the wet folds and occasionally popping it into my hole as he molested me. No part of me would be spared. He'd fondle my breasts, tease my nipples to aching erection, pull my hair, scratch my neck and smack my bottom. By then I'd be panting with lust, unable to hold back, wiggling my bottom for more even as I begged him to get it over with.

He'd ignore me, enjoying my body as he continued to grope, exploring my bottom, holding my cheeks wide to inspect the hole between and telling me how rude my little brown anus looked. Perhaps he'd finger it, spitting between my cheeks. Maybe he'd even lick my ring, with his bristly beard tickling in my crease, before pushing a finger up into my rectum. By then I'd be really begging, not to get it over with, but to be fucked, hard. He'd oblige, jamming his erection to the hilt in my pussy . . .

No. He'd have my bottom hole ready, and that's where he'd put his cock. I wouldn't realise until too late, and up it would go, the full length squeezed slowly up my back passage as I wriggled and cursed and swore at him, calling him a pig and a dirty bastard and worse for abusing me anally. Only I wouldn't mean it. I wouldn't even be fighting properly, unable to stop myself from enjoying every instant of having his cock fed up my bottom.

I had to do it. My long-handled hairbrush was in my bedside drawer. I hardly knew what I was doing as I scrabbled for it, pulling it out and immediately slipping the handle around behind me and up my pussy. For a few moments I enjoyed fucking myself, before pulling it free and wiping the sticky, slippery tip on my bumhole. It felt deliciously dirty, and dirtier still as I pushed and felt my anus spread to the pressure. Again I spent a moment working it in and out, with my eyes closed in bliss, before getting back on all fours, only now with the

47

brush sticking up rudely from between my open cheeks, the handle pushed deep up my bottom, imagining it was Dr Treadle's cock.

He would well and truly bugger me, using my rectum as a slide-box for his dirty cock as I hissed and spat like a she cat on the floor. Only I wouldn't be able to hold the pretence. Long before he'd come up my bottom I'd be masturbating furiously, to make myself come on his cock, bringing myself to peak after peak as my buggered ring contracted on his intruding penis, just as I was coming for real, and as my ring was contracting on the hairbrush handle.

My face was pressed to my bed, and I bit hard on the coverlet to stop myself screaming as I came. In my head I was in just the same position, only on the floor of Dr Treadle's room with the full length of his erection wedged deep in my rectum. I was still coming as I reached back to grab the hairbrush, working it firmly in and out of my poor, buggered bottom hole as I thought of how I'd be used, and I was still moving it as I slumped slowly down on the bed.

There was no point in trying to deny what I'd done, or why I'd done it. It was all in my own head, from start to finish, and if my reaction owed something to the way Tierney and others had treated me during my first year, then that was something I would just have to put up with. Not that I was going to tell anybody, and at the end of the day I'd thoroughly enjoyed myself. By the time I'd calmed down the most irritating thing was the thought of how my behaviour would have accorded so exactly with the way Sarah Finch thought of me.

I was going to prove her wrong, preferably ending up with her grovelling naked at my feet, although for the time being that was a little ambitious. First I had to secure my position as president of the Rattaners, and I was beginning to assemble my armoury. Reconditioning sounded an excellent idea, and I didn't share Dr

Treadle's doubts as to whether it would work. He, after all, was a scientist, so naturally given to questioning everything until proof was absolute.

The reconditioning option was definitely a reserve. Introducing Eliza Abbot had to be my first option. Until then, I simply had to do my best to exert my authority over the others and hope that when we voted either I would win or there would be another stalemate. That would be at the party, probably before we began to play.

Laura's invitation card simply said 'Black Tie', but Duncan was the only one of us to whom the instruction had any real meaning. Each of the eight women due to attend the Rattaners' party would be dressed in her own, highly specific, style. Laura would almost certainly indulge her obsession with military uniforms, and put Pippa into a subordinate version of whatever she chose. Sarah and Portia were less predictable, although riding gear was a favourite and certainly looked good on both of them. The others I could instruct, or leave them to give me a pleasant surprise.

Jasmine and Caroline made most of their income from making ball-gowns, waistcoats and so forth for the richer students, the rest from stripping at the Red Ox and a few of Oxford's other less salubrious pubs. Most of their house in the Cowley Road was given over to dress-making, and they shared my love of corsetry, which was how we'd met. Without exploiting their submission to me too much, I could get more or less what I wanted made for the party.

I needed to impress, to dominate, not just the submissive girls, who would quite happily go down to me even if I was in sloppy jeans and a T-shirt, or stark naked, but Laura and, above all, Sarah. Not that I would be dominating them physically, of course, but in a mental sense, and for that I really needed to go to town.

It was more than simply image. I know full well that there is a deep spark of submission in my nature, and if I dress in revealing clothing, that is how I feel. To dress in clothing that accentuates my dominance has the reverse effect, changing the way I feel about myself, my attitude to others and theirs to me.

From the point of view of image, my age was against me, especially to Sarah's way of thinking, but what I did have was height. Barefoot I was two inches or so taller than Sarah and well above Laura. Inevitably Sarah would be in heels, but two could play at that game. Possibly I could even make myself appear older.

When I went up to Jasmine's on the Sunday afternoon the three of us agreed that the keynote should be black. I already had the beautiful black silk corset they'd made me in my first year, and I did want to show it off, although that was somewhat at odds with the image I needed. Caroline, who provided most of the skill and imagination for them, provided the answer. She could make me a floor-length skirt in black satin, pinched at the waist to the narrowest measurement of my corset and cut to give it volume at the back and hem. That way my corset would show and, while my shoulders would be bare, I could also have long gloves, a hat and a veil.

Just hearing her describe it had me enraptured and I ordered it immediately, promising to pay the cost of the material at minimum. Before going home I spanked both of them, kneeling together on the workroom floor with their bare bottoms pushed up, before making them go head to tail and bring each other to orgasm. It was the least I could do.

I could have stayed the night and thoroughly indulged myself with both of them but, since before my birthday party, my private feelings had come to focus more and more on Katie. Throughout the week I'd kept telling myself I should cycle up to Foxson to see her.

Something had always got in the way, but underneath I knew I was concerned that for all her behaviour over tea at Sarah's flat, she might not fully return my feelings. Now was the time to go.

Just the thoughts in my head and the feel of my pussy against the bicycle seat were enough to keep me aroused as I made my way up the Marston Ferry Road, but as I went I grew increasingly nervous. I needn't have worried. No sooner had Katie opened the door to me than my welcoming peck had turned to an open-mouthed kiss. I kicked the door shut and let her melt against me, my hands moving down to cup the round-ness of her bottom. If we hadn't heard somebody in the passage I'd have had her then and there, but the door wasn't locked and we quickly disentangled ourselves from each other, sharing a guilty glance as the footsteps came closer.

Whoever it was moved on, but the moment was broken and I felt reassured, so accepted her offer of coffee and sat down in her armchair. Being in a modern, post-graduate college, her room was very different from mine, a simple square with the whole of one side a huge picture window looking out over a quad of sorts, with accommodation on three sides and the fourth only a single storey high and facing the Cherwell.

She had a fine view out across the fields towards Shotover, but also of at least a hundred other students' rooms, three storeys of them, all with the same huge picture windows, so that the face of the building was almost entirely glass. Every single one would have been able to watch us kissing, and where I'd put my hands.

'Sorry if I got a bit carried away,' I told her. 'I didn't realise it was so easy to see into your room.'

'Don't be,' she answered. 'I don't mind.'

'What about your neighbours?'

'I don't suppose anybody was looking, and I'm not ashamed if they were.'

For all her bold words she was blushing, and went to close her curtains as soon as she'd put the coffee in the mugs. She was in jeans, as usual, tight around her small but distinctly cheeky bottom, and a loose blouse that clung to her apple-sized breasts. Just watching her move was a delight, both her body and her pretty, freckled face, as if she was constantly embarrassed by her sexuality.

'I hope I wasn't too rude with you at Sarah's?' I asked.

She immediately went pink as she answered.

'No, no, not at all. It . . . it was just what I needed. You know I need to be handled that way to bring me out of myself.'

I nodded, pleased by her reaction and her blend of embarrassment and self-conscious boldness.

'I've just been down to Jasmine and Caroline in the Cowley Road,' I went on. 'They're making my outfit for Saturday, part of it anyway. What are you going to wear?'

'I'm not sure,' she answered. 'Maybe just my undies. I don't want to be such a rabbit.'

'No. You be a rabbit, Katie. It's one of the things I love about you.'

She flushed with pleasure at my words, casting me a shy smile as she poured boiling water into our mugs. I relaxed, wondering how I could have doubted her affection for an instant. When the coffee was ready I took it, blowing to cool it down as she went to sit at her desk.

'Do you still have your Line Ladies costume?' I suggested. 'Are you still a member for that matter?'

'Oh, yes,' she answered, with a giggle in her voice. 'Why, do you want me to wear it?'

'Maybe. It's very cute, in a vulgar sort of way. You look good in it anyway.'

'Thanks, so did you in yours . . . whoops, sorry!'

'Are you angling for a spanking, Katie West?'

'Not here, Isabelle, please. The walls are like paper.'

She'd really thought I was going to do it, seriously flustered. I laughed.

'You didn't seem to mind risking being seen kissing me?'

'Well, no, but that's different, isn't it. Lesbianism's ... you know, fashionable almost, but having my bottom spanked.'

The way she said it, with so much relish and yet so much embarrassment, almost got it done. I wasn't even sure if her mistake had been deliberate, reminding me of my brief and intensely humiliating association with the Line Ladies folk-dancing club where we'd met. Tierney, as part of his efforts to make me eager to please, had pretended that they were a society much like the Rattaners, and like an idiot I'd fallen for it. The memory of asking the perfectly straight and highly respectable Lady Emmeline Young, who ran the club, for a panties-down spanking was going to stay with me forever.

'I ought to,' I told her, 'because you deserve it, and with the curtains open so everyone can watch your cheeks wiggle while you're punished, but I'll be kind and let you off, this time.'

She was now bright pink, her deep embarrassment only encouraging me as I went on.

'Yes, that would be just the thing for you, Katie, a bare-bottom spanking in front of the window, so that all your colleagues get to see your panties taken down and your bottom smacked. What do you suppose they'd think, Katie? What do you suppose they'd think if I did it properly, and made you come?'

'Isabelle, please,' she hissed. 'The walls.'

'Go and get into your Line Ladies gear and I'll let you off,' I promised.

She nodded, eager to please, immediately put her coffee down and scampered across to her wardrobe. I settled down to watch, enjoying the show as she undressed with hurried embarrassment. Her panties were much like the ones I'd stuck up her bottom hole, only with little green apples instead of cherries, the pattern and the full cut making her bottom seem more delectably rounded than ever. She kept them on, also her bra and a pair of short white socks, before arranging her outfit on the bed.

The temptation to spank her was growing all the time, perhaps with her panties stuffed in her mouth to quieten her down, although the thought of her embarrassment at other people hearing was part of the thrill. I held back, conscious that the sound of my palm on her flesh would be highly suspicious if not a dead giveaway, and not really wanting to give her a reputation for being a pervert with her friends and colleagues, because I knew that was how most of them would see it.

Instead I contented myself with watching her dress. Even if it was theoretically a dance costume, her cowgirl outfit made her look very submissive indeed, at least to me. Her flared white jeans had a silver pattern running down the outside of each leg and on the seat, stretched taut by her chubby little bottom. The Stars and Stripes shirt was merely vulgar, but with the top three buttons undone it left plenty of soft pink cleavage on show. Tooled leather boots and a wide-brimmed cowgirl hat in white leather completed the ensemble, leaving her looking extraordinarily cute, but also ridiculous in a deliciously erotic way.

Once she put her hat on she posed, her expression flickering between happiness for my approval and embarrassment as she put her hands on her hips and twirled around. I nodded, more tempted than ever to smack her bottom, which was almost impossible to resist.

'Do you think the others will like it?' she asked. 'Or just think I look silly?'

'Both,' I answered her, truthfully. 'They'll certainly want to play with you.'

Her response was a nervous nod, sweet and shy, but at the same time acquiescence to being given to another woman, or perhaps to Duncan. I had to do something with her or I would burst. It had to be quiet and, as I glanced around the room, I realised there was something I could do.

'Come here,' I ordered gently. 'On your knees.'

She got down immediately, to shuffle forwards a little way, then dropping to all fours, crawling to me, her pretty face peering up from beneath the rim of the ridiculous hat, full of shame, uncertainty and longing. I lay back in my chair, sipping coffee and trying to look cool as I considered my options, even though I was trembling with need for her.

'Turn around,' I ordered. 'Take down your trousers, nice and slowly.'

'Are . . . are you going to beat me?'

'Shut up and do as you're told.'

She nodded and turned, looking down as she fiddled with her trousers, then back over her shoulder. Her thumbs went into the waistband as she stuck her bottom out, a rude display even in her tight white trousers, and very rude indeed once she'd pushed them slowly down, her bottom now a fat ball of girl flesh in her straining panties.

'Good,' I told her. 'Now your knickers.'

Again she nodded, as her thumbs went into the waistband of the pretty, apple-patterned panties. She was blushing as she began to push them down, slowly, as I had ordered, exposing her chubby cheeks and the deep cleft between inch by inch, until first the rude pink star of her anus was on show and, at last, the fat, golden-furred fig of her sex, deeply split to show a wet centre.

'Good girl. Now stay like that.'

She obeyed, gripping her lowered garments around her thighs with her bottom thrust well out for my inspection. I got up, walking across to her chest of drawers, on top of which she'd made a neat arrangement of framed pictures, a vase of flowers and a big dark-orange candle in a black-iron stick. I turned to smile at her as I picked it up. Her mouth came open a little, her gaze full of apprehension.

'Do you have any matches, Katie?'

'In . . . in my top drawer. I think you'd better lock the door too.'

'Of course.'

I locked us in and took the matches, making sure she could see as I lit the candle. A rich scent filled the air as it began to burn, something like oranges, but spicier. I pulled one sleeve up, lifting the candle above my arm and waiting until the wax had begun to melt before tilting it to allow a single drop to fall on my skin. It stung, a tiny shock of pain, but by no means unendurable.

'Not too bad, about right really,' I remarked as I stepped back towards where Katie still squatted with her bottom stuck out behind. 'No squealing now, OK? You're not a pig, despite a certain resemblance.'

'I'll try,' she promised, her voice faltering. 'Don't spoil my clothes, please?'

'Yes, good point. I don't suppose your cherry-patterned ones were much use after last week.'

She shook her head.

'Stick your bottom right out then,' I instructed.

She obeyed, tucking her shirt tail up and adjusting herself to leave her cheeks splayed wide in front of me, over the carpet rather than her lowered clothing, and ruder than ever, with her bumhole pushed right out as if awaiting a buggering. I put a file under her and lifted the candle, poising it above her bottom as the molten wax grew slowly into a fat orange bead. She was trembling, little shivers passing through her meaty bottom cheeks, her anus twitching, but only when the first sob broke from between her lips did I tilt the candle.

Katie gasped as the hot wax splashed on her skin, a reaction that sent a jolt of cruel pleasure right through me. Even as it hardened she was panting, making her body heave and her bottom cheeks open and close, her anus too, pulsing as if she was trying to suck with her ring. I tipped another drop of wax and again she flinched, but she held her rude pose, her bottom offered for my amusement.

My mouth was curved up into a delighted grin that wouldn't go away as I began to spot her naked bottom with splashes of the deep-orange wax. As each one hit she jerked and gasped, with her breathing growing ever deeper and her bottom ever more agitated. Soon both plump cheeks were liberally splashed with wax, like icing on a cake. I began to pick out areas of bare flesh and moved the candle a little closer, making her pained reaction more urgent still. Soon both her cheeks were so well coated that wax was dripping on wax, and only the soft pink valley of her crease remained.

I began to drip the wax into it, and her gasps immediately turned to squeaks of fright. Still she stayed as she was, even as I moved lower, the brilliant orange droplets splashing onto the chubby curves between her cheeks, to explode on her skin, closer and closer to my target, and at last, right on the twitching pink star of her anus. A gagging noise broke from her throat, her bottom went tight and, as the wax dried in her anus to form a little orange plug, she began to sob.

She was shaking badly, but she didn't move and, despite a pang of guilt, I continued, dripping the wax into her open crease until her anus was clogged with it, higher too, to coat the soft turn of her cheeks, until her whole bottom was a shiny, wax-coated ball. Only then did I take pity, with the candle half-burnt, but still long enough to hold, and to use on her.

I blew it out and immediately slipped the thick smooth shaft between her thighs, pushing at the moist hole of her sex, and up. She gave a deep sigh as I began to fuck her, her head now hung low, her breathing deep and even. Keeping the candle well in, I slid my hand underneath her, to cup her sex in much the way Duncan had mine as he brought me off across his knee. Katie's response was a muffled 'thank you' as my finger settled between her sex lips.

She was puffy with excitement and soaking wet, the candle going in and out with ease, her scent thick in the air. I had to come too, and knew I should really take my pleasure first, but I was enjoying myself too much to stop. As the contractions of her bottom cheeks became harder and rhythmic the wax began to crack, making her bottom look for all the world as if she'd been glazed in honey and roasted.

I was grinning at the image, thinking of her as a suckling pig, as she started to come, gasping and mewling out her ecstasy as I fucked her and rubbed hard on her pussy. She cried out, her muscles locking to shower me with bits of wax, and again, her whole body shaking in orgasm. Only when her thighs began to slide slowly apart did I stop rubbing and leave her to slump slowly to the floor, mumbling broken thanks for what I'd done to her.

'We're not finished yet, you greedy little pig,' I told her.

She didn't answer, but nodded her understanding. I knew I could do anything I liked with her, and didn't intend to hold back. Leaving the candle where it was, so deep in her pussy only the tip showed between her lips, I quickly rolled her over. Her face was flushed, shiny with sweat, her blonde hair dishevelled with her fringe plastered to her forehead, her mouth a little open.

I wasted no time, undoing my jeans and pushing them right down, my panties too, and off with my shoes. Naked from the waist down, I quickly straddled her, her pretty face showing a brief moment of surprise before disappearing underneath me. I made myself comfortable, wiggling my bottom into her face to leave her mouth to my pussy and her nose pressed onto my bottom hole.

She made a gulping noise, just once, and she began to lick, lapping eagerly, or perhaps with an urgent desire to make me come and spare herself the indignity of being smothered in bottom flesh. I didn't care which it was, only that she was mine to enjoy, and quickly grabbed her legs, holding onto them as I rode her, with her bottom rolled up to show her wax-smeared cheeks, her pussy with the candle end sticking out of her hole and her well-plugged anus.

I knew she was willing to lick my bottom, if I made her, but it was a delightful surprise when she took hold of my cheeks and buried her tongue in my anus as deep as it would go. My orgasm had already begun to rise up, and I closed my eyes, shivering in ecstasy as my beautiful, sweet Katie probed my bottom hole with her tongue. I'd really used her, making her dress in her ridiculous cowgirl outfit, making her strip for my amusement, waxing her bottom, sitting on her face. In response she'd not merely licked me to ecstasy, but stuck her tongue up my bottom, for her own pleasure as well as mine and, as I reached down to finished myself off with my fingers while she did it, I was feeling completely and utterly in love with her.

Four

Second week seemed to take forever. I'd spent Sunday night with Katie, not really caring about anything except each other, and had woken late on Monday morning at a time I should really have been at a lecture. She had been still asleep, nestled into my arms, and my attempt to wake her with a kiss had ended up with us head to tail on the bed to bring each other to what had to be maybe our eighth or ninth orgasms. It was lunchtime before I had left, but as I cycled back I told myself that I would not allow my social life to spoil my work.

I had applied myself for the rest of the week, spending more time in the Bodleian than ever before. Only in the evenings had I allowed myself time off, to have my new black skirt fitted and to visit Katie. We had agreed that sleeping together during the week was probably a bad idea, but that didn't stop us thoroughly indulging ourselves, our sole regret being that I couldn't risk more in the way of spanking than holding her down across my knee and gently patting her bottom.

On Friday Duncan had complimented me on my essay, and it was my turn to have my knickers taken down. It had felt odd after being so dominant with Katie, but if anything I had enjoyed it even more for the change of role, mouthing eagerly on his cock and balls as I masturbated, once my bottom had been properly warmed. I had also told him where the Rattaners' meeting was going to be, and he had agreed to drive up to Witney, taking Katie and me as well as Jasmine and Caroline.

Whatever my misgivings about who ran the Rattaners, I had to admit that Laura's house was the prefect place to meet. Not only was it safely away from Oxford and yet close enough to be practical, but it was secluded and fitted out with our shared tastes in mind. She had bought it at a property auction, a curious construction based around an old railway carriage still standing on the original track of a long dead branch line. A hedge and the corrugated iron front hid it almost completely from view, and with fields and rough pasture to either side and a steep, wooded bank behind there was no way to see into the actual carriage from beyond the garden.

The extension was completely innocuous, providing no hint of her tastes at all, but the carriage itself was a very different matter. It was the ancient, compartmented type, with a long passage on the near side leading to the original loo, still functional. Of the six compartments, the first housed her collection of military uniforms. The second was used for her extraordinary range of implements designed to be applied to her playmates' bottoms, from custom-made whips to kitchen spoons. The third was exactly as it had been while the carriage was in service, but reupholstered and made an interesting if rather specialised small playroom. The last three had been knocked together to make her large playroom, boasting a pillory, a cage, a whipping trestle, and a cross, all fitted with chains and cuffs for restraining those who needed it.

All of us had been there, at my birthday party, but that had been two months before, and I was keen to have a more leisurely look, both at her uniforms and the implements of punishment. First I wanted to change, because I couldn't wait to get into the beautiful clothes Jasmine and Caroline had made for me. Leaving the others to drink coffee in Laura's extension, I took Caroline and Katie into the small playroom to be my maids.

'You'll need a foundation for your corset,' Caroline told me as we entered the compartment. 'I've brought a black silk camisole which should do.'

'You shouldn't have,' I said, but I didn't mean it, taking the smooth, heavy silk garment from her hand and running my fingers over it.

'Don't worry about it,' she replied. 'Now, if Mistress would be so kind as to remove her clothes? Everything please.'

I smiled and gave a polite inclination of my head, pushing back my worry about how I was going to pay for everything as I slipped into role. Caroline went to pull the blinds down on the outside window, then the inner one, as if I was about to strip in an old-fashioned railway compartment and might be seen by some passing man. It was a small gesture, but perfect for my headspace as I began to undress, adding a naughty touch.

Both of them watched me strip, Caroline with an open smile, Katie bright-eyed and fidgeting, for all that they'd both seen me naked a dozen times. I took every last stitch off, with no reason for modesty, leaving myself stark naked as I came to stand between the twin rows of seats, my hands on my hips.

'Well?' I demanded.

'Your hair first, Mistress,' Caroline answered. 'If you would be kind enough to squat down.'

'I shall sit, thank you, Caroline,' I told her, with just a touch of frost in my voice.

Katie gave a nervous giggle as I sat down, allowing Caroline to wind my hair up on top of my head in an approximation of the Edwardian style and fix it in place with pins. I could see myself in the mirror opposite, at least my face and my bare shoulders, first looking my age with my long hair tumbling down out of view, then very different. With my hair up my neck seemed longer, my face less soft, a fresh-faced girl transformed into a rather cold, somewhat stern young lady.

'You look beautiful,' Katie breathed as I gave her a cool smile.

'I've barely begun,' Caroline answered her, 'but sure, I've never known a woman who could look so dominant stark naked.'

She laughed, and I swatted her well-upholstered backside for her as she stood up.

'Yes, please,' she responded.

'Later,' I told her. 'My camisole, please.'

'Stockings first, Mistress,' she said.

'You have stockings?'

'But of course, Mistress.'

I nodded complacently. It was obviously unthinkable that I go without stockings under my dress. She took them from her bag, and I extended a foot as she got down on her knees to roll one on up my leg, with Katie watching apparently entranced. With both my stockings on I stood up, already feeling intensely sexual.

'My camisole, girl,' I ordered as Caroline burrowed into her bag.

She passed it to me and I slipped into it, shivering slightly at the feel of soft, heavy silk on my skin. It had cups but no shoulder straps, leaving my breasts lightly encased in twin froths of lace. Caroline gave a satisfied nod to see how well she'd fitted me and reached into the bag once more for my corset.

'Katie,' she stated, and clicked her fingers.

Katie came behind me as I lifted my arms to let them put the corset around me. The laces were loose, but I still had to breathe in as Caroline did up the fastenings with Katie holding it in place. Immediately I felt encased, poised and powerful, and more so as Caroline came behind me and began to walk her fingers down my laces, tightening them bit by bit while instructing Katie where to hold on.

When my waist was already pulled well in, I took a firm grip on the luggage rail, holding tight as Caroline pulled me down to a slender minimum. She and Jasmine had corset trained me the year before, but I was a little out of practice, and found myself breathing in short gasps and a little light-headed by the time she was done.

'Perfect,' Caroline announced as she tied my laces off. 'You were right, Isa, it would have been a real shame not to show this off. I am the best.'

'Yes, but very immodest,' I chided her. 'Now my skirt, please.'

Katie was by the door, and passed my skirt across on its hanger. I let Caroline put it on, covering my legs and bottom in shimmering satin that hid everything and yet hinted at the shape of my cheeks as I moved. My gloves followed, each pulled on by Caroline, and my boots, which she put on with me seated, lacing each one up as she knelt at my feet. Last came my hat and veil, which fixed to my corset laces at the back to hold it in place, and I was ready.

I stood up, feeling supremely confident and intensely dominant, imperious even, encased in satin and silk and gauze from head to toe, and lifted to six foot two in my blocked-heeled boots. As I stepped from the compartment I was towering over both Katie and Caroline by about a foot, which was entirely as it should have been.

Katie retreated back to the compartment to get dressed, Caroline staying with me to show off her creation as I stepped down to join the others in the extension. Everybody had arrived, most of them already dressed. Duncan, in immaculate black tie as if he'd been attending a college dinner, smiled and clapped politely at my entrance. Portia gave a little purr that earned her a slapped leg from Sarah, who nevertheless turned me a nod of genuine appreciation that brought a flush of pride to my face.

Fortunately my veil prevented her from seeing how pleased I was to have her approval, an entirely involuntary reaction. Both she and Portia were in riding gear as I'd expected: Sarah in pinks with her hair up under a hard hat, Portia in just jodhpurs and a loose blouse under which her fullish breasts were quite clearly naked. A riding crop of plaited black leather with a horn handle hung at Sarah's waist.

Jasmine had seen me being fitted, and her nod of appreciation was more for Caroline than me, something I promised myself to correct her for later in the evening. Laura, who had greeted us in baggy fatigues with sergeant's stripes on her arms, joined Duncan in clapping, and as I saw Pippa I realised what lay behind Laura's choice of uniform. Like her mistress, she was in fatigues, but very definitely dressed down. Her camouflaged suit was belted tight at the waist, but turned down at the shoulder, to leave her breasts showing beneath a string vest of pale dull green. Her trousers were loose around her lower legs, but tight around her thighs and hips, presumably her bottom too, the result of squeezing a womanly figure into clothing designed for a man. Like Laura, she also had on shiny black boots and a forage cap marked with a tuft of yellow feathers.

It was Pippa I was after as part of my campaign, but that didn't mean I wasn't going to enjoy punishing her. She and Laura were sitting together on the skirting, which was topped with cushions, and I joined them, sitting carefully in the tight confines of my corset, which kept me bolt upright. I accepted a glass of wine from Duncan, who seemed to have taken on the role of butler, and began to sip it as Jasmine and Caroline scuttled away to get dressed. We were going to vote first, but I couldn't see anything changing, and concentrated on helping Laura tease Pippa with remarks about what might be done to her.

Katie was soon back, not only in her ridiculous cowgirl outfit, but with a rope made up as a lasso fixed around her waist so that I could keep a firm hold on her. I caught it as she came in and pulled her down onto my knee, where she perched, pink faced and self-conscious as the others admired her outfit and made appropriate remarks. Her bottom felt full and heavy in my lap, also warm, and I began to toy with her, stroking the roundness of her cheeks through the taut white fabric of her jeans. It was going to be a good night, the atmosphere already building, and everyone in the mood to enjoy themselves.

When Jasmine and Caroline came back I had to smile. Jasmine was in relatively conventional clothes for her: a purple waspie corset that left her breasts bare and her bottom nicely displayed beneath a jut of stiff lace at the rear, bright purple panties, stockings and high spike heels linked with a thin chain so that she could take only the tiniest steps. Caroline looked comic, but arousing in the same way Katie did, in a gaudy yellow-and-red-striped one piece cut to leave her huge breasts and her big wobbly bottom bare at front and rear. Both looked delightfully spankable, perhaps spankable enough to persuade Sarah to let me have Portia for a while.

'I think we should have our vote now,' I stated as soon as everyone had sat down, 'although if nobody has changed their minds?'

I looked around the room. Sarah glanced at Laura.

'I'll stand if I have people's support,' Laura said.

'You're clearly the sensible choice,' Sarah responded, and Portia nodded. 'What do you think, Jasmine, Caroline? Wouldn't it be sensible to let Laura organise things, as we're using her house?'

'Yes, maybe,' Jasmine replied and I felt a lump start in my throat, 'but my bottom line is still that Isabelle got us together and so it's really her club.'

Caroline simply nodded, but Pippa spoke up. 'I've been thinking about it. Why don't we make Laura our secretary, with responsibility for organising events and have Isabelle as president?'

I made to speak, but I wasn't quite sure what to say. It solved everything, except that it didn't leave me in charge, but if I voiced my true feelings I was really going to look a brat. Laura spoke up before I could find the right words.

'That seems ideal. Isabelle?'

Sarah was looking at me, one corner of her mouth flickering into a knowing, amused smile. I shrugged, although I was boiling inside and very glad she couldn't see my face properly.

'Um . . . yes,' I finally managed, 'that seems to make sense, at least for now . . .'

I trailed off, wishing I could stop myself from sounding quite so sulky. It wasn't at all what I wanted, but there was no denying it was the right decision, at least as long as we were holding our parties at Laura's house. Possibly I'd be able to find another, better venue, but until then I could only go along with it.

'Good, I'm glad that's settled,' Laura remarked.

'Exactly,' Sarah agreed. 'It's so important that everyone knows where they stand.'

I knew what she meant: that my position as president was a mere sinecure, an inconsequential post handed out to keep me quiet, much like allowing a spoilt child to go in the front seat of a car to shut her up. The temptation to march over to her, drag her across my knee, take down her jodhpurs and panties and spank her fat bottom until she absolutely howled was close to overwhelming. Physically, I might just have been able to do it, but it was out of the question. Such an act would have been completely and utterly inappropriate. All I could do was swallow my feelings and await my chance, while I was determined not to let it spoil my evening.

'That's settled then,' I said, doing my best to sound happy and to get a grip on things. 'Next, does anybody have suggestions for rules?'

Laura reached for a red clipboard on a nearby shelf. I'd been too busy, with work and with Katie, to give much thought to the issue, and felt a fresh touch of chagrin for Laura's efficiency.

'Sarah and I spoke in the week,' she said as I leant across to glance at the neatly printed list running down the top page on her clipboard. 'We both feel there should be a few major ones, serious rules with serious penalties, such as telling outsiders about us or bringing inappropriate men, and also minor ones.'

'Just playful, really,' Pippa added, 'such as a spanking for being late, or having to go nude for the rest of the evening if you use your stop word.'

'Maybe,' I answered her, amused but doubtful. 'We'll have to agree each one though.'

'Sure,' she said.

'Everyone can make suggestions,' I stated, intent on regaining my control, 'and send them to Laura. We finalise them at the next meeting.'

'We should agree the main rules now,' Sarah urged.

'Fair enough,' I agreed.

'Do these apply equally to everyone?' Portia asked.

'The major ones, yes, of course,' I answered.

'And the minor ones,' she insisted.

'We'll see,' I said. 'For now, our major rules. First of all, nobody is to admit the existence of the Rattaners to an outsider.'

'How do we find new members then?' Portia asked.

'Women can be tested first,' Sarah said, 'and brought in if three, or maybe four, of us agree. With men, we need everybody's agreement.'

'Both those should stand as major rules,' Laura added.

I nodded, content with both suggestions. Nothing else came to mind.

'That seems to be the most important thing,' I said. 'We'll make a formal list next time.'

Laura had been going to continue but contented herself with a nod.

'And the penalties?' Jasmine asked.

'Court martial,' Laura suggested, 'with three judges to decide what is to be done. We mustn't expel anyone, or we risk breaking up the society, but the punishment should be harsh enough to act as a deterrent.'

'I agree,' Sarah responded.

After a moment's pause I nodded. It made sense, and it was essential that we kept ourselves to ourselves. I'd taken enough risks in my first year, and suffered for my efforts. Now the society was up and running it was time to shield ourselves from the outside world, admitting only people we were completely sure of. I also had no desire at all to break the major rules.

'That's enough discussion for me,' I stated firmly, cutting Portia off as she was about to speak. 'Caroline, Jasmine, what do you think you're doing, letting poor Duncan serve the wine?'

'Sorry, Mistress,' they replied, in chorus, Jasmine quickly moving to take the bottle from Duncan.

Caroline made for where Laura had set out a buffet of filled vol-au-vents, devils-on-horseback and cocktail sausages on her kitchen worktop, but I shook my head.

'Sorry's not good enough. You should know how to behave without having to be asked. Come here, both of you. Caroline, bring a tray of those sausages.'

Both came immediately, Caroline dropping a neat curtsey as she offered me the sausages. I made her wait, amused by her pose and the way it left her big bare bottom stuck out to the room.

Taking Katie's lasso, I quickly tied her hands behind her back, looping the thick soft cord twice around her wrists, securing it and winding the rest around her waist before tying it off. As I tugged the knot tight she gave a little squeak of pain.

'Be quiet,' I instructed. 'You can count yourself lucky you're not hog-tied. Now go and stand by the carriage steps, quietly.'

She got up, trotting rather awkwardly across to the little steps leading up to the door of the railway carriage, where she stood as ordered, slightly pink faced and with her back to the room. Caroline had held her pose and I selected two of the cocktail sausages from the tray.

'Turn around,' I ordered. 'You too, Jasmine.'

Both obeyed, Jasmine with meek obedience, Caroline throwing the sausages a worried glance. I smiled back.

'Stick your bottoms out. Knickers down, Jasmine.'

Her thumbs went straight to her waistband and down they came, presenting me with her slim pale bottom, her firm little cheeks far enough open to show the tight dimple of her anus and her pussy lips between. Caroline was already bare, and fleshy enough to keep her rudest details hidden, although the thick black curls of her pussy fur showed well enough.

I gave each bare bottom six firm swats, making their flesh jiggle and drawing out squeaks of alarm. Both were left a little flushed, the crests of their cheeks pink with finger marks, Jasmine still, Caroline quivering with apprehension. Taking a sausage, I leant forwards, to ease it into Jasmine's moist, inviting pussy hole. She sighed as it went in, and again as I used a finger to push it well up.

Caroline gave a little whimper as she saw what I'd done, but she kept her bottom well out. I had to hold her cheeks open with two fingers to see what I was doing, but I managed it, sliding her sausage well up her before finishing with another slap to each fat cheek.

'Now stand up,' I ordered.

They obeyed, Jasmine quickly pulling her purple panties up around her bottom, and would have begun to serve the others, only I wagged a finger at them.

'Uh, uh, not just yet. As you're so keen to have others wait on you, you may have a sausage each first. Each other's sausages, to be exact.'

Caroline made a face, Jasmine merely hung her head, but both squatted down to delve between their thighs, each extracting a now juice-smeared cocktail sausage from her pussy. Jasmine went first, obediently opening her mouth to let Caroline pop the sausage in, chewing and swallowing before offering hers. Caroline took it between her lips, deliberately sucking as if it was a little cock before eating it.

'Don't show off,' I chided her. 'Very well, you may serve, and I hope that's taught you that in future you're to do so immediately, without waiting to be told.'

I sat back, feeling a great deal better as they began to take the bottles and trays around. Pippa was sent to join them and, with her hands tied, there was nothing Katie could do anyway, but Portia stayed as she was, holding her glass out for white wine and taking three devils-on-horseback at once. Sarah was talking to Duncan and didn't seem to notice, but it wasn't a chance I was about to pass up.

'Isn't your tart rather getting above herself, Sarah?' I remarked, causing her to turn abruptly, her face showing irritation for a brief instant before she managed to put on a cool smile.

Portia threw me a dirty look, but she was caught red handed, her knees crossed, her glass to her nose as she drew in the scent of the Sauvignon Jasmine had poured her and the three devils-on-horseback in her other hand. Sarah hesitated, knowing Portia was deliberately taunting her but not wanting to take the cue from me.

'I shall deal with her presently,' she said after a moment. 'I do beg your pardon, Duncan. What were you saying before I was so rudely interrupted?'

I felt the blood rise to my cheeks, making me grateful for my veil a third time, but no suitable retort came to

71

me. Ignoring Sarah, I turned to Laura, intent on my earlier plan despite the new complexion Pippa's suggestion had put on things.

'Would you like to put Katie through her paces?' I offered, knowing full well that if she accepted she would be honour bound to let me have Pippa.

She answered without hesitation. 'I'd love to. How's her training coming along?'

'Very well,' I replied, ignoring the apprehensive look Katie was giving me over her shoulder. 'I don't get much opportunity to spank her – too noisy – so I've taken to using wax to punish her.'

'On her breasts or on her bottom?'

'Her bottom, so far.'

'You should do her breasts. In fact, there's a little trick I'd like to show you, if that's OK?'

'Be my guest. Katie, come to Mistress Laura. You're to do whatever she says.'

Katie nodded, blushing dark as she stumbled across to where we were sitting. I sat back, sipping my wine, content to watch my girlfriend put through her paces. Laura looked tough, and Katie was openly apprehensive as she was ordered to her knees and got clumsily down. The others had also settled down to enjoy the show: Sarah beside Duncan with Portia snuggled up to her, Pippa intent and plainly excited at the prospect of watching her Mistress torment Katie, and perhaps for what she would get in her turn. Both Jasmine and Caroline had stopped serving, but began again as I snapped my fingers at them.

Laura's face was set in a cruel smile as she leant forwards and began to undo more of the buttons of Katie's Stars and Stripes blouse. With a further three open, Laura pulled the sides apart and gently lifted Katie's breasts free of her bra, sitting them in the open material with her nipples sticking up like her little pink snout of a nose. A touch to each brought the little buds fully erect, and Laura stood up.

'Wax,' she said, as she crossed to the carriage door, 'is not just wax. Excuse me a moment.'

She stepped from the room, leaving Katie looking rather sorry for herself with her erect nipples quivering slightly to the trembling of her body. I reached out to stroke her hair and she smiled, both grateful and rueful, so I began to tease her breasts, stroking the smooth pale skin and gently pinching her nipples. Laura was soon back, the carriage door opening behind me, and I saw Katie's eyes go wide.

I turned, to find Laura carrying three candles. One was huge, as thick as my wrist and at least a foot long despite being somewhat burnt down, made of deep-red wax marked with tiny flecks. The others were plain at the base and stripy further up, black and white, each band about half a centimetre thick, which Laura put to one side as she sat down again. Katie's eyes were riveted to the big candle as Laura extracted a box of matches from the breast pocket of her fatigues and lit it. I laughed.

'I don't think she's going to fuck you with it, darling. Although if you'd like to, Laura . . .'

'No, no,' Laura confirmed, 'that wasn't what I was thinking. Now, hold very still, Katie, and stick those tits out.'

Laura reached out as Katie pushed her chest forwards, to cup one plump little breast in a hand. Katie's trembling became abruptly stronger as the big candle was moved above her breast and tilted carefully sideways. I saw the first drop of wax form a bead and fall, splashing red on Katie's skin to make her gasp and jerk. She closed her eyes, shivering badly, but held still, allowing a second drop and a third to fall on her naked flesh.

I was growing quickly aroused at Katie's pained reaction, as fast as if I'd been the one tormenting her, her little shivers and the way her breasts jerked to the contraction of her muscles a joy to watch. Drop after drop fell, slowly coating the upper surface of one breast, and then the other, but her nipples were left bare. Only when both plump little globes where thickly coated with dark-red wax did Laura go back to the first, this time to do the achingly stiff nipple.

Katie cried out in pain as the first drop touched her sensitive flesh, and again with the next, but still she held her place, allowing Laura to slowly encase her nipple in wax. With one done, Katie's breathing had grown ragged and her head was thrown back, her eyes closed but her mouth wide. Her shaking had grown worse than ever, her chest was heaving and the skin of her neck was flushed pink, a sure sign she needed her sex attended to.

I knew Laura, and that would come, but not until the waxing was finished. Lifting Katie's second breast, Laura began applying drip after drip until the stiff little nipple was completely coated and Katie was gasping and shaking her head with the pain. Her reaction was more intense even than when I'd waxed her anus, to my surprise, and I wondered how Laura had done it.

'Does the wax melt at a higher temperature than usual?' I asked as she finally blew the candle out.

'No,' Laura answered, 'quite low. The little flecks you can see are ground chilli pepper. That's why the wax is red too. Even when it's cooled completely it burns, and it continues to burn. Right, Katie, let's have that fanny out. I suspect you need some attention. Pippa, you may have the privilege of licking Katie. If that's OK with you, Isabelle?'

'Fine. Lift your bottom, Katie, Pippa'll need to get your trousers down, but stay in that position.'

Laura gave a dry chuckle at my remark. Katie nodded, still trembling violently, making her wax-covered breasts quiver and jump as she rose a little higher on her knees. Pippa got down, quickly undoing the button of Katie's white cowgirl jeans and easing

74

them down back and front, first to show off the big white panties with their pattern of rosy peaches, more like little fat bottoms than even the cherries or the apples, then bare skin as those came down in turn.

As I'd intended, Pippa had little choice about how she did her licking. With Katie kneeling up, the only feasible thing to do was get down on the floor and slide in underneath, bottom to face. Even with Katie's thighs parted as far as they would go, Pippa was left with her head firmly trapped in her playmate's lowered knickers. Katie settled a little as the licking began, her plump soft cheeks spreading in Pippa's face, her eyes closed in a rapture that was clearly still pained.

Laura reached out to take one of Katie's breasts in each hand, gently manipulating them to make sure the wax wasn't forgotten. Not that it was likely. In one or two places where bits had chipped off, I could see how red the skin beneath had become, and they were distinctly swollen. Yet however much it hurt, there was no doubting the effect on Katie. She had soon begun to wiggle her bottom in Pippa's face, and to sigh out loud, then to moan, and finally reach a shuddering, gasping orgasm.

'I trust you'll say thank you to Mistress Laura properly, Katie?' I asked as the two girls began to untangle themselves.

'Later, thank you,' Laura said. 'I thought you might like to amuse yourself with Pippa?'

'I would, yes,' I assured her as she picked up the two stripy candles by her side.

'Do as you please with her, of course,' she went on, 'but these are rather fun. You make her bend over and have her push them in, back and front, but not all the way. Each band can represent something, a tin of dog food for instance –'

'No, please! Laura!' Pippa interrupted.

'Shut up, Private, nobody asked for your opinion,' Laura said casually, 'although unfortunately I don't have any dog food. Sorry, Isabelle, as I was saying, each black band can represent something, whatever it might be, any punishment you can think of so long as it can be broken down into bits. You then light the candles and start to beat her, generally aiming between them. For each black band that melts away, she's let off one unit, but if she drops either of the candles she gets the full punishment.'

'How very ingenious,' Sarah remarked, to which Portia responded with a sulky grunt. 'Where do you get the candles?'

'I make them myself,' Laura answered, 'but the really clever bit is this. The deeper she pushes the candles up, the more easily she can hold them, but of course that makes it harder for her because the stripes are nearer her skin. You have to be careful, of course.'

'Of course,' I agreed, 'but it's a great game. Come on, Pippa, trousers down and touch your toes.'

Pippa gave me a sulky look but stood to undo her belt and push down her fatigues, taking the plain white panties she had on underneath with them to bare her full pale bottom to me. She was wonderfully round behind, although softer and fleshier than Katie, her cheeks well tucked under, a mature woman's bottom, a thought that added a certain something to my pleasure at the prospect of tormenting her.

'Pop them in,' I instructed, taking the stripy candles from Laura and holding them out.

I was smiling cheerfully, and ignored Pippa's grimace as she took the candles. For all her maturity and experience, she was blushing as she reached back to ease the first in up her pussy, but her eyes closed in pleasure as she filled her hole. I thought she'd leave it up, but instead she spent a moment fucking herself before easing the candle free and putting the now juicy base to her bumhole. I watched the little pink ring spread with the grin on my face growing to manic delight, and it was all I could do not to rub my hands together in glee as she pushed it deep, but not too deep.

With the first candle wedged firmly in her anus, she slid the second up her pussy, again not too deep, so that with a little courage she would be able to avoid whatever unpleasant punishment I selected for her completely, but only so long as she could hold them in up her holes. It had already occurred to me that the more excited she was the harder she would find it to keep her holes tight, especially her pussy, something I was determined to take advantage of.

'Kneel on a chair,' I instructed her. 'Make yourself comfortable.'

She made for an armchair, shuffling across the room in her lowered garments with the candles wiggling between her tightly clenched bum cheeks. I was enjoying myself immensely as I stood up, determined not only to make her drop the candles, but to choose something really awful as her punishment.

My instinct would have been to make each band worth a stroke of some heavy implement: a cane or tawse perhaps. Yet I was going to beat her anyway, and she was quite a brave girl, but her reaction to the prospect of being made to eat dog food had been delightfully, and amusingly, sharp. I waited until she had arranged herself as comfortably as was possible, kneeling in the armchair with her bottom stuck high and the candles protruding from her twin holes, then spoke.

'Well, Pippa, what are we going to do with you? It's a shame Laura doesn't have any dog food in stock, because watching you eat it would have been highly amusing. What shall it be then? The tawse? No, why bother when you've already been caned. Some of Laura's peculiar wax on those fat breasts? Hmm ... a little hard to quantify, and Katie has just been given the same treatment. Ah yes, I know, each band can

77

represent a glass of your own pee, or mine, if you can't make the full ten glasses.'

She turned her head immediately.

'Oh, Isabelle, please! Not that!' she begged.

'Don't listen to her, Isabelle,' Laura remarked. 'She drinks pee easily enough if she has to. Oh, and one other rule. If you put a candle out while you're beating her, or hit it at all, she gets off.'

I nodded, happy to accept the condition and sure I could cope with it. Pippa was still looking at me, and she'd didn't look happy at all. I was going to relent, but an even more amusing idea occurred to me.

'You don't like the taste of your own pee?' I asked. 'No?'

'No,' she answered firmly.

'Do you really think I care? Do you really think it matters what you do or do not like?'

She didn't speak, but shook her head, her mouth set in a miserable grimace. I was sure her reaction was genuine, and half expected her to use her stop word, but it never came.

'I'm glad you understand that,' I went on, 'but this one time I'll give you a choice. You can drink your pee, or, if you prefer, take the same amount as an enema, with soapy water.'

I glanced at Sarah as I spoke, hoping my veil would conceal my eyes. As Portia had told me, Sarah had been made to take enemas with soapy water before her punishments from Eliza Abbott, ostensibly in case she had an embarrassing accident in her pain, but really just to humiliate her. If looks could kill I would have dropped dead on the spot, but I paid no attention to her whatsoever, folding my arms across my chest as I waited for Pippa's decision.

'Oh God,' she said and sighed, 'you are such a little bitch, Isabelle . . .'

'I beg your pardon.'

'Sorry! Sorry! Sorry! I didn't mean to say that. Don't make it any worse for me, please?'

'After that little outburst, I don't see I have a choice. What do you think, Laura?'

'If you don't punish her, I certainly will,' Laura replied.

'You see?' I addressed Pippa. 'There really is no choice. Each band is now worth two units.'

Pippa's face fell as I spoke, but she didn't answer me, biting her lip as she struggled to make her choice. After a while I began to tap my foot.

'Shall we make that three units per band?' I suggested.

'No, please,' she answered. 'I've decided. I'll have the pee . . . no, the enema . . . no, the pee, the pee.'

'The pee?' I echoed. 'Are you sure.'

'Yes,' she said sighing again, 'quite sure, Mistress Isabelle.'

There was a touch of sarcasm in her voice, but I ignored it. I knew she liked her punishments sudden and unexpected, what Laura called shock treatment, and possibly she was trying to goad me. I had no intention of falling for it, because I knew that the higher I made her and the less attention I paid to her tricks, the more she would respect me. At least, that was how it worked between her and Laura.

'Glasses of pee it is then,' I confirmed. 'Would you like a little water before your beating begins? A couple of litres perhaps?'

'Wine, please,' she answered.

'Jasmine, feed Pippa as much wine as she can hold,' I instructed. 'I think this calls for a specialised implement. A malacca or a dragon perhaps. Stay where you are, Pippa, and don't you dare move until I come back.'

Pippa gave a sullen nod as Jasmine began to uncork a fresh bottle of the Sauvignon. Laura had all sorts of canes, neatly arranged in the compartment she had set aside for her toys. I made for it, slowly, determined not to spoil the dominant elegance of my look by showing my eagerness.

The canes were hung from one of the baggage racks: thick ones, thin ones, long ones, short ones, straight ones and ones with crooked handles like the sort they used to use in English schools – all of different types and treated or finished in different ways. I took a moment to make my selection, choosing a slender, black dragon cane, heavy and stiff, the perfect instrument for the sort of precision work I needed to apply to Pippa's bottom.

As I took it down and turned for the door, a movement outside caught my eye. I turned sharply around, and caught it, just for one instant: a pale face at the window, jerking back as soon as he saw I was looking. It nearly made me jump out of my skin, but my feelings were more of anger than shock as I wrenched open the sliding panel of the window and thrust my head out. I'd recognised the face – Stan Tierney.

All I caught was a glimpse of movement in among the bushes behind the carriage, and a snigger. I was going to shout out, but stopped myself in time. If they, and there was at least one other, made a nuisance of themselves it was going to reflect badly on me, very badly, because I knew them and I'd get the blame. It would also be a blatant breach of the club rules, rules I'd just helped decide on and agreed to. My chances of taking proper control of the Rattaners would become non-existent. I had to make them go away, and quickly, which meant going outside to speak to them

Moving quickly back to the door into Laura's extension, I composed myself before opening it. Everyone was as before, waiting for me: Pippa tipped up in rude and ridiculous display as she drank wine from a cup held by Jasmine, the others on their seats. I fanned my face with my hand, as if hot, before speaking as calmly as I could manage.

'I feel the need for a breath of fresh air, if you'll excuse me. Pippa, stay as you are. Duncan, if you would be so kind to look after Katie for me.'

'My pleasure,' he answered.

I gave a gentle inclination of my head and retreated. I'd been dreading somebody wanting to come outside with me, but no one seemed inclined to follow. Walking quickly to the end of the carriage, I opened the door and peered out. The lights from the extension cast a dull glow across the garden, but the hedge was lost in blackness. I climbed down, awkward in my long dress, but I was grateful for it as I pushed through the long nettles growing between the sleepers. After a dozen paces, I stopped to listen. There was nothing, but I spoke in a hiss.

'Stan Tierney! I saw you. Come out of there now!'

There was a rustle, a whisper, and Big Dave emerged from the shadows, a sheepish grin doing very little to soften the look of his threatening bulk. Tierney followed, looking even more shifty, then Mo, a Chinese man who worked on the line at Cowley with Big Dave and was also a regular from the Red Ox. They were plainly embarrassed, but there was a good deal of lust and aggression there too. I stood my ground.

'What are you doing?' I demanded. 'How did you know we'd be here?'

'We ain't stupid, love,' Tierney answered, 'not like some stuck-up college girls would like to think.'

'You followed us, I suppose. Never mind that anyway. You have to go, now.'

'Go?' he drawled. 'But the party's just getting started.'

'Yeah,' Big Dave put in, Mo hanging back with his round, face split by a big, dirty grin.

I drew my breath in.

'Will you just go away, please!'

'Why should we?' Tierney demanded, as unreasonable as ever.

'Because . . . because you're not invited, for a start!' I answered, struggling to keep my voice down.

'Why not?' Big Dave asked, echoed by Mo.

'Because . . . because –' I managed, struggling to find words to express my outrage at his attitude, only to be interrupted by Tierney.

'We want to join in, that's all,' he protested.

'Yeah, we was all right last time, wasn't we?' Dave added.

I struggled to explain, trying desperately to be reasonable and to control my temper.

'Yes, of course you were, you were great, but . . . but it's not like that.'

'What is it like then?' he demanded.

'Well . . . well,' I tried, 'I don't want you here for a start, Tierney, not after the way you've treated me. I don't mind you, so much, Dave, but . . . but, we really don't want any men at all.'

'Dr Appledore's here, ain't he?' Tierney pointed out.

'Well, yes,' I admitted, 'but . . .'

'Like that is it?' Dave demanded, and the aggression was rising in his voice. 'All right for him but not for us ordinary blokes?'

'No,' I insisted. 'It's not like that at all.'

'Fucking looks like it from here!' he answered.

'She's always been like that,' Tierney assured him, 'a right stuck-up little bitch . . .'

'Yeah,' Dave took over, 'and like all the rest, when she wants it she's a dirty tart, worse.'

'That isn't fair,' I protested, now struggling to keep my voice firm and hold back the tears welling in my eyes. 'Please, would you just go away? We'll talk about it another time.'

'Sure,' Tierney sneered, 'and you'll be back up on your high horse, giving it all that about how it's not right what we're doing and all.'

'No,' I answered, although he'd hit on exactly what I'd been meaning to do.

He gave a snort, expressing both contempt and disbelief.

'What's the problem, anyway, that's what I want to know?' Big Dave demanded. 'Carrie and Jas are up for it, ain't they? Tell you what, let us in and they can suck us off. Then we'll fuck off home, all right?'

'Sounds good to me,' Tierney agreed.

'No,' I answered.

'We just want our cocks sucked,' Dave protested.

I threw my hands up in exasperation, now completely flustered and about to cry. There was no question in my mind that if the others found out the men had followed us who would get the blame – me. Perhaps Jasmine and Caroline too, but that wouldn't matter. I'd get court martialled. Both Tierney and Big Dave had started forwards, and there was only one thing for it.

'No, wait, I . . . I'll suck your cocks if you promise to go away. OK?'

Even as the words tumbled from my mouth I was choking with shame. They stopped, Tierney leering, Big Dave looking thoroughly pleased with himself.

'Yeah, all right,' Dave said.

'Sound good to me,' Mo agreed.

'Yeah, a bit of cock sucking'll be good for you,' Tierney said and laughed. 'Bring you down a peg or two.'

'Not here,' I said, sighing. 'Somebody might see us.'

'In the car's best,' Dave suggested.

I nodded weakly. They took my arms, steering me into the shadows, not towards Laura's gate, but across the lawn, Mo bringing up the rear. As we reached the hedge, Tierney flicked on a miniature torch, illuminating a gap. They had it all worked out, maybe even in advance. After all, Big Dave had been before, so why not?

My skirt caught in the hedge, but they dragged me through, into the lane and a couple of hundred yards down it, to where a red car was parked far enough away from Laura's to make sure the engine noise didn't arouse suspicion.

'You're a scheming bastard, Tierney,' I told him as Mo opened the car door.

The interior light came on, casting a dull yellow glow over the three of them, a scene that made me think of the three trolls from *The Hobbit*.

'For that I'm going to make you suck my balls,' Tierney answered. 'I'm first, lads.'

'Says who?' Dave responded.

'Yeah,' Mo agreed. 'Say's who?'

'I found her,' Tierney argued, jerking his thumb towards me.

'And?' Mo retorted.

'She should choose,' Dave suggested.

'Why?' both the others demanded as one.

''Cause it ain't proper, otherwise,' Dave responded, 'ain't gentlemanly.'

'We ain't fucking gentlemen, Dave,' Mo answered him.

'My tart, I get first dibs, simple,' Tierney insisted.

'I am not your tart!' I snapped. 'Just get on with it, will you. Toss a coin for me or something.'

'Yeah, all right,' Dave agreed.

'How's that work?' Mo queried. 'There are three of us.'

'Just give me a coin,' I said and sighed.

Dave pulled a fifty-pence piece from his pocket and I took it, no doubt looking as sulky as I felt, but hopefully covering the shameful arousal inside me. It wasn't fair, the way I couldn't help my own reactions, but it was going to make it easier as I helped them decide my fate.

I sat down in the passenger seat, where I could see, and flipped the coin, catching it on the back of my hand. The answer didn't matter much. It wasn't whether I had to suck or not, but who I had to suck first. That didn't dilute my feelings as I looked up to the three of them, now standing around the open door.

'Call,' I asked.

'Heads,' Tierney answered, ''cause that's what we're going to get.'

The others laughed. I revealed the coin.

'Tails. Now you, Mo.'

I flipped again. He called heads and it was heads. Dave also got it right. Tierney failed again, Mo succeeded, Dave failed.

'Done,' I announced, struggling to speak for the lump in my throat. 'Mo, then David, then you, Tierney.'

'Stan'll do fine,' he answered, 'seeing how you're about to suck my prick. Oh, and I'm going to spank your arse for you too, not 'cause I'm into that stuff, but you are, and I said I'd do you before the end of term. Yeah, that's right, Isabelle, I'm going to spank your arse.'

He said each of the last three words slowly and clearly, in the half-amused, half-vindictive tone I'd come to dread the year before. It had been much the same then, attending to him as the best of a bad option. Now I was back where he wanted me, obliged to serve, to allow myself to be used for his amusement and to satisfy his gross lust.

I climbed into the back, full of shame and consternation, telling myself over and over that I should back out, but quite unable to do it. My mouth was set in a rueful grimace as Mo got in beside me, a big, ugly grin plastered across his face. He wasted no time, pulling open his trousers and pushing down the front of a pair of grubby blue Y-fronts to flop out his cock and balls.

He was thick and short, the glossy tip of his helmet already poking out from his unpleasantly fleshy foreskin. I looked at it, thinking of how often I'd told myself I'd never suck cock again unless it was by my own, clear choice. That no longer mattered. He wanted it sucked, and I had to do the sucking.

'Come on, you little tart, it won't be the first time, and we both know it,' he said as I hesitated.

'I know,' I admitted, lifted my veil and went down on his cock.

He tasted of oil and grease and man, strongly, making me gag and swallow quickly to get it down. I felt his hand as he slipped it under me, taking hold of a breast, but I didn't try to stop him. Anything that helped to get it over quickly was good, and yet it was impossible to fight against my rising arousal as his thick clumsy fingers groped at me and his cock grew slowly bigger in my mouth. I was being made to submit, in a sense, and I couldn't help my reaction.

By the time he was hard he'd got my breasts out of my corset, both dangling free beneath me with the nipples erect and sensitive as his fat fingers loitered on my bare skin. He was so thick my jaw was agape, but short enough to let me get him all in, with his helmet now a bulbous plug to my throat. I took his balls in my hand, stroking them as I told myself it was just to make him come more quickly.

He began to grunt, and to fuck my head, jamming himself up into my mouth as I struggled to suck him. My head was taken and forced down, my eyes popped as his helmet was jammed into my gullet, his fingers closed hard on the breast he was fondling, and he'd come. It erupted into my throat, making me gag, and if he hadn't had his cock so deep it would have gone everywhere.

Even as he pulled back I was choking, but I couldn't risk it in my face, and was forced to swallow. My face screwed up as the slimy, foul-tasting mess slid down my throat, but I had no choice but to eat it, and did. He gave a final, pleased grunt as he finally let go of my breast and head, allowing me to lift up.

'Nice one,' he said. 'Not so bad, was it?'

I couldn't find an answer, and he was no sooner gone than Big Dave was squeezing into the seat.

'Tits out, nice,' he remarked as he saw that I'd had my breasts exposed.

Like Mo, he wasted no time with preliminaries, grinning at me as he released his cock from his fly, not even bothering to undo his trousers properly, so that the meaty wrinkled shaft was sticking up on its own. Generally, he'd been kinder than the others, which made it just a little less humiliating as I bent to take the great ugly thing in my mouth.

'Kneel up on the seat, darling,' he drawled as I began to suck. 'I fancy a grope of your arse.'

Once again as I obeyed I was telling myself it was only because whatever made them quicker was to the good. Bringing my knees up onto the seat, it took me a moment to get into position in the cramped space, and I was left with my bum stuck high and my head right down as I took him in my mouth again. His hand immediately settled on the seat of my beautiful long skirt, first groping, then beginning to pull at the material.

I hid a sigh, but let him do it, concentrating on my sucking as my dress was bunched up and turned over onto my back. He wanted me bare too, fumbling with the seat of my camisole in a vain effort to pull down what he must have thought were French knickers. He was going to grope me anyway, maybe tear the pretty, brand new garment, so I briefly pulled my head up from his cock.

'There are poppers between my legs, David.'

'Cheers, Isa,' he answered, and his huge fingers went to my crotch, pinching the fabric and my flesh too.

I winced, but I'd already taken him back in my mouth and said nothing.

'Dirty bitch, like I said,' Tierney's voice sounded from outside the car. 'Stick a cock in her mouth and she's anybody's.'

Mo laughed and I closed my eyes, feeling utterly helpless and thoroughly ashamed of myself, because I was enjoying not only the cock in my mouth as he grew rapidly to erection, but the feel of his big hard fingers on my now naked bottom. He didn't hold back either, fondling my cheeks and between, using a fingertip to tickle my anus and, after a moment, stuffing another roughly up my pussy.

I sucked harder, praying I wouldn't lose control completely and that I could make him come before he decided to fuck me. My hand closed on his shaft and I was masturbating him into my mouth, urgently, as his finger pushed in and out of my embarrassingly wet hole.

'She's ready this one,' Dave said, chuckling after a moment, 'well up for it.'

'Fuck her then,' Tierney drawled from outside, 'we can spit-roast the stuck-up little bitch.'

'Yeah, nice,' Dave answered, and my head was pulled from his cock.

As he scrambled out of the car, I was shaking my head, but I didn't mean it. It was all too much. I was meant to be caning Pippa. Instead I was down on my knees on the back seat of a car, my mouth full of the taste of cock and sperm, my bottom bare behind me. The sense of chagrin was unbearable, quickly bringing the tears to my eyes, but there was nothing to be done about it. It had got to me, leaving me ripe for cock, which was just what I was going to get.

When Tierney got into the car with his trousers already down and his cock and balls hanging from the slit of his dirty grey underpants I took him straight in my mouth. I'd always felt it unfair that the short wizened Tierney should have such a nice cock, big and smooth and well formed, the sort of cock that should have belonged to a handsome young man, not a grubby old one. He was already half stiff, and I was sucking eagerly as I felt the car shift to Dave's weight.

'Do my bollocks now,' Tierney demanded, and he pulled my head up, feeding the fat wrinkly sac to me as Dave began to grope my bottom once more.

As I began to roll Tierney's balls in my mouth my bottom was spread wide, my cheeks held open between Dave's thumbs and his cock was pushed for my hole. It touched my anus and, for one awful moment, I thought he was going to bugger me, unlubricated, before he slipped lower and his full length was jammed roughly up my pussy.

Dave grunted and took me by the hips. Tierney lifted my head once more, dislodging my hat, and I was getting what they'd told me I would, a cock in each end, like a pig on a spit. Not a roast pig though, an eager, dirty little pig, wiggling her bottom on one cock and mouthing rudely on the other as they used me. I wanted to come, but I was kneeling on my skirt and I couldn't get at myself, adding intense frustration to my burning feelings.

They'd made me offer to suck their cocks. They'd had me toss a coin to see who could go first. They'd pulled out my breasts and stripped my bottom. They'd groped me and fingered me and finally fucked me, making a pig roast of me, when at that very moment I should have been punishing Pippa, elegant and dominant in my beautiful clothes, not grovelling half-naked on the back seat of a car as two men used me back and front.

Tierney came and, for the second time in a few minutes, my mouth was filled with sperm. I swallowed frantically, and was still sucking it up from his cock as Big Dave grunted and jerked himself free. I felt the hot fluid spatter on my skin and I knew he'd come all over my bottom, probably soiling my pretty camisole as well, and my skirt. I had to stay as I was, sobbing with frustration as the sperm began to trickle down over my upturned bottom, and beg for help.

'Please ... please could you clean me up a little, Dave? If I get caught ...'

'Sure, love,' he answered, not waiting for an explanation.

Mo said something. Tierney laughed and, a moment later, something soft and oddly slippery touched my bottom, wiping up the sperm as I caught a familiar scent.

'What are you using?' I managed.

'Mo's car rag,' Dave answered me. 'It's a bit oily, I'm afraid.'

'Thank you very much,' I responded, but if they even heard the sarcasm in my voice not one of them paid any attention.

I thought I'd at least got away with the spanking, but no. Tierney came behind me while my bottom was still being wiped and gave me a dozen slaps, not even hard ones. Not that it mattered how hard they were. What mattered was that he'd said he'd spank my bottom before the term was out and I was getting it within just a few days, adding a final agonising touch to my shame.

A few minutes more and I was at least outwardly decent, although I was sure my bottom was smeared with oil. They kept their word, to my immense relief, but I stayed in the lane until I could no longer hear the engine of Mo's car, just to be certain. Only then did I turn back for the house, and went to the loo to check my appearance and make a half-hearted attempt to wipe my bottom properly before joining the others.

I had completely disgraced myself, but I'd done what I had to do, which was at least some consolation. Unfortunately it had also taken rather a long time, so long I was surprised nobody had come out to look for me. They had – Katie and Duncan – but I explained I'd felt dizzy and taken a walk along the lane to get some fresh air and they accepted it.

Pippa was exactly as I'd left her and she gave me a look of bitter reproach as I came in. I ignored her, flexing my cane as I stepped behind her, took careful

90

aim across the tuck of her cheeks, directly between the two candles, lifted the thin black rod, and brought it down . . .

. . . catching the candle up her bottom and putting the flame out. Sarah laughed.

Five

The rest of the Rattaners' evening had been a brilliant success, at least for everybody except me. I couldn't get what had been done to me out of my head, unsure if I wanted to come over it or cry about it, and I didn't dare let anyone see my bottom because I was sure my cheeks were still smeared with oil, which would have taken a bit of explaining. I had to pretend I felt faint, and had spent the rest of the evening sitting on Laura's bed with my corset unlaced and Katie attending to me while the others enjoyed themselves.

Despite everything I felt a certain pride at having defused the situation, but if they could do it once, they could do it again, and I was sure they would. It was extremely awkward, because the next time they might not be put off, while I couldn't very well demand a change of venue without good reason, and I couldn't give my reason without Sarah demanding I be punished.

I was obviously going to have to go up to the Red Ox and sort it out, and before our next meeting. That was in three weeks, at the end of fifth week, and there was a great deal I needed to do first. There was Eliza Abbot, who I was determined to contact if only for a chance of wiping the smug expression off Sarah's face once and for all, and preferably watching her being given an enema and soundly spanked.

It was also well worth while trying to find a new venue, but no easy task. The only real disadvantage of Laura's was that the men from the Red Ox knew about it, but I needed to keep that quiet. It was perhaps a little far from Oxford, but that was a minor inconvenience. To even be worth considering, a venue had to be more conveniently sited, private, secluded and a good place to have parties from the point of view of rooms and equipment.

I'd put my meeting with Dr Treadle and what he'd told me about reconditioning to the back of my mind, so much so that when I happened to find him standing at an adjoining set of shelves in Blackwell's on the Tuesday afternoon it took me a moment to realise what he was talking about.

'And how is Dr Watson's theory bearing out?'

'I'm sorry? Oh . . . yes, I see, that Dr Watson . . .'

'Yes, the famous ethologist, not Sherlock Holmes' amanuensis.'

'Of course . . . er . . . I haven't really had a chance to discuss it with Sarah yet, not in any depth. It's rather an awkward subject.'

'So I would imagine. She is understandably sensitive.'

He shook his head and I smiled encouragingly, hoping he might provide some new pearl of wisdom.

'I always knew Eliza was something of a virago,' he went on, 'but I would never have guessed she went to such extremes. Remarkable.'

'Yes,' I agreed, 'although who knows what people get up to behind closed doors.'

'Indeed so,' he replied, 'especially, as the gentleman upon whom we have just remarked observed, in lonely country houses.'

'Er . . . you've lost me, I'm afraid.'

'Sherlock Holmes, who remarked to Dr Watson that the country was a sinister place because in a remote house nobody could hear you scream, or words to that effect. Quite wrong, of course, because in the country

everybody knows everybody else's business, more so
then than now.'

'Do you think so?'

'Absolutely. The view from my study window, for
instance, is of the fields rising to Whytham Wood, and
it's unusual if there's so much as a tractor to be seen. In
the nineteenth century the same scene would have been
crawling with labourers.'

'I suppose that's true, now you mention it. You don't
live in then?'

'No, no. I purchased a house soon after taking up my
post, rather cheaply, as the ring road runs more or less
through the bottom of my garden.'

'That's a shame.'

'It is quite a long garden. You should pay me a visit.
Perhaps for tea one afternoon?'

'That would be delightful, thank you.'

'My pleasure, I assure you. Shall we say Thursday?'

I had accepted Dr Treadle's invitation, but I was very
much in two minds about him. There had been a distinct
twinkle in his eye as he treated me to tea and cake at
the Twistleton after meeting in Blackwell's, and he had
made more than one remark that might have been
interpreted as suggestive. It occurred to me that he
might have realised I hadn't simply been being polite
after we'd met before and might be considering whether
I could be taken advantage of.

Yet it was impossible not to be intrigued, and not
only because of my guilty, secretive penchant for being
manhandled by dirty old men. His house had to be at
least a possible venue, a lot closer than Laura's, but
perhaps as secluded, even with the main road so close.
At the very least it was worth investigating. Besides that,
he was affable, civilised and, as a middle-aged bachelor,
presumably fairly easy to keep happy, infinitely prefer-
able to Stan Tierney.

I considered taking Katie, in order to defuse the situation, but decided against it. One way or the other, I was sure I could look after myself, and if it did come to the crunch, he was hardly likely to be very different from Duncan, whose demands I was only too happy to accommodate. Besides, she hadn't been invited, so it would be rude.

In order to leave for Portsmouth early on the Friday I had rescheduled my tutorial with Duncan for the Thursday afternoon, so I left St George's shortly after three o'clock with a hot bottom and a warm glow all through. It was a fair way to Whytham, right across the top of town and out across the Thames at Wolvercote, but it was a beautiful autumn day, and I enjoyed the ride, especially once I was out of town with the meadows to either side and the woods rising in front of me.

Dr Treadle's house proved easy to find, a little way south of the village, standing on its own, and I stopped in admiration. It was built of red brick, and had a distinctly Gothic flavour, with high gables and tall chimney stacks, along with a round tower built into one corner. The brickwork was old, with flowers growing in cracks in the mortar and along the top of a crumbling wall, which faced the road and apparently enclosed part of the garden.

As he'd said, the drawback was the proximity of the ring road, but he'd exaggerated when he said it cut through the bottom of his garden, which ended at a pretty stream, with the embankment only rising another fifty yards beyond. It was noisy though, and easy to see that before the road was built the location would have been idyllic, with a view across the Thames water meadows to the spires of Oxford beyond. Despite the road, it was easy to imagine the house as the location of a Rattaners' party.

I pushed my bike the last few yards to his door and chained it up before ringing the bell. Dr Treadle answered it almost immediately, perhaps having seen me in the road. He looked as dapper as ever, in a suit of distinctly old-fashioned cut and a cravat of bright-blue silk over an open-necked shirt. Knowing how formal he could be, I'd dressed smartly myself, in a yellow woollen skirt and a crisp white blouse, not the easiest outfit to cycle in, but I was glad of my choice as I entered the house.

Unlike his office, it was immaculately tidy, and also eccentric in the extreme, at least by modern standards. The first thing that caught my eye as I entered the hall was a case of stuffed birds, not the exotic, brightly plumaged species I'd have expected, but a dozen coal tits, seemingly frozen in a quarrel.

'Studliness,' he remarked cryptically, noting my interest, but my gaze had already moved on to the stuffed ostrich standing by the base of the stairs.

Dr Treadle chuckled.

'Meet Esmond,' he said, for all the world as if introducing me to a friend.

He stepped towards the ostrich and I followed, astonished to find such a thing in a private house. It was male, I could tell, not only because it was called Esmond, but from the striking black and white plumage. The head was well over a foot above mine, with the beady glass eyes giving a look of fixed outrage.

'Magnificent, isn't he?' Dr Treadle stated, and reached out to the bird's tail.

With a single, delicate twitch of his fingers he extracted one of the long, feathery plumes, holding it out as he went on.

'An extraordinary piece of design, the feather, do you not think? Flight, insulation, display, camouflage; extraordinary versatility, while there are of course uses to which it may be put that the birds never intended.'

As he finished he brushed the long plume across my cheek, very gently, but tickling so much I flinched and gave a little involuntary giggle. He didn't do it a second time, but his eyes were bright with mischief and he was smiling as he replaced the feather. Clearly Esmond could be plucked and set right at will, which seemed more than a little peculiar, while there was no mistaking the implications of brushing the feather against my cheek. It was a small thing, nothing even the most prim of girls would have made a fuss over, but physical contact for all that, and strangely intimate because it had made me giggle, a tiny surrender of self control.

'Tea awaits us,' he stated, moving on towards where a panelled door stood open at the far side of the hall.

I took a last glance around, at the stuffed birds and the heavy gilt frames holding old pictures of a snowy owl, martins over a windswept marsh and a man with an immense beard – all set against the dark wood panelling. Had I been in my corset and Victorian underwear I might have looked a touch improper, but by no means out of place. Only the telephone provided the slightest hint of modernity, and that looked as if it was pre-war.

The room he led me into was also panelled in dark wood, but only two-thirds of the way up the walls, with a picture rail and elaborate sculpted plasterwork above and on the ceiling. Bookcases covered a good deal of the wall space, the centre of the floor was occupied by a rug woven in strong tones of red, deep blue and gold and a set of old but fine leather-upholstered furniture was arranged around a low table. Large arched windows set with red-stained glass in fleurs-de-lys at the top allowed the room to be bathed in warm, richly coloured sunlight.

He had clearly expected me to be punctual. Tea was already set out on the table: a pot, two cups with teaspoons, two plates with knives, a jug of cream and a bowl full of sugar lumps, were all arranged on a silver tray, which in turn rested on a lace trimmed white cloth.

To one side was a cake stand, bearing exactly the same sort of lemon sponge I had chosen at the Twistleton. A plate held half-a-dozen slices of thinly cut brown bread, already buttered.

It was impossible not to be enthralled by the atmosphere of the house, by his solicitude and by his eccentricity, which I found both intriguing and refreshing. My cheek still tingled to the touch of the ostrich feather as I sat down, and I had already decided that if I was to be seduced, Dr Treadle's technique had a great deal to be said for it.

'Bread and butter?' he offered, extending the plate.

'Thank you.'

I took a slice, remembering how my grandmother had been the same, insistent that my cousins and I took a slice of brown bread and butter before indulging in anything so decadent as cake or biscuits. Dr Treadle evidently belonged to the same school of thought, displaying a genteel etiquette half a century or more out of date. I even wondered if I should cut the bread with my knife, and waited until he had taken a neat bite from the corner of his own piece before starting mine.

He continued the ritual of serving tea, in a manner of which Granny would have entirely approved. I accepted my cup, sipping the hot fragrant liquid as he explained to me about the coal tits, and how the amount of black on their breasts related to the pecking order among the males. The nervousness I'd felt cycling up had vanished completely, leaving me relaxed and happy to accept whatever the occasion brought. In the timeless, refined atmosphere he had created, even the problems of the Rattaners seemed, if not unimportant, a game.

We stretched tea out to nearly an hour, our conversation at first polite and a trifle guarded, but slowly growing more open. He did most of the talking, full of stories about his life, his travels and Oxford, frequently illustrated with asides on the behaviour of birds. He wasn't always easy to follow, and assumed I had a great deal of knowledge I didn't, so I listened, sipped my tea and ate lemon cake, genuinely interested, and all the more so when Eliza Abbot came into the conversation.

I kept my white lies to a minimum, implying that while my mother and she had been at school the relationship had been somewhat one sided. Only when he gave an understanding nod in response did I realise the implications of what I'd said, and nearly choked on my lemon cake before I could recover myself.

He paid no attention and continued happily with his description of how they'd met, as postgraduates, some thirty years before. She sounded terrifying, even as a young woman, absolutely forthright, 100 per cent certain of herself and her sexuality. It seemed that her unashamed advocacy of open lesbianism as a valid lifestyle had been so ferocious that what opposition there was had melted before her. Before she had accepted her post as a junior lecturer she had managed to get a lesbian stand accepted as normal at freshers' fair, something that apparently would have been unthinkable only a few years earlier.

Yet for all her openness it seemed she had kept her dark side firmly to herself, with the sole exception of Sarah. Dr Treadle had never suspected anything of the sort, although he'd been well aware that her blue-stocking exterior hid a somewhat wicked, even malign, sense of humour. She had apparently admitted to having been what used to be called a 'madcap' at school, and had only avoided expulsion due to her brilliant academic record after sneaking out at night to paint the founder's statue purple.

He also remembered Sarah, but only as a very quiet girl who barely ever spoke and gave the impression that she found even making eye contact with a man almost physically painful. The conversation moved back to her as we finished tea.

'I recall seeing her on one occasion when I happened to call in at Eliza's rooms when she was at St Mary's. I don't suppose you know the Wallace Block there, but where it joins onto the main buildings there is a maze of roofs. Eliza's room looked out over them, and Sarah was sunbathing on the leads. At least, I imagine it was Sarah. She was in a bikini, skimpy perhaps, but quite decent, yet I've never seen anybody cover up quite so fast in my life, or blush so hard.'

'I can guess why,' I said and laughed, completely off guard.

'And may I share the secret?' he asked, lifting one grey eyebrow.

I hesitated, but only for a moment. After all, he already knew about her conditioning.

'I imagine she'd had her bottom spanked.'

'Good heavens! Really?'

'Really,' I answered, amused by the tone of his voice, full of shock but also fascination.

I decided to tease a little.

'Eliza used to spank her regularly,' I went on, 'and always on the bare bottom. They had a little ritual.'

'Indeed?'

He was fascinated, completely hooked, and it was completely beyond me not to tell him.

'Yes,' I told him, relishing every word, 'Eliza used to spank Sarah, always on the bare bottom, and usually after giving her an enema.'

'An enema? Great heavens!'

'Yes, supposedly for hygiene reasons, but that was just an excuse. In practice it was to humiliate her.'

'To humiliate her?'

'Yes. That was an essential part of their ritual. First Sarah would be told to strip naked, then she would be given her enema and soundly spanked. As you know, Eliza is a sadist, and took pleasure in treating Sarah badly . . .'

100

'. . . by acts that as a masochistic Sarah enjoyed?'

'Exactly.'

'Who would have thought.'

'Now you see why she kept it secret. Lesbianism is one thing, but . . .'

'Absolutely. And, um . . . ah . . . without wishing to intrude, am I to assume that Sarah and yourself are now in a relationship?'

'Just good friends,' I answered, unwilling to admit more, let alone attempt to explain the full complexities of our relationship.

'I see,' he said, 'and she now finds the excesses of her youth an inconvenience, most specifically the conditioned reflex, which, I can see, cannot possibly have been done without not only her consent, but her active participation.'

'Sarah was willing, yes, completely willing, and she doesn't regret what she did at all. It's more that nowadays she prefers to give rather than take, spankings that is.'

He shook his head and I wondered if I'd gone too far. His face was very red indeed, and he seemed to be beyond speech, yet the rather conspicuous bulge in the front of his trousers suggested that however shocked he was, his reaction was far from prudish. He saw where I was looking and went redder still, hastily positioning his teacup over the evidence of his arousal as he spoke.

'I must apologise, but I confess that I am more than a little flustered.'

'Don't apologise,' I answered him. 'It's entirely understandable. In fact . . .'

I hesitated. It was the crucial moment, an offer to play with his cock sure to break down what barriers remained between us. After that, anything would be possible. There was a lump in my throat, a knot in my stomach and my sense of erotic humiliation was rising sharply, but it had to be done.

'In fact,' I continued, 'if you like, I might be able to help you relieve that.'

It wasn't the most romantic of propositions, but it didn't need to be. I wasn't offering a loving relationship but simply sex, for the sake of his comfort as much as anything else. He swallowed, perhaps wondering if I really meant it, or was teasing, even acting in bad intent.

'I mean what I say,' I assured him. 'I've obviously made you excited, and it's only fair to help. Come on, let me get your cock out for you.'

He nodded weakly and put his cup and saucer down, exposing the bulge of what looked like quite a healthy-sized erection. I put my plate down and was about to get down on my knees when he spoke again, his voice halting and severely flustered.

'You are ... ah ... really a most generous young lady, Isabelle, but please ... I wouldn't dream of having you do anything you didn't –'

'Don't be silly, Dr Treadle,' I interrupted him. 'It's no trouble at all.'

'Ah ... um ... yes, well in that case I ... that is to say, what I would really like to do, if it's not too much to ask, would be to ...'

He hesitated, obviously embarrassed, and I gave him an encouraging smile, hoping it would be something I could cope with.

'... tickle you,' he finally finished.

'Tickle me?' I echoed.

'Yes. Perhaps with a feather?'

I hesitated, taken aback.

'Yes, I suppose so ... all right, if you like. Just tickle me?'

'Exactly that, although it would need to be, I think, on the bare?'

'Yes, naturally. So, what part of me would you like to tickle, my feet?'

'A delight ... but, um ... ah ... perhaps, if, of course, you don't mind ... your ah ... um ... chest?'

I laughed, starting to regain my composure.

'If you like,' I replied, 'but is that really all? I really don't mind giving you a hand with your cock. In fact, I'd like to.'

'Thank you. What a delightful offer, and perhaps . . . yes, if you are of a mind. Afterwards?'

'If you like.'

'I do, very much. Shall we retire upstairs?'

I'd been halfway down to my knees, and really quite keen to suck his cock in the quiet reserved atmosphere of his drawing room. The bedroom is where sex is supposed to happen, which makes it less naughty, like fucking in missionary position rather than on all fours or some other rude pose.

'Here will do very nicely,' I told him, putting my fingers to the buttons of my blouse as I sat back in my chair. 'Are you going to fetch a feather from Esmond then?'

'Yes . . . absolutely, in just a moment,' he answered, his eyes fixed firmly on the open neck of my blouse.

I smiled, rather enjoying his attention as I began to undo my buttons. There is something about having a man, or a woman, completely and utterly enthralled that is both amusing and highly arousing. Yet from the expression on Dr Treadle's face what I had agreed to allow him to do was going to make him my worshipful slave for life, which was a pity, as whatever my attitude to other girls, I do prefer men who take control.

His gaze remained firmly level as he watched me undo myself. As each button came open his eyes flickered a little, and when I opened the sides of my blouse to show my bra he gave a little sigh. Merely lifting my bra seemed inappropriate, impossibly slovenly in such genteel surroundings, so I reached back to undo the catch and slipped it off out of one sleeve. My hair had fallen across my chest and I tossed it back before fully opening my blouse to show him my bare breasts.

'Beautiful,' he said sighing. He then rose and hastened from the room.

I felt naughty, but also slightly silly, not the sense of being in an utterly ridiculous pose I get when bent bare bottom across a man's knee, but just that the situation was a touch foolish. It was, in a very English and very eccentric way: sitting at tea with my breasts showing, waiting for a middle-aged don to tickle me with a feather.

His smile had become a manic grin when he returned, holding up not one, but two of Esmond's long, fluffy tail feathers. I pushed my breasts out as he came to stand in front of me, keen to play his game, however bizarre. In response he smacked his lips, twiddled the ostrich feathers between his fingers and applied them to my skin, right on my nipples.

My muscles jerked instinctively and my mouth came open in a little 'O' of shock; my hands went to my breasts automatically, to shield them from the unbearable tickling sensation, even as I burst into a fit of completely involuntary giggles. He stood back, his eyes glittering, his teeth bared in a rictus grin.

'Sorry,' I managed, baring myself once more.

'No, no,' he answered, in childish delight, 'that is precisely the right reaction, my dear. Once again, if I might?'

I nodded and once more pushed my breasts out. My nipples had started to go hard, and my flesh was twitching in anticipation of the unbearable tickling sensation even before the feathers had touched my skin. When they did I was giggling on the instant, and kicking my feet on the carpet in a desperate effort not to shield myself which lasted all of a few seconds.

'Oh joy,' he breathed as I finally gave in, curling up with my hands clasped to my chest and shaking my head in desperation.

Again I exposed myself, this time biting my lip and wiggling my toes as I put myself on offer, my breasts pushed well up, my now stiff nipples standing to attention for him. Smiling, he moved one feather close, just brushing a nipple.

'Tickle, tickle,' he said chortling as I winced. 'How lovely you are, Isabelle.'

I forced a smile, wondering how I could possibly have seen his desire to tickle me as anything other than controlling, dominant. Just the touch of the feathers reduced me to utter helplessness, while I had begun to feel distinctly warm between my thighs.

'Once more,' he said happily, only now it was an instruction and not a request.

Bravely I thrust out my chest. He began to tickle, chuckling to himself and repeating the word over and over as I began to squirm and stamp my feet. I took it for maybe fifteen seconds before once more curling up in helpless laughter. As he stood back once more he gave a sigh of deepest satisfaction. The bulge in his trousers was as big as ever, and I was keen to play and reached out to touch. I could feel the shape of his cock, long if not that thick, but before I could pull his zip down he wagged a finger at me.

'Patience, my dear, patience,' he chided, his voice now full of confidence. 'If, perhaps, I might be permitted to tickle your bottom first? On the bare.'

'On the bare, of course,' I answered, trying to hide a sigh.

I was turned on, but it made me feel so out of control and, like being spanked, there was something in me that wanted it, and another part that didn't. The difference was that being spanked was an important part of me, while being tickled wasn't. Yet it was only fair to play, and I quickly turned over on the chair, kneeling in the seat with my elbows on the back and my chin rested on one hand.

'I'm all yours,' I told him.

Once again he twiddled his fingers in sheer exuberant joy, before reaching forwards to push the feathers into my hair, together and behind one ear as if I were a squaw in a game of cowboys and Indians. Feeling more foolish than ever, I waited patiently as he fumbled my skirt up my thighs and over my bottom, letting out another one of his satisfied sighs as the seat of my panties came on show. They were white and full cut, spanking panties for Duncan, and I wondered if my cheeks were still red at the sides.

'How tasteful,' he remarked, applying a gentle pat to the taut white cotton of my knickers, 'and such a pretty bottom. Pert, yes, decidedly pert. I take it I may pull your knickers down? Bare is bare, is it not?'

'Thank you,' I answered. 'Yes, you can pull my knickers down.'

He didn't do it immediately, but stuck his thumbs into my waistband and paused, savouring the moment before he levered my panties slowly down over my bottom. I was sure I'd still be red, and that he'd realise I'd been fairly freshly spanked, and sure enough, as my knickers were inverted around my thighs, he gave a low chuckle and took a pinch of my flesh.

'You seem a trifle rosy, my dear,' he stated. 'Am I to infer that you enjoy the same treatment to your delightful posterior as young Sarah?'

'Yes,' I admitted. I hesitated and then decided to tell him with a flush of deliciously erotic shame: 'My tutor spanks me.'

'Your tutor spanks you?' he echoed. 'Splendid, and so he should. Who says undergraduates don't have the right stuff in them these days, eh?'

I didn't answer, but hung my head, my feelings building fast, and wishing that instead of tickling me he was about to punish me, maybe spank me, maybe apply a half-dozen cuts of the cane to my naked, vulnerable bottom. I was vulnerable too, very vulnerable, with my bottom pushed well down and my panties right down so I showed behind, the air cool on my moist, pouted pussy

106

lips, my bottom hole twitching a little in anticipation of the ostrich feathers, sure he would tickle between my cheeks.

'There we are then,' he announced, taking the feathers from my hair, 'a perfect bottom, all rosy too. Now, if you would be so kind as to stick it out a little more?'

A sob escaped my throat as I pulled my back in, allowing my cheeks to open properly and making a yet ruder display of my anus, as always hoping he'd realise I was naturally brown and not dirty. He said nothing, but stood back a little, drinking in the view of my exposed body, every intimate detail on plain show. After a moment I looked back, to discover that he'd taken his cock out, long, pale and fully erect in his hand as he nursed himself and feasted his eyes on my body.

'You . . . you can have me if you like,' I managed. 'I don't mind.'

'I shall,' he answered, 'but not yet. Tickle, tickle, my dear.'

He'd already reached out with the feathers and, as he spoke, he drew them up between my thighs and my bottom cheeks. I was giggling immediately, unable to hold myself, or, after just a few seconds, not to reach back and cover my bottom. It was too much, making my pussy twitch, and my bladder tighten, so that after all the tea I'd drunk I was seriously worried I might have an accident, which would have been hideously embarrassing.

'Sorry,' I told him, taking my hands away, 'try again.'

Once more the feathers were applied to my bottom, tickling in my crease to set my anus clenching in helpless response and my feet kicking in the chair as I struggled to take it. I couldn't, reaching back to protect myself in just seconds, and I was unable to stop giggling even when he took the feather away.

'You react wonderfully,' he chuckled. 'Now, if you would excuse me . . .'

He trailed off, and I realised he was going to fuck me as he dropped the feathers onto the tea tray and took a firm grip on my hips. I set my knees a touch further apart, glad the tickling was over and eager for sex. His cock touched my pussy, a little low, then just right, sliding deep in up my slippery hole with a single push. Immediately I was moaning in pleasure, more than content to be fucked in the thoroughly rude kneeling position, with my bum on full show as he enjoyed me. I was even going to masturbate, intent on coming while he was inside me, but no sooner had my fingers found the wet purse of my sex than he had pulled out.

'Don't stop!' I protested. 'You haven't come, have you?'

'Oh no,' he assured me, 'not yet. So impatient, you young girls.'

I sighed as he picked the feathers up again. My cheeks tightened, involuntarily and, an instant later, I was giggling and kicking in the chair, only to once more fail and reach back to protect myself. He gave an amused cough.

'Sorry,' I said, yet again. 'I can't help it. I don't know, perhaps if you held my hands behind up my back?'

'A trifle inconvenient,' he answered, giving his cock shaft a few tugs to show why, 'and yet, perhaps ... Might I tie your hands, just lightly?'

I hesitated, but it was impossible to imagine him abusing my trust and I nodded. He gave a happy chuckle and moved to the side of the room to unfasten a curtain tie, soft dark green rope almost as thick as my wrists, which I crossed obediently behind my back as he came close. Good to his word, he merely twisted the tie several times around, trapping my hands, but only so long as I didn't fight too much. With the ends twisted together I was helpless enough though, at least for his purposes.

'If I start to beg or anything, just ignore me,' I told him, 'but if I say the word "red", stop immediately.'

He gave a nod of understanding.

Again he got behind me, again my cheeks clenched even before the feathers touched my skin and again they were applied full between my cheeks, to my pussy lips and my bumhole and my inner thighs. I was twitching and kicking on the instant, giggling stupidly too, but this time I couldn't protect myself, my hands merely jerking in my bonds and I began to lose control.

'Tickle! Tickle!' he crowed, in abandoned delight, as I began to squirm in desperation, now wriggling my bottom and tossing my hair.

It was nearly as bad as being spanked in bondage, with all the consternation and sense of utter helplessness, and if there was no pain as such, the jerking of my muscles and the effect of my uncontrollable giggling wasn't far off. There was no let up either, no time to catch my breath. He kept the feather right between my cheeks, creating a constant, maddening tickling sensation from which there was no escape.

In no time I was thrashing in desperation and begging him to stop, broken words between fits of hysterical giggling, and still he tickled. I began to squirm my bottom about, frantic to get just an instant of relief, but he seemed to follow my every movement, even as I began to buck up and down, no doubt a completely ludicrous sight, but about which I could do absolutely nothing.

It just happened, completely unexpectedly. One moment I was wriggling like an eel in the chair, and the next I lost control of my bladder, exploding a great gush of pee backwards from my pussy, all over Dr Treadle, his exquisite carpet, his chair and his tea things. He stopped immediately, and I was babbling apologies and sobbing my heart out, but I couldn't stop it, spurt after spurt of piddle erupting from my sex in time to hard, helpless contractions of my body.

I didn't even realise I was coming, at first, but I was, my pussy in contraction as hard and unstoppable as ever, even with pee squirting out. As my hands finally slipped free of the restraining cord they went straight to my sex and I was rubbing myself with a truly demented urgency, finally locking my pee off as I brought myself to peak after peak after peak. Even as I climaxed I was burning with shame for my own behaviour, but I didn't stop. I couldn't stop.

Nor could Dr Treadle, grabbing me by the hips and pushing the full length of his erection up me from behind, to fuck me at a furious pace, deep in, grunting and gasping as his front smacked into my cheeks over and over. He came in no time, my last few, hard contractions on his cock as he held it deep up me, and the sperm bubbled out over my sex. Only when I'd quite finished did he pull back, to leave me gasping in the chair with his come trickling down among the hairs of my pussy and falling in clots to the carpet. Even when I'd begun to get my breath back I couldn't think of anything to say, nor bear to look at the mess I'd made. At last he spoke.

'Oh dearie me, how unfortunate.'

Six

'Unfortunate' seemed to me an understatement to say the least, but Dr Treadle had been determined to put a brave face on it. We cleared up together, as best we could, and no permanent damage had been done, while if anything the shared disaster served to cement a bond between us rather than the reverse. When I left we were on the best of terms, and I felt good enough about it to describe the incident to a giggling Katie, who immediately insisted on being tickled herself.

After the inevitable bout of sex we went out to eat and returned to her rooms shortly before midnight. As I was going to Portsmouth the next day anyway, I decided to break my rule and stayed over. We kissed and cuddled until the early hours, and brought each other to orgasm time after time, in several inventive ways.

I was tired in the morning, and the temptation to roll over and go back to sleep was huge. Fortunately Katie managed to get herself up and dosed me with black coffee, so I was on my way to the station by half past nine. I'd told her what I was doing, and she had been alarmed, as she was sure I'd just end up having to accept a punishment from Sarah, or even Sarah and Eliza together. My response had been that it was a risk I was prepared to take, although I didn't feel quite so brave.

The journey hadn't looked all that long on the map, but it took all morning, first to Reading and then south on a train that seemed determined to stop at every tiny wayside station. Having caught up on a little sleep, I then had plenty of time to think, and grew gradually more nervous. Again and again I told myself that the worst thing that could happen would be for Eliza Abbott to simply tell me to go away, and that mattered. It also wasn't strictly true, because there had to be at least a small chance that she would tell me to go away and then get in touch with Sarah.

Sarah's attitude would be fairly predictable. She might be genuinely angry, she might not, depending on what Eliza Abbott would say. In any case she would pretend to be angry, and do her best to find an excuse to have me put in front of a court martial. I might be able to wriggle out of it, I might not, but if it did happen she was sure to be one of the judges and she would really go to town on me. Worst of all, I knew full well that once she'd got me where she wanted, I would be completely unable to resist my own feelings.

I was so engrossed in my thoughts that I managed to miss the main station completely and had to get off at Portsmouth Harbour instead. Having come so far, there was no question about not going through with it, despite my rising nervousness as I made my way to the university and her department. It was a typical red brick and glass construction, but quite smart, with a reception of sorts, where a man was drinking coffee behind a desk.

'Could you direct me to Professor Abbott's room?' I asked.

'Certainly,' he answered, surprisingly formal. 'Are you with the Commission?'

'Commission? I'm a student.'

'Oh . . . right, of course. Room three-hundred-and-forty-two.'

It proved to be room forty-two on the third floor, and not actually her room at all, but a large meeting room, sparsely furnished save for a long table surrounded by chairs upholstered in bright-red cloth. All but a few of these were occupied, and with four exceptions by men, mostly in suits. Of the four women three were definitely under fifty. The fourth wasn't. She was also at the head of the table, very clearly in charge, and undoubtedly Professor Abbott.

I had no intention of breaking in on what was obviously some high-level meeting – the Commission the man at reception had referred to – but the window in the door was big enough to let me see Eliza Abbott clearly even without putting my face to it, giving me a chance to study her at leisure.

She was of middling height, certainly shorter than either Sarah or myself, and of slight build, yet there was a definite presence about her. Her hair was steel grey, undyed, but dressed in a severe and distinctly old-fashioned style. She wore glasses, adding an extra touch to a face that would have done justice to the most reactionary of school-ma'ams, as did her long, bony fingers. Even her charcoal-grey trouser suit suggested both severity and more than a little masculinity. She well earned Dr Treadle's description of her as a virago.

I'd known more or less what to expect, but to see her in the flesh really brought it home, especially as I had to wait half an hour before the meeting began to break up. When it did, she was detained by one of the men, and they remained in earnest conversation even after the others had filed from the room. I stayed put, hoping he'd come out and leave her to herself, but once she had ordered her papers they turned to the door together.

'Excuse me, Professor Abbott?' I said as they came out into the corridor, evidently intending to walk straight past me. 'Sorry, but could you spare me a moment.'

'I am somewhat busy,' she answered, not irritably, but in a tone that made it very clear I came well down her list of priorities.

I was not to be so easily put off.

'I've come from Oxford. I'm a friend of Sarah Finch.'

That stopped her, so suddenly she nearly dropped her papers. Her companion had also stopped, and was looking at me with a trace of annoyance. She turned to him.

'I do apologise, Sir Kenneth. Perhaps we can continue our conversation over lunch?'

It was polite, but it was a dismissal, and the man accepted it. Only when he was out of earshot did she address me.

'You say you're a friend of Sarah's?'

'Yes,' I answered, taken aback by her tone of voice, which was on the edge of being aggressive.

Tucking her papers under one arm, she pulled a mobile phone from her handbag.

'You will excuse me if I ring Sarah to confirm this.'

'Ring Sarah? No, no, no! Don't do that . . .'

She looked up at me, and I felt myself start to wilt, but realised that for whatever reason she thought I was somehow misrepresenting myself.

'I know,' I said hastily. 'Ring Dr Treadle. He'll vouch for me. Ask about Isabelle Colraine.'

'Isadore Treadle?' she asked, now more puzzled than cross.

'Yes,' I assured her. 'He's a friend of mine too. I had tea with him only yesterday.'

She nodded, but didn't reply. I waited as she rang a number, evidently the lab in Oxford, who put her through to his extension. Given what had happened the day before and the increasingly amused tone of her responses as they spoke, I was becoming more and more embarrassed, but when she broke the connection her voice had softened, although was still very much matter-of-fact.

'I am sorry if I appeared unduly suspicious, but for all I know you could have been some horrible creature from the press. At present, I must join the Consultative Commission for lunch, but I can see you if you are in the Gravediggers on Highland Road at two o'clock precisely.'

I would have spoken further but she was already moving on down the passage. For a moment I stood where I was, slightly bemused by her abrupt, decisive manner and wondering what had been said on the phone. Whatever it was it had amused her, and clearly I'd been given the green light, and not surprisingly, although allowing Dr Treadle to tickle me until I wet myself was hardly the image I'd intended to present.

It seemed unlikely he'd have made quite so intimate an admission, but I was still pink faced as I made my way back to the street. I had at least made contact, and she'd hadn't told me to get lost immediately, even if things weren't going quite my way. It was easy to imagine her as a friend of Dr Treadle's, which was hopeful. They shared many of the same old-fashioned attitudes: in their dress, in their manner of speech and perhaps also in the way they looked out at the world.

The Gravediggers proved to be a pub, rather to my relief, in Southsea, a fair way from the university. I ordered a double malt whisky, which I not only needed, but felt I'd earned, and also lunch. As I ate, all sorts of worries went through my brain. Could she have decided to ring Sarah after all? What would be the consequences if she had? How much had Dr Treadle told her, and what was her reaction likely to be? Did she find me attractive and, if so, what was she likely to do about it?

Once I'd finished lunch a second whisky helped me to put a bolder face on matters, and I'd just ordered a third when, at exactly two o'clock, Eliza Abbott appeared in the doorway. She saw me immediately, but ordered a mineral water at the bar before coming to my table.

'It seems I am a friend of your mother's?' she remarked as she sat down, immediately discomfiting me.

'Oh,' I managed. 'Um . . . yes. Sorry.'

'You are in fact a friend of Sarah's, rather a close friend to judge by Isadore's remarks?'

'Yes, absolutely.'

'So you wished to meet me?'

'Yes.'

She sat back, her mouth now curved into a definite smile. I smiled back, cautiously confident.

'Yet you specifically do not wish me to call Sarah?' she went on. 'Why not?'

I was ready for that one, and it was the opening I'd been hoping for.

'I want to give her a surprise,' I answered. 'We have a club, you see, in Oxford, Sarah, myself and a few others, all women, and I thought it might be rather fun if you could join us one evening.'

'A club?' she mused. 'If it's the sort of club you seem to be implying it is, then Sarah's being very bold these days.'

'I suspect it's exactly the sort of club you're imagining,' I told her, still just a touch cautious as she seemed keen to skirt around the issue, 'but Sarah didn't set it up. I did.'

Her eyebrows rose a fraction in a manner that reminded me irresistibly of Dr Treadle.

'You would seem to be a very forceful young lady,' she went on. 'May I ask how old you are?'

'Twenty,' I admitted. 'I'm in my second year at St George's.'

'And yet you have managed to set up a club for women of, shall we say, a certain persuasion? No doubt things are a little more relaxed now than in my day, but still . . .'

She trailed off, and I couldn't help but smile, basking in her approval for all my slight sense of annoyance that I wanted to impress her so badly. Her eyes met mine and I felt myself start to melt, yet also began to fidget, suddenly uneasy. There was something deeply compelling in her gaze, and it was very easy to understand how Sarah had fallen so completely under her spell.

'I assume the club is both clandestine and private?' she asked.

'Absolutely,' I assured her.

'Absolutely?' she queried.

'Um ... yes,' I answered, sure she couldn't possibly know about the Red Ox men. 'We have only eight members, and election is by majority vote after an initial meeting –'

She lifted a finger and I shut up.

'And Isadore?' she asked.

'Dr Treadle ... ah, yes,' I replied. 'He doesn't know anything about the club. I just wanted to ask him about conditioned reflexes, because Sarah ... um ... it's all rather complicated, but he doesn't know anything about the club, and I'm sure he'd be discreet anyway.'

'No doubt at all, although to judge by his remarks on the phone, he now knows rather more about my relationship with Sarah than I had chosen to divulge myself. Is that true?'

I hung my head, feeling thoroughly ashamed of myself, because she was making it abundantly clear where my loyalty should have been. She went on.

'Am I to understand, Isabelle, that you told Isadore Treadle about my personal life, specifically about my little game with Sarah as regards her reflexive response?'

'Um ... yes, sorry,' I admitted.

She drew a sigh.

'Isabelle. If one wishes to be unconventional in a way of which society disapproves, one has two choices, to fight one's cause, or to keep very, very quiet about it. I have chosen the latter course. Do you intend to fight the cause?'

'No.'

For a moment I thought I'd failed, and that she was going to give me a few kind words nd tell me she was

117

now too public a figure to take the risks involved, but then she spoke.

'Good. In that case I might consider joining you one evening, although you must appreciate my need for caution.'

'Absolutely.'

She gave a thoughtful nod.

'We meet in a secluded house near Witney,' I went on, keen to impress her with our discretion. 'The owner sends out invitations as if to a dinner party, so that nothing incriminating ever gets written down. We even stay off the web.'

Again she nodded, clearly weighing my claims.

'There are only eight of us, as I said,' I continued, 'and nobody can be invited without the approval of four other members –'

'And in my case?' she asked.

'I'm sure we can make an exception,' I answered, aware I was fawning, but I just couldn't help it.

Just as when I'd first met Laura, I was rapidly developing a crush on Eliza Abbott. I found myself blushing and went on hastily.

'Sarah may not know you're coming, but she can be said to have already approved you, while I can introduce you to my girlfriend, and my two slaves, before we go to the party.'

Now I was blushing more than ever, aware that I was showing off to her, and that awareness of my own reaction only making it worse.

'Your slaves?' she queried, surprised. 'Do you take a dominant role then?'

I hesitated, knowing her opinions on age and dominance, because she had passed them on to Sarah. However eager to please, I had to assert myself, but it wasn't easy.

'Yes,' I answered her, frantically hedging my bets, 'I am dominant by nature, although I do appreciate the idea of senior women giving discipline to their juniors. Just think of me as older than I look.'

'There is a little more to it than simple seniority,' she said, her tone now a touch frosty. 'It is not something to be taken lightly, when you wish to take pleasure in the control of another person. Maturity is essential, while one must also learn. No woman who has not been in a relationship as the sexually submissive partner can possibly understand what it means to dominate another —'

'No, no, I'm not like that at all,' I hastened to correct her, 'I do enjoy submission, and have done so, to Sarah for instance. I'm regularly spanked.'

I'd put on a big smile, trying to bring some humour into the situation. She responded, lifting one eyebrow as she replied. 'So I should hope.'

I found myself blushing again, with pride, but also embarrassment at my desperate need to please. Instead of asserting my right to my own sexuality I was trying to make excuses, and admitting things I'd intended to keep firmly to myself. Suddenly I wasn't sure if I'd done the right thing at all, imagining myself being put across her knee, which I knew I'd enjoy, but in front of Sarah and the others at a party. My cheeks were crimson as I struggled to explain myself.

'Yes, of course, but it's um . . . all rather complicated. With the society, you see, I need to stay dominant for . . . for the sake of my girlfriend, Katie, and Caroline and Jasmine. They want me as their Mistress, you see, and they don't like to see me punished, or on my knees or anything. I think the other dominant women would lose respect for me too, if I did . . .'

I trailed off, but what I was saying wasn't strictly accurate, more a justification of the stand I'd chosen to take. Laura respected me precisely because I did submit occasionally, just as she did, while Sarah merely regarded me as an uppity brat. I finished rather lamely,

'So I take discipline from somebody else . . . a man, and he is older than me, much older than me.'

She was looking at me, and I smiled weakly in return, as in place of the critical expression I'd expected, she looked amused.

'I think I understand,' she remarked.

'Thank you,' I answered, ignoring the hint of condescension in her tone.

She took a polite sip of her mineral water and I swallowed a gulp of whisky. Her poise was absolute, while I felt more nervous than ever, my sole consolation being that Sarah would no doubt feel even worse in due course, when Eliza stepped unannounced into a Rattaners' party.

'I have an appointment at three-thirty,' she said after a while, 'but perhaps you would like to continue this conversation later this afternoon?'

'Yes, absolutely.'

'Good. I'm at number eight Brother's Grove, just around the corner.'

She was already rising as she spoke, and left with a slight smile, with her mineral water standing barely touched on the table. I finished my whisky and followed, first checking to see which her road was and then walking down towards the sea. The front was quite crowded, with plenty of people enjoying the autumn sunshine and a noisy funfair not far along the shore. In no mood for other people, I set off in the opposite direction, towards where the shingle beach was almost deserted and I could sit on a groyne and think.

Drunk and also vulnerable, my mood swung between elation and concern that I'd bitten off more than I could chew. Eliza Abbot was extremely forceful, and also took things rather seriously. It was very easy to see her agreeing with Sarah's viewpoint, and even Laura looking up to her. If so, rather than finding an ally, I would have to work harder than ever to maintain my position.

One thing was certain. I could not manipulate Eliza Abbott. She clearly saw me as inexperienced, although presumably also forceful. Possibly I could influence her, a little, but I had clearly set in motion a chain of events over which I now had very little control. Trying to put a brave face on it, I told myself it would be well worthwhile if only I got to watch Sarah dominated.

I started back towards her house long before I really needed to, and there was nobody in when I got there. Ten minutes later she appeared, as brisk and formal as ever, walking rapidly down the street with a bag in one hand. She greeted me and opened the door, allowing me to follow her into a spotless kitchen. I accepted her suggestion of tea and was presently sitting at the table sipping at a china cup, much as I had the day before with Dr Treadle.

She did most of the talking, at first of neutral things, her work and times back at Oxford. I listened politely and put in an occasional remark of my own, but only when we had finished tea and she had taken the tray out did our conversation return to my reason for being there, and to Sarah.

'Do you know how Sarah and I parted?' she asked.

'When you took up your post here?' I suggested.

'Not entirely,' she answered. 'She wanted to, shall we say, spread her wings, and specifically to dominate other women, but found herself unable to do so while she was my partner.'

'No offence, but I think I can understand that,' I said, imagining what it would have been like for Sarah.

'Even exchanging letters regularly apparently made it hard for her to exert herself,' Eliza went on.

I nodded, rather pleased. It was just what I wanted to hear, and I could hope that, like me, Sarah's inevitable consternation would come with an arousal too strong to be denied. I wondered if I could help matters along a little after all.

'I'm sure seeing you again will do her a lot of good,' I ventured. 'She does rather give herself airs and graces.'

'Airs and graces,' Eliza said thoughtfully. 'I can imagine it.'

'And I can imagine you know how to deal with airs and graces?' I suggested.

She looked at me over her glasses, a questioning glance. I felt my stomach tighten.

'I do, yes,' she assured me, 'also other faults.'

'Other faults?' I asked, knowing full well she was now playing with me but unsure what I could be accused of.

'Precisely how much did you tell Isadore Treadle?' she asked. 'The truth, please.'

I could hardly avoid it, because for all I knew he'd already told her, either during their first phone conversation or a subsequent one. Still I hesitated before answering.

'Um . . . that you'd given Sarah a conditioned reflex to pee herself,' I managed after a while, again hesitating before I continued, 'and, um . . . that you used to spank Sarah, and . . . um . . . that's all, really.'

Eliza raised an eyebrow at me. I grimaced.

'And is that what Sarah told you?' she asked.

'Not Sarah,' I admitted. 'Her girlfriend, Portia.'

'I see,' Eliza went on. 'So, let me be sure I have everything correct. This Portia told you, presumably in confidence, about my relationship with Sarah, including at least some of the more intimate details. This information you then passed on to Dr Treadle, who is not only a man but an old friend and a work colleague of mine. Furthermore, you have come down here with the express purpose of inviting me up to Oxford to give Sarah a surprise. Presumably you'd like me to dominate Sarah?'

'Yes,' I answered, but in the smallest of voices.

'I see,' she repeated, 'and do you consider your behaviour to have been good?'

'No,' I admitted, quieter still.

'No,' she said, 'it is not good, Isabelle.'

'I've been a brat, I know, but –' I began, only for her to cut me off.

'A brat? Yes, you have, haven't you? You have been a deceitful, disloyal, scheming, thoroughly wicked little brat.'

'I . . . I suppose so . . . That's a bit harsh.'

'Harsh? In what particular?'

'Um . . . I don't know.'

'Not harsh then?'

'No.'

'And is that the behaviour of a dominant woman?'

'No.'

'Why then do you present yourself as such?'

'I . . . I . . . it's who I am.'

'No, Isabelle, it is who you wish to be. You have a long way to go before you get there. Now perhaps you begin to understand my philosophy?'

I could only manage a bitter grimace, my lips pursed in mute acceptance of what she was saying. There was a rebellious voice in the back of my head, screaming at me to assert myself, the same voice that made me what I was, a brat. Eliza nodded, perhaps sensing the conflict in my head and where it was leading.

'And what do you think should be done about your behaviour?' she asked, her voice suddenly full of amusement, because she knew I was trapped by my own feelings.

I opened my mouth, but no words came, unable to admit the truth, that I needed, and deserved, punishment. Once more she lifted an eyebrow, waiting for my response. At last I managed it.

'I . . . ah . . . I'd be willing to take a spanking.'

'Willing to take a spanking?' she echoed. 'Would it not be better to admit that you deserve a spanking?'

'I . . . I suppose so . . . OK, I deserve a spanking. I suppose you're going to do it?'

123

'I might,' she responded, 'although realising you deserve it is the most important thing. Perhaps I should postpone it, to allow poor Sarah to appreciate that justice had been done?'

'No! I mean, no, please, Eliza . . . Professor Abbott. That would not be fair.'

'It seems eminently fair to me, Isabelle. What you need, my girl, is a stern lesson, do you not, and what better time to administer it than in front of the woman you have wronged? Don't worry, I'll do it privately so that your girlfriend needn't know.'

'Yes, but . . .' I managed, now close to tears, 'but . . . look, not that, please? Do me now, and I promise to be a good girl, to do anything I'm told.'

'Do you want me to?'

'Yes,' I mumbled, now irrevocably caught.

'I am very glad to hear it,' she said. 'And yes, I will come to Oxford, as you are willing to accept the consequences of your behaviour, and coincidentally prove to me for certain that you are genuine. Otherwise, I would not have done. Come.'

She extended her hand, and I took it, rather surprised as she led me towards the hall, picking up her shopping on the way. I'd expected to be upended then and there, but gave no resistance as I was led upstairs. If she felt that the bedroom was the proper place for discipline, then it was not my place to object. My place was to be put across her knee and spanked.

We reached a landing, carpeted in rich blue, across which I could see into the bedroom, where an embroidered coverlet lay turned down at one corner over an immaculately made bed. To my surprise she went to another door, opening it to reveal black and white tiles. It was the bathroom and, as I realised the implications of her choice, I felt my stomach go tight and hesitated, tugging slightly on her hand.

'Is there some difficulty?' she asked, and put the shopping bag down.

As the bag came to rest on the floor the top fell open a little, exposing a large, red hot-water bottle, the price tag still attached to the handle. Lower, a circular impression suggested a coiled tube. I found myself stammering and treading my feet, my sense of helpless frustration skyrocketing as I became fully certain of her intentions. I was to be given an enema before my spanking.

'I ... um ... look, Eliza ... Professor Abbot,' I managed, stumbling at every word. 'I don't ... I mean ... I ... Must you?'

Her response was a mild, amused smile, but I could see exactly what Dr Treadle had meant about her malign sense of humour. She was thoroughly enjoying my embarrassment, and by trying to fight I was only going to make it worse for myself. There was absolute confidence in her voice as she answered.

'You can, naturally, decline, but you must decline entirely, or not at all. Which is it to be?'

I knew the answer, and so did she, yet I still stood there fidgeting and wriggling my toes, and when I did answer it was with a mute shrug. She took my hand once more and gave a gentle pull, leading me into the bathroom. It was as neat and as old fashioned as the rest of the house: white porcelain, black and white tiles, brass fittings. There was a chair too, also black and white, and she sat down, crossing her legs as I went to stand awkwardly in the middle of the floor.

'Undress,' she instructed, casual yet assertive.

My face was hot with blushes as I began to strip. Not only had I met her just hours before and was now to go stark naked before accepting a deeply humiliating punishment, but my image of her was still the forceful, no-nonsense academic who chaired important committees, making the thought of going nude in front of her infinitely more embarrassing.

Her attitude didn't help either, as she watched me without emotion as I peeled off. For some reason it seemed appropriate to fold each item of clothing as I removed it, and to place them neatly on a wicker laundry basket by the door. By the time I was down to my underwear I was shaking badly, and I fumbled at my bra catch several times before it came loose.

With my breasts showing I risked a glance to see if she appreciated my figure, but she was still watching me with that same cool, unreadable smile. It wasn't like stripping for sex at all, more undressing for an intimate doctor's examination, and all the more embarrassing for that. As I pushed my panties to the floor I was biting my lip in raw consternation, with my face and chest flushed pink. In the faint hope that she would react to me I placed my panties carefully on top of my other clothes and stood to attention, my hands on my head, my feet a little apart, naked and vulnerable in front of her. She merely gave a complacent nod and reached for the hot-water bottle.

Only as I took it did I realise that there was a valve in the top. It was no ordinary hot-water bottle, but designed specifically to hold an enema as the contents drained into some unfortunate girl's rectum. She'd obviously just bought it, which meant she'd known all along that I would submit, perhaps from the moment I'd made it plain who I was.

I was trying to keep the rueful expression off my face as I took it from her, but it was no good. For all my efforts to conceal the submissive side of my nature and accentuate the dominant, more experienced women of the same tastes always seem to see through me. It had happened again, and now not only was I going to be spanked, but I had to take a tube up my bottom first, an added humiliation far, far worse than simple exposure and punishment.

'Run the sink,' she instructed, 'with lukewarm water, into which you are to rub a little soap.'

All I could manage was a dumb nod of acceptance as I obeyed my instructions. Already my bottom hole had begun to twitch, and I was wondering how it was going to feel and if she'd allow me any modesty at all or make me adopt some awful position to take it. Supposedly, she had always claimed it was for hygienic reasons, which might just mean she would spare me . . .

'When the water is ready,' she stated as I began to rub the soap bar under the tap, 'you are to hang the bottle up from the shower rail and attach this hose. I will lubricate you myself.'

I winced, my hopes destroyed. Not only would I have to adopt a rude position, but she was going to finger my bottom too, and probably insert the long white nozzle I could see at the tip of the hose. With the sink ready, I submerged the bottle, allowing a trickle of water to run into it before lifting it up. Eliza merely coughed and I submerged it again, this time allowing it to fill properly. She nodded.

'Believe me,' she said, 'I know every little trick you girls play, and it won't do you a bit of good. Now hang up the bottle.'

There was a rubber hook at the base of the bottle and I used it to attach the horrible thing to the shower rail. It felt obscene, rubbery and turgid, and looked as bad, with the water making it bulge out into a fat pear shape. Ruefully, I attached the tube and made sure it was tight, sealing my own fate, before turning to her with my head bowed.

'Fetch the cream,' she instructed, and pointed to her shopping bag.

It was right next to her, forcing me to bend across her legs, and I was only a little surprised when she tripped me skilfully and tucked me down across her lap, bottom up. An involuntary sob escaped me as I burrowed for the cream, and another as she took it from me. Her grip on my waist tightened. I felt her hands on my bare skin

127

as she unscrewed the lid and popped the seal, before a long worm of cool squashy cream was laid between my half-open bottom cheeks. I winced, a mistake, as it made my cheeks tighten and squeezed the cream between them. Eliza gave a little sigh.

'Silly girl,' she remarked. 'Push it up, and open your legs a little, this is no time for false modesty.'

I obeyed, my face hotter than ever as I went up on my toes and spread my feet to let my bottom come properly open, offering my anus to her touch. More cream was applied between my cheeks, this time directly onto my hole, an image of which was burning in my mind, brown and wrinkly, topped with a blob of cream. Her finger touched, smearing the cool slippery stuff around my ring, into the little hole and up, deep in me, drawing a sigh of helpless pleasure from my lips.

Her response was to begin to slide her finger in and out and, after a moment, to insert a second, and a third, this time making me gasp and pop my eyes as my ring stretched wide. My mouth stayed open too, as she pushed up, so deep I thought she was going to fist my bottom hole and I began to wriggle and plead.

'No, Eliza, please . . . I don't think I can take that, I really don't.'

'Sh,' she chided, and pulled her fingers free, leaving me gaping behind, my bumhole soft and slippery, feeling loose enough to take a horse.

Her fingers pushed back in again, this time easily, and deep, until I felt her knuckles pushing at my straining ring. I began to gasp and kick my feet, sure she was going to make me take her whole hand, but again she stopped and withdrew, leaving me more open than ever. Her grip changed, I saw her hand go down by my head, into the bag, to pull up an inflatable rubber bulb with a hole running through it, now slack.

I'd imagined, naively, that she'd simply pop the nozzle up my bottom and probably make me hold it in, but as I saw the awful thing I realised I was to be well and truly plugged, and why she'd opened me so wide. With a fresh sigh of resignation I hung my head down, letting her have her fun with my bottom hole as the rounded tip of the bulb pressed to my slippery flesh.

She slid it in up my slippery hole, halfway, picked up the nozzle and pushed it firmly into place, leaving me connected, bumhole to enema bag, the bulb now right in. I felt it immediately as she began to pump on the valve, filling the plug with air to make it swell in my rectum. My mouth came gradually wide with my bumhole as the awful straining sensation grew, until I was gasping and clenching my ring.

It felt as if I was about to have the most dreadful accident, and no amount of logic would tell my bottom hole that I was in fact safely plugged and not about to soil myself in front of Eliza. She kept pumping too, until I was gasping for breath at the sheer enormity of the thing wedged in my rectum, but at last a slap on my cheeks signalled that I should rise, and she spoke.

'Get up, Isabelle. Go and sit on the loo.'

She rose with me and stepped to where the bag hung from the shower rail. I sat as ordered, my thighs well apart, on the toilet in front of her as she looked calmly down, enjoying my discomfort. One of my thighs had started to twitch in reaction and wouldn't stop. Both my nipples were rock hard, my pussy embarrassingly wet and open, if nothing like as wet and open as my bumhole.

'Here we go,' she said cheerfully, and pressed the valve.

At first I felt nothing, until the water began to ooze down to touch the inside of my anal ring. Then I felt plenty, and realised the full horror of a soapy-water enema. It stung, crazily, bringing a hot pain to my already straining bumhole. Next came the pressure as my rectum began to fill, an odd, bloated feeling which mixed with the stinging sensation to set me wiggling my toes and made me very glad indeed I was seated on the loo. As my belly began to swell it grew rapidly worse, the soap stinging my poor, over-stretched bumhole more and more, the strain growing, and the awful sense of urgency. Soon my teeth were clenched and my breathing had started to get deep, the weight inside me close to unbearable.

My hands went to my stomach, holding the little fat ball of my belly as it slowly grew, with the water gurgling and bubbling inside me. I wanted to let it out, desperately, but I was too well plugged. My anus began to spasm and I was gasping and shaking my head, but still my belly grew fatter and heavier, while the enema bag barely seemed to have changed shape. At last I began to beg.

'Please, Eliza, that's all I can take, really . . .'

'Nonsense,' she answered, the kindness in her voice failing to mask her satisfaction as I began to wriggle.

'I mean it,' I panted, clutching my swollen belly, 'I really can't hold it . . . I can't –'

I broke off, my teeth gritted against the pressure, but still with my bumhole clamped tight on the plug in an effort to keep it in. It was no good though, my hole too slippery, too open, the stinging too strong and, as my mouth came open in a long gasp, the bulb began to push out and I was babbling.

'It's coming! I can't hold on . . . I can't . . . I . . .'

With a last, despairing grunt I let go. The bulb shot out of my bottom hole, and the water with it, in a great, noisy rush. I was sobbing and gasping as my belly deflated, shaking with reaction and emotion, full of shame and helpless excitement. Even though she'd done it to me and was enjoying every second of my anguish, I still felt impossibly rude and dirty for doing it in front of her, both the enema and what came afterwards, and taking it so badly. Only when I'd stopped did I dare to look up, through eyes now hazy with tears. Eliza Abbot stood above me, calm and a little amused, as ever.

'What a fuss you do make,' she remarked. 'I'm going to enjoy you, Isabelle. Uh uh, don't get up, not yet. You'll find you haven't quite finished.'

I gave a nod of acquiescence and, sure enough, I hadn't, which would have brought my embarrassment to a whole new level if she hadn't warned me. Not that doing my toilet in front of her was exactly free of shame, but I was feeling pathetically grateful. I waited, still trembling a little, until at last I was sure. Eliza had gone out of the room by then, and I wasn't quite sure what to do, so called out to her.

'I'm ready, Eliza. What should I do?'

'Into the shower with you then,' she answered me, and a moment later appeared in the doorway, 'and pay particular attention to your bottom.'

She watched as I showered, seated throughout, without a word, even as I dried my bottom and pussy, making myself presentable for punishment. Only when I was once more standing naked at the centre of the bathroom floor did she bring me forwards with a crook of her finger. My stomach felt weak, I was acutely conscious of my nudity and I was feeling very meek. As I stepped close to her I'd never in my life felt so ready to have my bottom smacked.

'Now,' she remarked, 'we needn't worry about any nasty little accidents during your spanking, need we?'

'No,' I managed.

'Good, then I think you had better get across my knee, don't you?'

'Yes.'

I went, very meek, very contrite, aware that I genuinely deserved what I was about to get. Her legs jutted out over the edge of the chair, and I bent myself over them in classic spanking position, my hands and feet braced on the floor, my bare bottom the highest

131

part of my body. There were no preliminaries, no teasing. She began at once, taking me around my waist and setting to work on my cheeks, one at a time. It was punishment, firm and stern, and all my emotions immediately came to the boil, my eyes filling with tears.

It was just, and my surrender was absolute, lying limp across her lap as my bottom was spanked, in the nude while she was fully, smartly dressed. Even as it got harder and I began to get into a state it still felt right, to lie as I was, naked across her knees, the soft wool of her trousers on my bare skin, my bottom warming to the stinging, admonishing slaps. I was being punished, as I should be, for behaving badly, for being a brat, and brats should be spanked.

Soon I was really blubbering, choking out my emotions with the tears running hot and wet down my face. There was no thought for my dignity, the way I was behaving or the display I was making of my pussy and bottom hole. I let my legs kick and shook my head about, bucking my bottom and spreading my thighs, wriggling pathetically, abandoned to the pain and the shame too.

She never said a single word, but she knew, waiting until I had surrendered every last shred of reserve and was beginning to let my arousal through. Only then did she abruptly catch my leg, pulling my thighs wide and cocking her knee up between them. With that her thigh was against my sex, pushed hard onto the cloth so that every smack to my bottom jammed my clitoris onto the wool.

I never even tried to stop it happening. The spanking grew harder. My wriggling grew more abandoned. Her grip tightened. I began to squirm myself against her leg. The spanking grew harder still and I was gasping and squealing, rubbing myself on her leg in wanton, selfish ecstasy as my cheeks bounced and danced to her hand. My dignity was utterly gone, broken, as I writhed naked in her grip with my bottom wobbling and my hips jerking back and forth.

My orgasm began to rise and I thought of how she'd treated me, so cool, so clinical, as I'd been made to strip nude, had my bottom hole lubricated and plugged, taken an enema with stinging, soapy water and expelled it in front of her, showered and dried, completely exposed, and lastly ... lastly, been turned across her knee and had my naughty bottom spanked until I was well and truly punished, before being brought off on her leg.

I screamed, once, before her hand was clapped over my mouth, only not empty, but with the bar of soap in it. My eyes popped, still coming and unable to stop myself as my mouth filled with the horrible sharp taste. I swallowed, bubbles burst from my nose and, as my orgasm hit a second, I felt a jolt of helpless submission stronger than anything she had yet given me. Even when I thought she'd at last given in to her feelings she'd still wanted to punish me, soaping my mouth even as I came to orgasm on her leg.

Seven

What Eliza Abbott had done to me proved very strong indeed. I knew what to expect, because after playing with very dominant women before I'd always found myself questioning my sexuality, but that didn't make it any easier to get over it. All the way back to Oxford I was thinking of what it would be like to be Dr Abbott's girlfriend, and feel the helpless, almost babyish, dependence she'd brought me to as I was punished.

Once I'd come, she'd stayed in charge for the rest of the evening. I hadn't been allowed to dress, but had gone nude, acting as her maid about the house. To my surprise she hadn't made me lick her, and to the best of my knowledge she hadn't come at all. Nor had she even once surrendered so much as an ounce of her control. Even at bedtime she'd gone into her room to change in private, before making me wash my mouth out with soap and giving me a blistering spanking with the bar still held between my teeth. I'd been made to come that way too, stripped of all dignity, squatting on the bathroom floor with my red bottom stuck in the air and soap bubbles frothing from my mouth and nose. She'd then sent me to bed, hot bottomed and shaking, to bring myself to a third orgasm under my fingers.

Even in the morning she'd been a little stern with me, but had also driven me to the station and kissed me goodbye, promising to come up for the first Rattaners' party she had time to attend. That was good, as I'd succeeded in what I'd set out to do, but the possible consequences were alarming to say the least. Sarah would get it, I was sure, and the thought was immensely satisfying, but whether it would be worth the cost was another matter.

Any idea I'd had of pretending I'd only been trying to do Sarah a favour was now out of the question. Eliza would see it as deceitful, with inevitable consequences for me. Sarah would back her, and Portia, perhaps Laura too, and I'd get dealt with, thoroughly. There was no question of resistance.

Then there was the matter of what Eliza would do to me if we became regular playmates, something I knew I wouldn't be able to resist either. Fortunately she was too far away to give me regular punishment evenings or anything, which was just as well for the way she made me feel. It would be bad enough to develop a need for an enema before my spankings, never mind her obsession with soap. What she'd done hinted at conditioning, and I could just imagine her finding the idea of making a girl associate orgasm and having her mouth washed out with soap amusing, an act typical of her cruel humour.

Back in Oxford I went straight to Foxson and Katie, determined to reassert myself. Unfortunately she was keen to know what I'd been up to, and something in the way Eliza had treated me seemed to have provoked an aversion to lying. I admitted I'd allowed myself to be spanked, leaving out only the most humiliating details. I'd wondered if it would put her off me, but to my surprise Katie was delighted, even insisting I retold her the story as we lay together and masturbated.

The next day, after a thoroughly rude night in bed telling each other stories and playing, I felt more uncertain than ever. I'd relied on Katie as a rock to support my dominance, and hadn't expected her to get off on the idea of me being punished by a yet more powerful and assertive woman. All week the mood stayed with me, but sooner or later I knew I'd have to face my third and most important task relating to the Rattaners – a visit to the Red Ox.

It was still over a week until the next party, so very easy to tell myself there was no hurry, but I knew I was just putting it off. Twice during the week I saw Stan Tierney while he was doing his duties at the Mill, but there was no point in speaking to him alone. It had to be all three of them, and perhaps others too, particularly the landlord of the Red Ox, Mike. On Friday Duncan gave me my normal combination of tutorial and spanking session, and afterwards, with a warm bottom and a feeling of repletion, I decided the time had come.

I knew they'd all be there, but the timing was tricky. If I arrived early they'd be sober, but they might not all be there and there would be plenty of other people around. If I arrived late, they'd be drunk, which had its own drawbacks. Only when I went to see Caroline and Jasmine did I discover a third problem. They were stripping that night, which meant it would be next to impossible to keep what I was up to private.

They also wanted me to come with them, for company and moral support rather than as part of the act, but I refused, knowing full well I'd have half the men in the place chanting for me to be put on stage if I turned up. Inevitably I'd get dragged into it, and the thought of doing striptease in front of a couple of hundred rowdy car plant workers and assorted hoi polloi was simply too much. They understood, but the incident left me feeling more vulnerable than ever as I sat over my essay that night, constantly thinking that I might, at the very same instant, have been peeling off my clothes for the amusement of a drunken, lecherous crowd of men.

In the end I gave up and cycled up to Foxson, to soothe my feelings in Katie's arms, or, more accurately, on her bottom with half a candle's worth of wax. I still had to go, and decided I would do it on Saturday, in the late morning before the football crowds began to turn up. It made sense and, after no more than a little dithering, I cycled up to Cowley. Approaching the Red Ox, it was impossible not to feel strongly emotional. So much had happened there, and although I'd sworn I'd never go near the place again time after time I always seemed to end up coming back. I also seemed to end up naked, and more often than not attending to one or more men's erections. All too probably that was what was going to happen again, but it was a price I would just have to pay.

After striptease night I was taking a risk that the men I needed to see would still be snoring in bed or getting over their hangovers, but I needn't have worried. The run-down, grubby exterior looked seedier than ever, and there was a deserted look to the place, but the door was open and the first person I saw was Mike, still tidying up from the night before.

'Isa? Now there's a surprise,' he greeted me. 'Here, boys, look who it is.'

I saw that Stan Tierney and Big Dave were drinking coffee together at a table to one side, also Jack, a greasy individual with a pot belly and a teddy-boy haircut made even more ridiculous by a spreading bald patch. Mo wasn't there, but he was the least important of them. There were one or two others about, who I didn't recognise.

'Coffee?' Mike offered as I came up to the bar.

'Thanks, that would be great,' I answered, eager to enlist his support as he was both the most honest and the most sensible among them.

Tierney had seen me, and nudged Big Dave as I approached. Jack also turned.

'Bit late, ain't you?' Jack joked.

'Late?' I queried.

137

'For the stripping,' he went on. 'But who gives a fuck. Better late than never, eh lads?'

The others laughed. I shook my head, determined not to be diverted from my purpose, and sat down.

'You would have been good last night, and all,' Tierney put in. 'Carrie and Jas got right down to it on stage, cunt licking, the works.'

'We need to talk about the Rattaners' club,' I stated, ignoring him.

'Oh, yeah?' Dave asked. 'Changed your mind?'

'No,' I said firmly. 'I haven't, and I need to be sure you won't try to harass us the next time.'

'Who's harassing anybody?' Tierney demanded. 'We helped you set it up, and we want to be in on it, that's all.'

'You did not help me,' I answered.

'Yes I did.'

'No you did not.'

'Yes I did.'

'No . . . oh for goodness sake, Tierney.'

'I don't see what the problem is,' Mike put in as he brought my coffee over. 'You know you love it.'

'It's not about me,' I said. 'We made a majority decision not to invite men, and I have to stick by it.'

'What about Dr Appledore?' Tierney demanded.

'He was a guest,' I answered him, not entirely untruthfully. 'It's a ladies' club, male guests are strictly invitation only.'

'Why can't we be guests?' Big Dave asked.

'I . . . I suppose you could, if everyone agrees to invite you, but I don't think that's very likely.'

Tierney grunted, still not wanting to accept what I was saying.

'I can propose you as guests,' I said, 'that's all, but according to our rules all eight of us have to agree, and we never will. Please don't feel left out, and don't think it's me either, or Jasmine and Caroline, but . . .'

'Tell you what, we'll play you for it,' Tierney suggested, completely ignoring what I'd been trying to tell him. 'You win, we keep our distance. We win, we get to come.'

'That's out of the question, and besides, if you think you're luring me into a card game . . .'

'Darts?'

'Very funny.'

'Snooker?'

I hesitated. There was a billiard table at home, and when I was younger I'd spent a great deal of time playing on it when stuck indoors on rainy days. Scotland being Scotland, there had been a lot of rainy days, and while I had no idea how my ability compared with anyone else's, it was at least a thought. If I won, I'd be rid of them, if not . . .

'I can't do it,' I said.

'It's your club, ain't it?' Big Dave asked. 'You can do as you like.'

His remark stung and I shrugged in answer.

'I think that's a great idea,' Jack put in, 'and how about your clothes come off with every black ball downed, to make it a bit more spicy?'

'Yeah, let's play,' Big Dave said. 'I'm up for that.'

'I'm sure you are!' I retorted. 'I'm not stripping.'

'But you'll play, yeah?' Tierney demanded.

'No, I told you,' I began, and stopped, wondering if there might not be a way out after all.

'I know,' Jack went on, oblivious to my refusal to strip, 'she can buy back points with her clothes, you know, a yellow for a shoe, up to a black for her panties. What d'you reckon?'

'Nice one,' Big Dave agreed.

'Yeah,' Tierney put in, 'and blow jobs and stuff –'

'Hang on, will you,' I interrupted. 'I didn't agree to any of that. I haven't even said I'd play, but I might, if you're fair about it and give me your words you'll leave us alone if I win.'

'Sure,' Tierney agreed immediately, the others voicing their agreement in chorus.

'Who would I be playing against?' I asked cautiously.

'We need Jerry really,' Big Dave suggested.

'Nobody else, one of you four,' I insisted, 'or Mo if he's around.'

'Yeah, Mo's good,' Mike put in. 'So you're up for it, Isa?'

'Maybe,' I said after a long pause, 'but I can't invite you, full stop.'

'What's the deal then?' Big Dave demanded.

'If I win you leave us alone, simple.'

'Yeah, sure,' Tierney sneered. 'Come on, Isa, you know you've got to put something on the table.'

I bit my lip, looking around the ring of expectant faces, hesitant. It was obvious what they wanted, what they always wanted, me. I could cope, as I had outside Laura's, even with so many, and could it be worse than a soapy enema? Unfortunately the answer was yes, but it didn't seem there was much of an alternative. I was about to expose myself to the risk of another round of cock sucking, only to realise that there was another possibility.

'Look,' I said, 'how about this. If I win, I have your word never to interfere with a Rattaners' party, or anything of the sort, ever again. If I lose, I promise to set you up a private party, with Caroline and Jasmine.'

'And you?' Jack demanded.

'I . . . I'll be there,' I promised, 'but don't expect too much.'

'How about that Katie?' Tierney demanded.

'Yeah,' Big Dave put in. 'She's nice she is, that Katie.'

I hesitated.

'Maybe Katie, if she wants to come. She probably won't.'

'And that stuck-up piece with the titties?' Dave suggested.

'Portia,' Mike reminded him.

'I very much doubt it,' I said, 'and I'm sure her girlfriend wouldn't want her to go anyway. Look, you don't even know it's going to happen yet.'

'Whatever,' Jack drawled. 'I'll ring Mo, yeah?'

He pulled out his mobile phone and I sat back, sipping coffee and wondering what I'd got myself into. I had to win, because even if I could handle the consequences of losing, I'd be back to square one, only with the added humiliation of having to service four or five men.

'Mo's coming over,' Jack announced after a brief conversation. 'Right, lads, let's set 'em up.'

I gulped down the rest of my coffee as the men rose. Mike proved to have made a few changes since the last time I'd been there, running a wood and glass partition across the floor to screen off the area in which the snooker table, the darts board and a wide-screen TV lived. It folded back, allowing the whole bar to watch football matches and so forth, but was currently closed.

It created a quiet area, which I was grateful for, and while the glass panes looked out into the main bar, it at least gave the illusion of privacy. Mike even locked it to make sure we weren't disturbed, and hung a PRIVATE PARTY notice on the outside. By then I'd selected a cue, and rubbed the chalk down to almost nothing in my eagerness to begin. It was a relatively small table, with ten red balls rather than fifteen, which had to increase the element of chance, and hopefully in my favour. Eventually Mo rolled up, looking somewhat the worse for wear. I waited a little more as they explained the deal to him, we tossed a coin to see who was going to break, I won, and it had begun.

I barely knew the rules, but that didn't seem likely to matter. Mo had a hangover and was merely a pub player anyway, while my long hours of solitary practice had to count. I broke well anyway, scattering the reds but leaving the white ball nestled against the far

141

cushion. Mo took his shot, full of confidence, but managed to leave a red ball directly over a pocket and the other wide open.

A professional might well have cleared the table from the position he'd left me in, even made a maximum break. I was hardly going to achieve that, but his bad play had filled me with confidence. The red went down easily, and I managed a black, only to leave the white ball directly behind the blue so that I was forced to play a safety shot.

Mo fluffed it completely and I was back on and eight points up. I added a ninth but missed a tricky pink. By then Mo had finished a pint of lager and I was struggling to hide a smile. If he kept on drinking that way I was going to win with ease. Sure enough, he failed to score yet again, and I managed a break of fourteen before coming off the table again. With twenty-three points and five reds gone I was beginning to relax, while Tierney and the others did not look at all happy.

The balls had fallen moderately well, and Mo at last managed to pot a red, but I still wasn't worried. A pink followed, and another red before he failed with an over-ambitious attempt on the black, and I was back on: twenty-three to eight. There was an easy red, but it meant climbing half onto the table, with one leg up and my bottom in a distinctly embarrassing position. Not that I cared too much, rather amused by the idea of teasing them when I was doing so well, but just as I was about to take my shot Jack spoke up.

'Look at that peach, eh, boys? Wouldn't mind potting the pink in that.'

'Nah, brown for me,' Tierney drawled, 'right up her shitter.'

His final crude word came just as my cue hit the white, which shot sideways, missed the red I'd been aiming at by about a yard and disappeared into a corner pocket.

'Foul. Four to Mo,' Mike said casually.

'Hey!' I protested. 'That's hardly fair, Tierney distracted me.'

'Shouldn't stick your arse out like that then, should you,' Jack said laughing.

'Can you just be quiet, please?' I demanded, turning on them.

'OK, OK, keep your knickers on, Isa,' Tierney responded, ''cause that way we get to pull 'em off!'

All five of them laughed, and I found myself blushing as I went back to my seat. Mo was already well down his second pint of lager, but I'd left the table wide open. He potted his first red, a black, a second red and a second black, now playing with a disturbingly fluid, confident motion as he took the lead: twenty-three to twenty-eight, with three reds left on the table. He potted the next, followed by a pink and my stomach had started to tighten, growing worse as the next red went down, and a black, then the last red. He missed the next shot, to my intense relief, but the score was twenty-three to forty-four, twenty-one behind, with twenty-seven on the table. I could still do it, just.

I had to put my leg up on the table again to have a chance at the yellow, but gave Tierney a warning glare before adopting my pose. It was still awkward, as I was intensely aware of their eyes on my bottom, but I managed it, only to have the white rebound, hit the green and begin to roll towards a pocket, very slowly, giving me time to watch in mounting horror before it tipped slowly over.

'Foul,' Mike remarked. 'Two to Isa, four to Mo. Twenty-five to forty-eight, twenty-five on the table.'

As I went back to my seat I felt numb. The green was lying directly over the middle pocket, a shot Mo could hardly miss, while the beer he'd put back, far from making him worse, seemed to have improved his game immeasurably. I could only watch, trying to hide my emotions, as he casually potted it, and I was done.

'Can't catch that!' he declared, raising his heavy arms over his head.

'You might foul,' I pointed out, sounding petulant even to myself.

'Nah!' he said and laughed.

Jack stood up and came over to Mo to whisper in his ear. Mo responded. Jack frowned and then nodded. Mo turned to me.

'Tell you what,' he offered, 'like Jack said, you can buy, with your clothes. Each bit puts a red back on the table.'

I felt my mouth purse into an involuntary pout, but I was already calculating in my head. The score was twenty-five to fifty-one, so one red and any colour would be enough. It was worth taking a shoe off.

'OK,' I said, sighing, 'I'll buy one red.'

'Hang on,' he responded, 'you ain't on yet.'

Jack whispered something else and Mo grinned, then took his shot, hitting the brown, but not even trying to pot it, and leaving the white snug against the top cushion. Obviously it was a deliberate ploy, made in the hope of getting me stripped down. I had no choice but to take my chances, and pulled off my shoe. Jack looked at me, shaking his head.

'Not your shoes, you daft bitch. We want a flash of your undies, at least. Go for your jumper, or your jeans.'

'Jeans,' Mo suggested, 'she ain't got the tit, but I love that arse.'

'Dead right,' Tierney agreed. 'Get 'em off, Isa!'

'It's only fair,' Mike put in. 'I mean, like, who wants to see your feet?'

'Some men like girls' feet,' I pointed out.

'Yeah, freaks,' Tierney answered me.

'Weird!' Big Dave said.

'No –' I began, suddenly eager to defend foot fetishists, but Mo interrupted. 'Your jeans Isa, or no show.'

144

'Come on, show us your knicks!' Jack called. 'Get 'em off, get 'em off . . .'

The others took up the chant and I found myself blushing furiously. Another group of men had come into the main bar, football fans in their yellow and blue colours eager for an early drink. They weren't looking, but they only had to glance through the glass windows in the partition to see me. It was bad enough being expected to show my knickers in front of men I knew, never mind strangers. Worse still, I'd borrowed a pair of Katie's colourful panties that morning, white with black and red spots, just to add a final touch to my indignity.

'Well?' Tierney demanded when I failed to respond to their chanting. 'Are they coming off or what?'

Still I hesitated, almost tempted to give in and set up the party for them, except that it would mean I had to come up with something else to stop them harassing us. At last I nodded.

'You know it makes sense,' Jack crowed as he saw I was going to do it.

All five of them were focussed on me as I pulled off my shoes and socks, even Mike, who'd given over the bar to someone else. I stood, my hands went to the button of my jeans and it was open. My zip came down, my thumbs went into my waistband, and I was doing it, peeling down my jeans in a public bar with five men leering at me and a good chance of being seen by another dozen.

'There we are,' I said and sighed as I put my clothes aside. 'I hope you're satisfied.'

'Not really,' Tierney answered me. 'We'd prefer your knicks off, too.'

I drew in my breath, reluctant to tempt fate by telling him it wasn't going to happen. Mike had placed a red ball back on the table, approximately where the top of the triangle would have been, and I paused to consider my options. I could try and pot it, then the black, and hope to clean up, or take it slowly, making safety shots in the hope Mo would make mistakes.

Jack was walking behind me with a fresh pint, and pinched my bottom through my knickers as he passed, breaking my train of thought and making me jump.

'Do you mind?' I snapped, turning on him.

'Not at all, you've got a lovely arse,' he answered.

'You . . .' I began, and stopped, to take a deep breath.

If I allowed them to rile me I was finished, and the longer I took the more chance they had, not to mention the more time I had to spend flashing my knickers to all and sundry. More football fans were pushing into the main bar, as well, and it could only be a matter of time before they noticed. I decided on the fast option.

I lined up my shot, carefully, blocking the remarks the men were making on my rear view from my mind. A firm, smooth drive and the red was in the corner pocket: twenty-six to fifty-one. The white ball had stopped exactly where I wanted it, allowing me to put the black down in the middle, and I had a serious chance: thirty-three to fifty-one, with twenty-two on the table. The brown was next, at the far end of the table, but not impossible. I missed and Mo was on.

'Take it easy, Mo,' Jack said, no longer even bothering to whisper. 'Remember, we want her out of those panties before you're done.'

Mo nodded, lined up his shot and knocked the brown down with an almost casual tap: thirty-three to fifty-five, and I was in trouble again. As I watched Mo give the white ball a barely perceptible nudge to roll it up against the blue I felt a lump start to swell in my throat. They were toying with me, teasing me, and yet I still had a chance and I knew I was going to take it.

Without a word I reached up under my jumper, unsnipped my bra and pulled it off down my sleeve, revealing nothing. They merely grinned, leering at my panties and top, keen to see more. I wasn't going to let them, not if I could help it. Mike replaced a red as before and I lined up carefully, determined to take the remaining twenty-four points, every one of which I needed.

'Fuck me, that bird's got no strides on!'

It was sudden, completely unexpected, from right behind me, and in a harsh, male voice, heavily accented. I miscued completely, sending the white ball hopping down the table to bump against the pink and knock it in. Only then did I turn around, to find two men staring in through the partition, both ogling me shamelessly.

'Foul, six to Mo,' Mike stated.

Even as he spoke the tears were welling in my eyes, of bitter frustration and anger too.

'That's not fair,' I wailed. 'They distracted me.'

'Sorry, Isa, that's just tough,' Mike responded and stuck his head around where the partition joined the bar. 'Look, lads, if you want to watch, fine, but keep it down, yeah?'

'No sweat, Mike,' the one who'd spoken first answered, his thick Antipodean accent tinged with amusement.

The other man simply raised his pint and both turned back to watch, their eyes full on me. I swallowed hard as I turned back to watch Mo, who was lining up on the red. He played his shot, another tap, the white barely touching, to leave me on with an easy pot. As he stood back he was grinning, and I knew why. At thirty-three to sixty-one he was twenty-eight ahead with just twenty-four on the table. If I wanted to play on my top had to come off, and the loud-mouthed Australian had begun to attract others, six men now peering in at the partition.

'Titties out, love!' Jack taunted, and I threw him an angry glare as I tugged up my jumper.

I was topless. Tierney made a rude gesture, and some of the men in the main bar began to clap. Fighting back

147

my tears, I ignored them, waiting until Mike had placed a second red on the table. From behind me came a crude exclamation of surprise, then a voice, this time local.

'Here, lads, they've got some bit of posh tottie in there, playing snooker an' she's just in her panties! What a laugh, eh?'

'Quiet, please!' Mike urged.

I heard the scrape of chairs being pushed back, other voices and exclamations as every person in the now crowded main bar came to the windows, pressing in to get a good view of me. They wouldn't shut up, either, laughing and joking, making remarks on how small my breasts were, on the length of my legs and the shape of my bottom, as if I was on display in a market. Struggling to ignore them, I calculated my chances. With an extra eight possible points on the table I could now score thirty-four, which gave me more leeway than before. Setting my teeth in determination, I bent to line up my shot, inevitably providing the crowd with a full show of my panty-covered bottom, to trigger a chorus of crude remarks.

'Nice arse, eh?'

'Yeah, slim but meaty.'

'Was she one of the strippers?'

'Dunno, but she should be. Shame about her knockers, that's all.'

'Sod that, I'd given her one.'

'Yeah, doggy style.'

Stan Tierney gave a dry chuckle, his wicked little eyes fixed right on my dangling breasts as I once more tried to line up. Again Mike asked for silence, but to no effect whatever. I closed my eyes, thinking of how I'd feel watching my beautiful, sweet Katie being made to suck Stan Tierney's cock, opened them again, took careful aim and made my shot.

It was perfect, putting the first red in the corner pocket and leaving me in an ideal position for the black.

Blocking out everything around me, I lined up and put it away with panache, again bringing the white ball back to a good position. To get at the next red I once more had to cock my leg up on the table, this time presenting my straining panty seat to the entire crowd. I did it anyway, their remarks a fuzz of sound behind me as I sank the ball and climbed down.

'Fifteen,' Mike stated, 'forty-eight to sixty-one.'

I needed all three balls to win, and the blue was difficult, so close to a cushion that the only chance I had of potting it was to make it bounce back across the table. That, or I could play safe, but with maybe sixty men now staring at my near-naked body I was beginning to get seriously nervous. I had to finish before they started getting ideas, or I'd be in real trouble.

'Buy a red ball, Mo!' Jack said, laughing.

'Fuck off, Jack,' he answered. 'Anyway, she ain't won yet.'

He was right, but it was no time to dither. I lined up as best I could, shot, and was delighted to see the blue ball bounce back, run smoothly across the table and disappear into the middle pocket, exactly as I'd intended. It was impossible not to feel pleased with myself, and I even heard one or two compliments on my play in among the jeers and laughter from the watching men.

The pink and black were both on their spots, straightforward shots, at least for a skilled player. I'd succeeded with harder combinations dozens of times, but never playing in just my panties with sixty men looking on. Taking a deep breath, I lined up, and pushed the pink towards an end pocket, intent on bringing the white ball back onto the black. As I stood back I saw I had the line perfectly, but not the speed. The pink ball was already slowing, and slowing, and slowing, rolling to the very lip of the pocket . . .

. . . and stopping, so close the curve of the ball was over the pocket. I put my hand over my eyes, groaning

149

in defeat. So close, yet to fail. Stripped to my knickers, yet to fail.

'Shame,' Mo stated, and casually slammed the pink down. 'My game, I reckon.'

'Fifty-three to sixty-seven,' Mike said. 'Mo's game.'

'Hang on,' Jack cut in, even as Mo lined up on the black to finish me off once and for all. 'I want her stripped down.'

'Yeah,' Tierney added. 'Get her stripped.'

'You got it,' Mo answered, and tapped the white up against the black.

I closed my eyes, my whole body shaking with consternation as every man in the Red Ox began to bay for my panties to come off. He was fourteen ahead, and I could do it, if I was prepared to go nude in front of them, to show everything, just as if I'd stripped for them, only worse, because I'd been slowly tricked and teased out of my clothes, and even if my knickers came off I might still lose. Yet if I didn't try, it had all been for nothing, and I'd find myself entertaining the five of them at Jasmine's into the bargain.

'OK,' I managed weakly. 'I'll do it.'

A great cheer went up as I pushed my knickers to the floor and stepped out of them. Mike was grinning and glancing at the thick bush of my pubic hair as he set the red ball out and, as I stepped back to consider my shot, Tierney's hand closed on my bare bottom. I slapped him away, drawing laughter from the men in the main bar and fresh blushes to my already beetroot-red face.

Mike had at least given me a reasonable shot on the red, but I was shaking badly as I lined up. I caught it well though, and felt a jolt of triumph run through me as it disappeared into the pocket. Two more pots and I'd win, while the black was in perfect line for the corner pocket. I was still careful, very careful, but away it went, and again a surge of triumph ran through me, only for the emotion to change to embarrassment as I watched the white ball come to a halt. It was in a fine position for the black, but one which meant I'd have to get my leg up on the table, with my rear view to the watching crowd.

There was simply no choice. Biting down my raging feelings, I got into position, steadying myself with my pussy spread wide and a good half of them also with a full view of my bottom hole, rude and brown and between my cheeks. I expected jeers, catcalls, filthy suggestions, the usual waggish remarks about whether I'd wiped properly. What I got was near silence, broken only by their breathing, a reaction more disturbing still as an image came to my mind, of me held down over the snooker table while sixty men took turns with me from behind.

I was wet. I knew it and they knew it, because they could see, while my nipples had been stiff since before I'd taken my top off. Yet I had to put it from my mind, my nudity and what might happen when I'd finished, win or lose. Telling myself that Mike wouldn't let it get out of hand, I took careful aim and shot, crying out in delight as the black ball disappeared down the hole.

'Sixty-eight to sixty-seven,' Mike declared. 'Isa's game.'

As he spoke I sank down into a chair, so overcome with relief that for a moment even being in the nude didn't matter. I'd done it, at considerable cost to my dignity, but I'd done it. They were now honour bound to leave the Rattaners alone, and I didn't even have to suffer any further degradations. Inevitably I felt so aroused in reaction that I'd have played on if I'd had to, taking whatever they suggested, and there was a touch of disappointment beneath my triumph, lending a wry edge to my smile as I got up, bowed to my audience and picked up my knickers.

Stan Tierney was shaking his head in disappointment as I pulled them up, my tension already beginning to drain away as I covered myself. Seeing that I was getting dressed, the crowd began to dissolve, with a few disappointed remarks, but no longer threatening. I was safe, and if I wanted to masturbate, it could wait until I was home, where I could imagine taking sixty men one after the other without the consequences.

'What d'you have to push it for, Jack?' Stan demanded. 'If Mo had taken the game, we'd have had her stripped down anyway, wouldn't we, at Jas's place?'

'Yeah, well, it was a laugh, weren't it,' Jack replied. 'Anyway, you're going to take us in the bogs, ain't you, Isa?'

'No I am not,' I answered him, genuinely outraged yet laughing at his sheer nerve.

'Give the poor boys a break, Isa,' Mike said, laughing.

'They've already had me stark naked,' I protested. 'Isn't that enough?'

'Bollocks to it,' Tierney sneered, 'she always was a bitch.'

'Shut up, Stan,' Big Dave said. 'I reckon she's a sport, stripping off and that. Come on, Isa, how about it? I'm fit to fucking bust here, with your arse right in my face and that, and it ain't like you ain't done it before.'

'No chance,' Tierney said, laughing. 'She only puts out when there's something in it for her, that one, or when she has to.'

'I do not,' I protested, pulling my jumper on.

Tierney answered with a snort of contempt and disbelief. He was beginning to annoy me, and I responded sharply, 'I do as I please, with decent, considerate men, but yes, to have sex with you I'd need to have to, believe me.'

With that as a parting shot I grabbed the rest of my clothes and ran from the room. There was a little storeroom where the girls changed on striptease nights, and I went to it, intending to change in peace. Only once

I'd closed the door behind me and sat down on a stack of boxes did I begin to wonder if it might not be an idea to snatch a sneaky orgasm then and there. I was still full of nerves, but without the men my arousal, which had been growing stronger minute by minute as the tension of the snooker game died away, was rapidly coming to the fore.

I needed to, but it was risky. Then again, the worst that could possibly happen was for Mike to catch me and make me suck his cock, and that wasn't going to do me any harm. In fact it would be good for me to have a cock in my mouth as I played with myself, meanwhile imagining having to give the same favour to a great crowd of rowdy, drunken men. The thought sent a shiver through me, and instead of putting on my jeans I placed them to one side and put my hand to the front of my panties. I was soaking wet, and it was only going to take a moment.

Mike would also tell Tierney, and the awful Jack, which would be very satisfying. They thought I'd run off in a tizzy, and would be green with envy to discover I'd given in to their friend but not to them. The thought made me chuckle, and I was about to slip my hand down the front of my panties when I heard a footstep in the passage outside. I froze, expecting the door to open, for Mike to come in, pull out his cock and tell me in no uncertain terms that I had to suck him.

Nothing happened and, after a moment, I pushed my hand in down my panties, no longer able to resist. I thought of what I'd done, made to strip as I played snooker, bit by bit, with the gathering crowd amused by the state I was in, enjoying my helpless frustration and biting shame as much as my body. I thought of how I would have looked, first with my panties showing, then topless, finally nude, my pussy and bumhole flaunted to the crowd. I thought of what might have happened if I'd needed extra points after going nude, perhaps playing with a ball shoved up my pussy, so as I bent into my rude pose the smooth red surface would have shown, bulging out of my gaping hole. I thought of what might have happened if the men had been bolder, being used by all five of them as the crowd cheered them on, or used by the crowd. That would have been best, if they'd just taken me, made me suck their cocks, fucked me over the table, one after another, all sixty of them, up my bottom too . . .

I heard the grating sound of a beer keg being rolled on the floor, stopped and stood up, embarrassed by the thought of the young barman catching me. Opening the door, I peeped out, to find Mike just a couple of feet away, manoeuvring the beer keg into a line of them. He saw me and looked up.

'There you are!' he said, laughing. 'The boys think you've locked yourself in the Ladies'.'

'Good,' I answered him. 'Look, I, um . . . didn't mean to seem prissy or anything. I'd have done it if Tierney, and Jack too, were . . . like I said, decent and considerate.'

He knew. The front of my panties was soaking and he must have been able to smell my excitement, because I could. I was full of embarrassment as his smile turned into a lewd grin. He answered me.

'I'm decent and considerate, aren't I?'

'Yes,' I replied, 'and . . . I suppose, if I've aroused you I don't mind . . . helping you a little.'

I moved back into the storeroom as he set the beer keg straight. He followed me as I sat where I had before, wiping his hands on his trousers before closing the door. Out came his cock, pulled free with the casual motion of a man who knows he's going to get it sucked. I opened wide, leaning forwards a little, to let him pop it in as I once more began to stroke my pussy. He tasted strong, and very male, lifting my sense of being thoroughly dealt with as I began to suck and to play with

154

his balls, all the while teasing myself through my wet panties.

It was better, far better, to actually do it with a cock in my mouth. I was in no hurry though. I wanted him to come first, right in my face, so I could imagine the men in bar using me as I brought myself off. Men like to spunk in girls' faces, maybe to show what they can do, to make their mark, maybe to soil us, to make us look used and dirty, which was exactly how I wanted to feel.

As Mike grew hard in my mouth I was getting rapidly more urgent. A few touches to my clitoris and I'd have been there, but I held back, keeping my hands outside my panty crotch and no more than teasing my flesh. By the time he was close to erect it was almost unbearable, my muscles already beginning to jump and tighten as I rose towards orgasm. When he began to wank into my mouth I knew he was close, and pulled him free, pushing my hand frantically into my panties as I spoke.

'In my face, Mike, do it in my face.'

He began to jerk harder, my fingers found my clitoris and I was almost there, holding back only so I could get my face spattered with his come as I imagined if from the crowd, cock after cock jerked off over my body, thrust deep into me too, cocks up my pussy and cocks up my bottom, but every single one finishing in my face, until I was plastered with sperm, sodden with sperm, blind with sperm . . .

'Nice, do I get a go?'

My eyes sprang open, at exactly the wrong moment. I caught only a glimpse of Big Dave standing in the doorway and Mike came, right in my face, exactly as I had asked him too, but with my eyes open as well as my mouth. The first streamer of sperm caught me from my cheek to my forehead and in one eye. I closed them, feeling the sperm squash out from under my eyelid, and was babbling for him to stop, only to have his cock thrust back in my open mouth. He finished off down my throat, holding me by the hair to stop me getting away, and I swallowed as best I could before he allowed me to pull back.

Dave already had his cock out. I hadn't come, my orgasm broken at the crucial moment by his interruption, but I could barely see through the eye Mike had spunked in and I was gasping for breath. Not that Dave cared, moving in on me as Mike stepped aside, his fat cock held out for sucking. I could hear the others, out in the passage, but I didn't care, too far gone to worry if they watched me suck Dave off, or made me do them too, all except Tierney.

'Come on, love, in yer gob,' Dave urged and took hold of my hair.

He pulled me in, pressing his big rubbery cock to my face. I raised a hand, trying to signal him to slow down, but the moment my mouth came open he'd pushed himself in and I was having my mouth used whether I liked it or not. Beyond him, Mo and Tierney had pushed into the room, with Jack behind in the open doorway, the crowded floor not permitting any more in. All three were watching as I began to suck Dave's cock, once more in control of myself.

'I knew she'd do it,' Tierney said, chortling.

'Yeah, dirty bitch,' Jack agreed.

'Aw, look, she's frigging her cunt,' Mo called. 'Go on, girl, show us some pink.'

My hand had gone back down my panties, my excitement too high to be denied. For all my shame I was going to do it, masturbating in front of them as I sucked on Big Dave's now hard cock. If anything it was that very shame that was going to make my orgasm so especially good. I pulled my panties aside to show Mo what he wanted, my open pussy, my pink, on display with my fingers working among the folds and my hole agape in excitement.

'There we are,' I gasped as Dave pulled out of my mouth to tug himself over my upturned face, 'look . . . look all you want . . .'

'I'll do more than fucking look!' he shouted, and pushed forwards.

Before I could stop him my ankles had been grabbed and my body thrown back onto the cases behind me. Dave cursed, I squeaked in alarm and then moaned as Mo's cock was driven deep in up my pussy hole.

'Watch what you're fucking doing, will you?' Dave snarled. 'I'm trying to get a blow job here.'

I opened my mouth, all too willing to suck as my body rocked to the rhythm of Mo's fucking. Dave climbed up on some beer cases, to push his erection at my face. I took hold of him and stuck my tongue out, licking at the salty, rubbery flesh. He looked huge, right up against my face, a fat, ugly pillar of flesh, yet so desirable. I popped it in, sucking on his fat helmet as Mo took my thighs and pushed himself deeper into me.

'Suck me properly,' Dave demanded. 'Stop tarting around.'

As he spoke he pushed his cock into my mouth, deep, making my eyes pop as the bulbous head squeezed into my throat. He reached down, grabbing me by the ears and forcing himself deeper still, grunting in pleasure as he began to fuck in my gullet, with me batting my hands uselessly against his massive body. I thought I was going to choke, but then he'd come, gasping in ecstasy and jamming himself deeper still. My throat went into helpless spasms, sperm exploded from my nose, all over his fat belly an instant before it pressed to my face, smearing the mess across my features. Again he grunted, pulling hard on my ears to hold himself deep before at last moving back, to wipe his slippery cock in my face.

'Messy bitch, ain't you?' he grumbled, looking down at his sperm-soiled top. 'Can't you just swallow it?'

I didn't answer, panting for breath with my whole body rocking to Mo's deep, firm pushes. Dave drew back, and only then did I realise just how many men were watching me get my fucking. Jack and Tierney had pressed into the room, climbing on beer cases, and more, men from the crowd, football fans and others, men I'd never seen before in my life, leering down on me as Mo's cock worked in my hole.

Hands reached down for me, Jack's and another man's, pulling up my jumper to get my breasts showing, groping me. Tierney was close too, his withered old face set in a lewd smirk as he began to pull down his fly over the straining bulk of his cock within. I shook my head.

'No, not you, Tierney, anyone, but not you.'

'Bollocks,' he answered, burrowing his hand into his fly.

'No!' I repeated, a gasp as Mo's cock was thrust hard up me.

My mouth went wide in reaction as Mo came up my pussy, and Tierney would have filled it, only a big football fan with a shaved head had pulled him back by the shoulders.

'You heard what the lady said,' the fan said, laughing, and he himself was pushing close, ignoring Tierney's protests.

I smiled and reached out, pulling down the new man's fly even as a fresh cock was thrust in up my pussy – Jack's. He'd been rude to me too, and I hadn't wanted to fuck with him, but it was too late, his cock already moving in my sperm-slick hole. It felt too good, just as I knew I'd have sucked Tierney once his lovely big cock had been put in my mouth.

At least I had the football fan instead, just as big and maybe longer, hot in my hand and then in my mouth as he swung a thigh across my body, kneeling on two stacks of beer as he fed me his penis. All I could see was his blue and yellow shirt above me and the thick cock shaft going into my mouth as he pushed right down into me, before drawing back, to let me suck, revelling in his cock as Jack pumped into me.

I was in a ring of leering male faces, men clambering onto the stacks and still more pushing behind, demanding to know what was going on, then crowing with lewd delight as they saw. Jack had my legs up and wide, holding my thighs in his arms, with my bare feet waving to the motion of his thrusts. The man in my mouth had his balls rubbing in my cleavage where he'd flopped them out of his trousers, the cloth of which was rubbing on my nipples. They'd done it, what I'd wanted, and I had to come, but I couldn't get to my pussy, while the thought of having to take every single one was as frightening as it was exciting. Not that it mattered how I felt. I was going to get it and that was that.

As the man on top of me grabbed his cock I knew he was going to come and the next instant he had, full in my face. I felt the hot sperm splash across my nose and cheeks before he popped his cock back in to let me suck him dry, swallowing down my mouthful of sperm. Jack had pulled out, but thrust in again, making me gasp as the man I'd sucked dismounted. I twisted my head, gaping for another cock, but so I could rub myself as I sucked.

Only then did I realise that it wasn't Jack in me at all, but another man, somebody I'd never seen before in my life, grinning down at my near naked body as he enjoyed my hole. He was fucking in another man's sperm, but he didn't seem to care, as wanton as I was as he held me wide for his cock. The others were no better, staring as the closest to me fed his erection into my mouth, and even as I began to suck I'd been spunked in one more time.

I pulled up my legs as the man's cock slipped from my pussy, to leave hot sperm trickling down between my cheeks and into my panties as the gusset snapped back into place. My pussy was on offer, three or four men jostling for position to take me up on it, with the seat of my panties the only thing between me and their cocks. One pushed forwards, his erection in his hand as he shouldered the others aside, and my knickers had been wrenched up my legs, exposing me fully. As he began to rub his cock head in the slippery valley between my bottom cheeks one of the others called out, a football fan in full blue and yellow kit. 'Here, check out her knickers, she's in enemy colours!'

A roar of laughter went up and a moment later my panties had been hauled roughly up my legs and off, leaving me kicking bare for an instant before my legs had been taken and several inches of hot fat cock driven in up my pussy. As my fucking began once again, the man with my panties was waving them in the air.

My hand had gone to my pussy, my legs were spread wide to the man inside me, I was sucking eagerly and I was going to bring myself off. I was barely aware of the men pulling at my panties, or of their laughter and shouts, save as a background to the glorious mixture of raw sex and erotic shame building in my head. Vaguely I was aware that the red and black on white had to be the team colours of the day's opposition, and that my wearing panties in those colours made it all the more fun to have me stripped and fucked on my back among the beer cases.

The man I was sucking came, filling my mouth with sperm even as my own muscles began to contract in orgasm. I rolled back, my mouth wide, staring up at the ring of men above me, their cocks out, wanking over me as I was fucked fast and furious. One had my knickers wrapped around his cock and he was rubbing himself in them, his helmet stretching out the coloured cotton. Another came, hot sperm spattering my belly and chest to give me more to rub into my tits and pussy. A third was standing right over me, his cock pointed at my head, and I never even realised what he was going to do until a great gush of hot yellow piss exploded in my face.

They were screaming and yelling in glee as I was pissed on, calling me an Imp bitch and a tart and a slut as my mouth came wide to catch the hot, pungent urine. Another let go, all over my tits, and I was coming, with urine bubbling out of the sides of my mouth and splashing over my naked body, spunk too, as they let themselves go completely. The man in my pussy pulled out, my legs were pushed up and again a cock shoved between, to my sperm-slick anal ring.

Calls went up to bugger me as two more men let go over my body, urinating in my face and over my breasts and belly. I felt my bottom hole spread to the man's helmet as my body went tight in ecstasy, and he was in, jamming himself deeper as his mates cried out in delight to see me get it up the bum. My ring tightened on his shaft, in powerful contraction, as I squirmed beneath them, in utter, grovelling defeat, stripped and used and pissed on and, finally, sodomised.

As my back arched in ecstasy I'd have screamed the Red Ox down if my mouth hadn't been full of pee, my head burning with the image of my spunk-sodden, piss-soiled body and the feel of the big penis pumping in my rectum. Even as I swallowed my horrid, delicious mouthful and sucked air into my lungs to let all my emotion out I was hit by an awful sense of instability.

For one awful moment I had no idea what was happening, before I realised that the cardboard boxes I was lying on had given way, sodden through. The man in my bottom came on top of me as I collapsed, and I was gripping his back as he buggered me fiercely, barely sensible, utterly soiled, but still triumphant. My last thought as the grunting football fan spunked in my rectum was that I might be in a sorry state, but I'd won my game, and I'd denied Stan Tierney.

Eight

It took me over a week to recover from what had happened at the Red Ox, but it was well worth it. They'd been pretty rough with me, and I was covered with little bruises and sore both in my pussy and up my bum, while my jaw ached so badly it hurt to speak for a day after. That didn't stop me masturbating myself silly as I lay on my bed in Cut Mill the next day, or again with Katie as I went over the story as we lay together in her Foxson room with our hands down each other's knickers. She was both delighted and terrified, telling me over and over again how brave I was and how scary it sounded, only to come over the thought of being given the same treatment herself.

The aftermath had been no fun at all, with Mike absolutely furious over the state of his storeroom, while it had taken him, Big Dave, Mo and half-a-dozen of the other regulars to calm the situation down and prevent me being made to service all sixty or so men. I'd been suitably grateful and promised to make it up to them, before making myself scarce and cycling back down the hill as fast as I dared, with no panties on and my jumper soaking after I'd been forced to rinse it while I washed myself in the Ladies'.

On the Monday I received Laura's invitation to the next Rattaners, as before on a gilt-edged card with my name neatly written across the middle, asking if I'd like to come to dinner. She'd chosen the Saturday night, and I immediately sent Eliza Abbott an equally carefully worded email to ask if she could come, although not without a good deal of trepidation. The next time I checked my mail she had not only accepted, but informed me that she would be coming up on the Friday evening and staying with Dr Treadle.

I was also invited to dinner, but in this case wasn't sure if she really meant dinner or not. As I walked up towards Foxson to have lunch with Katie I was somewhat ruefully imagining myself tied up, given a soapy enema and then tickled until I could hold it no more. I even told Katie, leaving us giggling together as we walked down to the cafeteria.

According to Rattaners' rules four of us had to confirm a new membership, four who had met and who approved of the woman in question. It was perhaps slightly stretching a point to introduce Eliza to Katie, Jasmine and Caroline before the party, but it had to be done or Sarah was sure to use it as an excuse to get me into trouble. The most sensible time seemed to be the Saturday at lunch, so I suggested to each of the four that we meet up at the Eagle and Lamb. Having made the arrangements I began to feel more confident, also pleased with myself, and stayed that way for the rest of the week.

As Eliza was coming it seemed unwise to invite Duncan, so I gave him a special treat, asking Katie to come down just as my tutorial was finishing. They'd played together at my birthday party and Katie was growing bolder with experience, so there was no difficulty in letting him put us over his knee in turn. With both our bottoms soundly spanked we got down on our knees, side by side, still bare behind, and gave his cock and balls a leisurely tongue bath before going head to tail on the floor while he masturbated over the sight of us together.

The experience left me in excellent trim for the evening, and I was hoping that Eliza and Dr Treadle, who I found it impossible to think of as Isadore, were going to take advantage of me. I'd been feeling unusually submissive ever since my trip to Portsmouth, and experienced only a trace of chagrin as I selected a pair of plain white panties and pulled a blue velvet dress on over them, with hold-up stockings, heels, but no bra.

It was hardly cycling gear, and too far to walk, so I called Jasmine and had her drop me off. Caroline came with her, and she was teasing me unmercifully about the way I was dressed as we drove across the city. Jasmine was more respectful, as usual, and didn't hesitate to obey when I told her to pull in to the side of the road beyond Wolvercote. There, with the evening traffic out of Oxford moving past, I put Caroline across my knee in the back of the car, took down her jeans and spanked her fat bottom through the seat of her panties, until she was laughing and crying at the same time.

By the time they dropped me at Dr Treadle's house I couldn't keep the smile off my face. Caroline got out of the car with me, helping to adjust the crumples on my dress, and inevitably making it an excuse to smack at my bottom, claiming there was a piece of thread she couldn't get off. I caught her wrist and she squeaked as I spun her round. One tiny motion and she'd have been over the bonnet of the car, in full view of the road, and she knew it, laughing and begging at the same time.

'No, Isabelle, not again. Come on, please, that's really not fair.'

'Perhaps not,' I admitted, 'but believe me, I am going to make such a spectacle of you tomorrow night.'

She was going to reply, but made a face instead, and I caught Eliza Abbott's crisp, even tones at the same moment I realised somebody was behind me.

'Not in the road, Isabelle,' she chided. 'Do you have no sense of propriety?'

'No, she doesn't,' Caroline answered, and stuck her tongue out at me.

'I do apologise for my brat's behaviour,' I addressed Eliza, desperately trying to show some authority. 'She's very undisciplined. Caroline, this is Professor Eliza Abbott, in front of whom you are going to be soundly disciplined. In fact, Eliza, perhaps you'd care to borrow her at the party tomorrow night?'

I'd been hoping for gracious acceptance of my offer, and therefore as Eliza's equal, but rather expecting a cutting put down, implying that Caroline and I should both be punished. Instead Eliza gave an urgent cough, and only then did I realise that Dr Treadle was standing in the shadows of the doorway.

'Are you planning a party, Eliza?' he asked, his face showing more amusement than genuine enquiry.

Eliza sighed and gave me a stern look before speaking.

'Yes, Isadore, we are having a party, as you have clearly already surmised. You'd better come in, Isabelle, although it might be considered polite to introduce Isadore and myself to both your friends.'

'Oh ... sorry,' I managed. 'This is Caroline, and Jasmine in the car. Professor Eliza Abbott, Sarah's ... Sarah's ... um ... and Dr Treadle.'

I was making a complete hash of it, made even worse by Jasmine's polite nod and bright smile as she leant across to greet them. My cheeks were burning, because I'd assumed Eliza would have told Dr Treadle what was going on, but she clearly hadn't, and now I had no idea who knew what or what I could or couldn't say. To judge by the look on her face I'd already committed an unpardonable sin, or rather a sin the pardon for which was probably going to involve soap in some way.

All I could do was kiss the girls goodbye and follow Eliza into the house, feeling much as if I was going to the scaffold. Eliza's manner was distinctly stiff as Dr

Treadle ushered us through, beyond the stuffed ostrich, into a room I hadn't been in before, panelled and furnished in austere comfort. A large oval dining table occupied much of the room, with chairs set around it and others against the walls. Several decanters stood on a sideboard, and I gratefully accepted a large whisky before attempting the apology that was so evidently needed.

'I'm very sorry about that, Eliza,' I said, as soon as I'd taken a swallow and Dr Treadle had disappeared through a further door to the kitchen. 'I shouldn't have been messing about with Caroline, and I should have been more careful with what I said.'

'So you should,' she said. 'Although Isadore had no doubt guessed that I might be here to do more than simply visit you, I had understood that the party was not to be mentioned, and therefore respected that decision.'

'Of course . . . thank you,' I managed, 'although I'm sure Dr Treadle –'

'Oh, Isadore is to be trusted,' she cut me off, 'but that is not the issue. If we are to be discreet, we must be discreet. Is that not so?'

'Yes,' I mumbled, 'of course.'

'Then let us say no more about it,' she went on, suddenly bright. 'You say Caroline is coming? Jasmine too?'

'So, er . . . it's OK to discuss it now?' I asked cautiously as Dr Treadle reappeared with his hands full of cutlery and table mats.

'The cat is rather out of the bag, is it not?' she answered.

I nodded, moving aside a little as Dr Treadle began to lay the table.

'They're both coming, yes, also my girlfriend, Katie, and Sarah, of course, with Portia. Also Laura, who's our hostess, and Pippa, her playmate.'

'All eight then, good. And how are we getting there?'

'In Jasmine's car. She lives on the Cowley Road, so perhaps if we stay in town after lunch tomorrow?'

'That would be ideal. One of the drawbacks of Portsmouth is that there are so few worthwhile shops. Is Annabelle's still in the High?'

'Yes,' I told her, relieved to have the conversation move away from the Rattaners to something less likely to land me in trouble.

The rest of the dinner party went smoothly. Dr Treadle was an excellent host, and provided a very English meal, as I might have expected: leek soup, small fillets of river trout, a roast leg of lamb served with mint sauce and treacle pudding. By the end my tummy was feeling distinctly full, making a round bulge beneath the blue velvet of my dress. I was also a trifle drunk, as an appropriate wine had been served with each course, two full bottles and two halves, which along with the whisky was quite enough. Any awkwardness there might have been between us had also dissolved and, as we retired to the drawing room, I was feeling relaxed and no longer on guard.

'Port?' Dr Treadle offered as I sat down in the same chair on which he'd tickled me.

'A small glass, thank you,' I answered, and accepted a large one.

He had already filled a glass for Eliza, and finished with his own before seating himself. We had avoided the topic of the Rattaners during dinner, but as we'd been finishing the treacle pudding they had begun to discuss conditioning, first in general and then in Sarah's case. As soon as she'd taken a sip of port, Eliza took up where she'd left off.

'She was eager to be obedient, but the choice, I confess, was mine. Her favourite thing had always been to achieve a sense of being unable to control the expression of her sexuality, a typical masochistic trait, and so it seemed a sensible choice. Certainly it was one she enjoyed a great deal, although I'm surprised to hear the conditioning has lasted so long. In general, conditioned reflexes fade with time, although slowly.'

'It probably has faded, at least a little,' I told her.

'You have tried this?' she asked.

'Yes,' I admitted.

'Given what you say of her new-found dominance, I'm surprised she permitted it.'

'I ... um ... I didn't actually ask,' I confessed. 'Portia had told me, you see, and it was a very merry evening, my birthday party as it happens, and Sarah was in tight jodhpurs, bending, and ... well, I couldn't resist it.'

I spread my hands, grinning. So was Dr Treadle, but not Eliza, although she failed to completely conceal the amusement in her voice as she answered me.

'You really have no self-discipline at all, do you, Isabelle? This is why it's so important that a woman who wishes to be sexually dominant with her partners needs to learn how it feels to be on the receiving end, preferably for several years. There is variation, certainly, but I would suggest thirty as a typical age for a woman to be considered responsible enough to hold the position you have clearly put yourself in with Caroline, Jasmine, and presumably also Katie.'

'But it's my nature,' I protested, blushing more for the absorbed interest of Dr Treadle than for what she was saying.

'It is also mine,' she responded, 'so be assured that I understand you, perhaps better than you do yourself.'

She was going to continue, but I got in quickly before she could decide I ought to be put across her knee in front of him, an order I wasn't sure I had the will to refuse.

'My idea was to help Sarah by reconditioning her,' I said. 'Do you think that would work?'

'No,' she answered flatly. 'If you mean by substituting her response to the command for another, I think it more likely that you would merely superimpose the two. After all, there is no reason that a single stimulus cannot produce two separate reflexes.'

Dr Treadle nodded wisely.

'Have you discussed this with Sarah?' Eliza asked.

'No,' I told her. 'I wanted to be sure of what I was doing first.'

'So you are not entirely irresponsible then,' she replied. 'Still, we can discuss it tomorrow night, and perhaps I can give her some useful advice.'

'I'd really rather you didn't mention it,' I said hastily. 'It was only an idea.'

'You imply that you'd rather I didn't mention your involvement?' she queried, lifting an eyebrow.

'Yes,' I admitted.

'I shall not enquire into your exact motives,' she went on, 'but I suspect they are not entirely altruistic?'

I hesitated, wondering whether to lie or provide her with further evidence that I was an irresponsible brat. Both of them were looking at me, and in Eliza's case it was as if she could see every secret detail of the workings of my mind.

'I, um . . . I only wanted to . . . to assert my authority a little,' I admitted, 'because it was me who set the club up, so I should run it. Sarah doesn't think so.'

'She wishes to run it herself?'

'No. She thinks Laura should. Laura's older than her, and we meet at her house.'

'On the face of it, hers would seem the sensible choice.'

'I know,' I said weakly, 'but I . . . I . . .'

'Put your emotions first, in place of common sense,' she answered for me. 'Sarah, by contrast, seems to have acted for the common good, perhaps surprising when I consider how she used to behave, but then I have said

169

all along, maturity is essential. Perhaps you begin to realise that?'

'Yes,' I admitted, reluctantly, because I was beginning to realise it was true, and that my instinctive rejection of it was merely further evidence of my immaturity, thus reinforcing her argument.

'I really do think,' she continued, 'that a period of training would be much the best thing for you. Do you agree?'

'Yes,' I answered, my voice little more than a whisper.

'That admission is in itself is a great step forwards, Isabelle,' she said, smiling. 'I'm only sorry I can't take on the task myself, but Portsmouth is really too far away.'

I responded with a smile, intended to express regret, but in reality born of relief.

The after-dinner conversation I'd had with Eliza Abbott would have been embarrassing enough at the best of times, never mind in front of Dr Treadle. He had said nothing, but had taken it all in, quietly amused, and undoubtedly aroused too. Nothing had happened between us, but as I'd sat in the cab they'd ordered for me back to town, I'd been imagining how once he was in bed he would masturbate over me, his head full of images of how I'd looked as he tickled my bare bottom until I wet myself in helpless laughter.

It had been too late to go to Foxson, and Katie wasn't expecting me, so I'd returned to St George's. In the morning there was a note from her in my pigeonhole to say she couldn't come to lunch at the Eagle and Lamb because her tutor had unexpectedly invited all his postgrads for drinks. It was a minor irritation, but there was nothing to be done about it and I put it from my mind, spending the morning putting together the framework for my essay on the Otmoor enclosure riots.

I set off with plenty of time, walking up the High Street and window shopping, so slowly that Jasmine and

Caroline caught up with me outside St Mary's. Lunch was a pleasant affair, if somewhat embarrassing, because Caroline insisted on telling Eliza how I'd brought the Rattaners together, including my ordeal with the Line Ladies and my introduction to Sarah and Portia, which had involved being whipped on horseback with a posy of flowers inserted into my anus.

Eliza was determined to spend the afternoon shopping, and I offered to accompany her: a mistake, as I ended up carrying her bags while she replenished her wardrobe from Oxford's more formal ladies' establishments. After what she'd said the night before it was all too easy to see myself in a role as her plaything and, effectively, her maid. The idea filled me with resentment, but was hard to resist, because everything about her brought out the submissive side of my nature.

She was also full of energy and insisted on walking from Carfax all the way to Jasmine's house. I was immensely glad to slump down in a chair once we got there, and ordered Jasmine to make coffee both because I needed it and to show off my authority. Jasmine obeyed, but I noticed she served Eliza first and was showing every bit as much deference to her as to me.

I was determined not to give in, despite my growing feeling that I really would be better off at Eliza's feet, as would the others, possibly excepting Laura. Therefore I really went to town on my outfit, choosing my black corset over Victorian-style combinations in heavy silk, thick black knee stockings, my black skirt, but this time with a high-necked Edwardian top, along with my hat, gloves, veil and, finally, the same boots I'd worn before. The complete effect was like body armour, in both a mental and physical sense, leaving me feeling strong and confident, although also severely restricted.

Jasmine had helped me, leaving Caroline to go through their various garments to see what Eliza could borrow. They had finished long before I was ready and

I came down to the kitchen to find Eliza sitting at the table in a simple grey dress, Victorian in style, completely unadorned, but with her hair wound into a severe bun. With her mature and naturally severe face it made her look like a nineteenth-century prison wardress, and a tough one at that. It was also loose and practical.

I felt comprehensively over dressed and my sense of dominance and strength immediately began to evaporate. Side by side we looked not like two dominant women dressed for a party, but more a Victorian prison wardress taking a genteel but sinful girl into custody. Still I managed to hold my poise, at least outwardly, ordering the girls to get dressed as quickly as possible and consoling myself with the thought that if I found Eliza terrifying, then Sarah was about to get the shock of her life.

The girls were soon down: Caroline in a manga-style sailor suit straining out over her ample figure both back and front; Jasmine in a long coat over nothing but yellow high-heels, yellow bikini bottoms and a collar to match. I made them show off, again wishing to exert my authority, a show Eliza accepted with a polite, amused smile, as if I was doing it in deference to her, which perhaps I was.

Caroline drove, Jasmine's outfit being somewhat impractical, first to a road near Foxson where we'd agreed to collect Katie, who was in her Line Ladies costume once more, which had the advantage of not being obviously sexual in nature. We then made for Witney, talking nervously together with the tension and excitement of the coming evening rising with every passing mile.

We were the last to arrive, Pippa answering the door to us in a smart military jacket, shirt, tie, cap, brilliant polished boots and snug khaki-green knickers but no trousers. Laura was within, in her major's uniform with a swagger stick under one arm, but to my delight Sarah was in the carriage, warming Portia's bottom for the coming evening. I could hear the smacks, which stopped as the door banged shut. Portia bounced in, stark naked, giggling happily and rubbing at her bare red bottom, followed by Sarah, cool and poised in jodhpurs and pinks, only to stop dead in her tracks, her mouth open wide as she focussed on Eliza.

It was a sight to see, worth the soapy enema, worth the spanking, worth every bit of shame and indignity and uncertainty I had suffered to bring it about. Sarah was completely and utterly taken aback, unable to move, unable to speak, all her poise shattered in one instant, and worse. As I struggled to restrain my grin I saw the taut 'V' of her jodhpur's crotch go abruptly dark, then begin to bubble with pee, a little yellow fountain gushing out to patter on the floor and trickle down the insides of her legs as she wet herself.

For a long moment she was simply too shocked to do anything about it, just standing, with little squirts of pee erupting from where the material of her jodhpurs was now plastered to her pussy lips. As her expression changed to acute humiliation a rush of guilt hit me, but it didn't stop me wanting to laugh, a reaction I could no longer hide, even behind my veil, clutching my mouth and tummy as painfully intense spasms tore through me. As Sarah made a desperate and futile clutch for her pussy, ridiculously late, I let go, clutching my sides in helpless reaction as if I'd been spreadeagled on Dr Treadle's bed with half a dozen of Esmond's feathers working between my legs.

'What's the matter?' Portia demanded. 'What's so funny, Isabelle? Sarah?'

Sarah's response was a gurgling noise and she ran for the loo. I finally managed to get myself at least partially under control, and gestured to Eliza.

'Portia, may I introduce you to Dr Eliza Abbott. Eliza, meet Portia Anson-Jones.'

Portia's mouth fell open, but unfortunately she didn't wet herself. I was still shaking with laughter, as was Caroline. Katie was trying to hold it back too, but looking worried, Jasmine was serene but amused, Pippa uncertain. Laura looked unhappy, and clearly disapproved of my open amusement, but Eliza herself was unreadable, maybe amused, maybe angry, maybe neither, her face quite still as she nodded to Portia, then Laura.

'Pleased to meet you,' she said, 'and my apologies if my arrival came as something of a shock. As some of you know, I was with Sarah some years ago, and I must say, it's a delight to meet so many like-minded people. From Isabelle's description, you must be Laura, our hostess?'

'Yes,' Laura answered, still somewhat nonplussed, 'er . . . and this is my friend Pippa, and I think you know everybody then? Would you like a glass of wine? Isabelle?'

'Yes, please,' I answered, and Pippa was sent to fetch it with a snap of Laura's fingers.

As with Jasmine, Pippa served Eliza first as if in response to some natural pecking order, although possibly only because she was a guest. I ordered Jasmine and Caroline to help serve as well and sat down on the bed with Katie by my side. Portia had gone to look after Sarah, who was presumably changing, and I settled down to enjoy the evening. Sarah's reaction was unpredictable, as she prided herself on keeping her reserve, but I felt I could rely on Eliza not giving away my intentions. To do so was to betray her own, and she had clearly found the idea of surprising Sarah amusing.

When Sarah came back she was in jeans, presumably with fresh knickers on underneath, and infinitely more composed. She went straight to where Eliza was sitting and kissed her on the cheek. Eliza's reaction was a friendly smile.

'I'm so sorry to have startled you like that, Sarah, dear. We expected you to be surprised, but we had no idea you'd have such a strong reaction.'

'Pleasantly surprised, of course,' I said quickly.

Sarah looked puzzled, turning to me and back to Eliza.

'What is the connection between you two, exactly? How did you manage to meet?'

'Isabelle felt I'd be a suitable member for your club,' Eliza responded.

'Just Isabelle?' Sarah replied, casting a suspicious glance at Portia, who had just come in.

'It was nothing to do with me,' Portia said quickly.

For a moment Sarah looked doubtful, and even as she went on her voice was noticeably less firm than usual.

'Oh well, never mind. I dare say Isabelle enjoyed her little joke, and I'm sure you'll fit in, Eliza. Portia, you can help the others serve, and you're to stay naked.'

I recognised the gesture, exactly the same as I'd made to show my dominance over the other girls. Clearly Sarah was flustered and, as her feelings were obviously very strong indeed, there had to be at least a chance of something really worthwhile happening. All I needed to do was set things in motion and with good luck she would end up across Eliza's lap, or possibly in the dungeon, tied, helpless and so high on submission that we could all share her. That would come later, hopefully, but it was at least my first chance to show that I wasn't completely useless.

'How about something to break the ice?' I suggested. 'A game, maybe. Katie, answer this question or you're going over my knee.'

The look of consternation on Katie's face as she realised she was to get the first punishment of the evening was a joy to behold. She knew full well my question would be something from my own speciality, which she wouldn't have a hope of answering. I waited to let what was about to happen sink in before making my choice.

'In what year was a proposal for the enclosure of common land torn from the church door in the village of Noke?'

She merely made a face, so I grabbed her by the scruff of her neck and hauled her across my lap, lifting her haunches to the room. Her bottom was truly magnificent in her tight white trousers, a perfect globe of cheeky flesh. She was already whimpering softly as I began to stroke the seat of her trousers, and I knew she'd soon be in tears. Sure enough, with everybody else watching in delight, she had begun to snivel before I'd got her trousers properly down off her bottom to show off the apricot-patterned panties beneath. They made her bottom look more lovely still, and again I spent a moment caressing her, as she began to cry softly into the bed.

'She always does this,' I explained, 'because she's such a baby, but watch.'

Taking a firm hold of her panties, I levered them down off her bottom, baring the full width of her meaty little cheeks to view. A couple of sharp tugs and both panties and jeans were around her knees, then stretched taut as I opened her thighs behind to show off the furry bulge of her pussy between her legs and the rude little knot of her tiny anal hole. She was limp, sobbing bitterly in complete surrender to me as I began to spank, just pats from my fingertips to make her skin sting and bring the colour to her cheeks.

With Eliza watching I was not only showing off my girlfriend's bottom, but my own ability, and I was determined to make Katie come. I knew she would, and that having her in tears was a good start, because only if she could really let out her feelings would she get there, and for Katie that meant crying. I wasn't going to touch either, just spank, save a quick touch to tickle

176

her anus and make sure she knew it was showing to her audience.

By the time her bottom was a warm rosy pink all over I knew she was as good as there, her sobs now broken, her breath coming in little urgent gasps. I'd been using my hand cupped, to make the smacks echo loud around the room, but now changed, applying the palm of my hand firmly to the fat tuck of her cheeks, right over her pussy. Just a few swats and her sobs changed to helpless, ecstatic grunting as the last of her reserve broke, just like the little pig she liked to be told she resembled. I spanked harder, her grunts grew louder and she was there, wriggling her bottom and gasping in ecstasy as I brought her off on the pleasure of spanking alone.

As Katie began to come down from her orgasm Caroline started to clap, then Jasmine and Pippa, Laura and Portia, even Sarah patted her hands together a couple of times in acknowledgement of our performance. Eliza merely smiled, but she was clearly impressed and I found myself smiling back, well pleased to bask in the warm glow of her approval.

'How amusing,' she said as Katie's shiver finally died away. 'We used to play a similar game, didn't we, Sarah? Although you never reacted quite like that.'

For one glorious moment I thought she was going to ask Sarah a question and give her the same treatment. From the look of panic on Sarah's face she clearly thought the same, but after a sip of wine, Eliza spoke to Katie, although to her bottom rather than her face as she was still over my lap.

'And may I say how beautiful you are, Katie dear.'

'Thank you,' Katie mumbled, then squeaked as I gave her another half-dozen rapid spanks, taking out a touch of jealousy at Eliza's comment.

It was hardly a worthy reaction, and I quickly stopped and kissed her cheeks instead, before letting her up. She snuggled close, her jeans and panties still in a

177

tangle around her thighs, kissed my cheek, and then whispered in my ear, 'Are you going to let Eliza give you a spanking?'

'Katie!' I hissed back.

'Pretty please? For your piggy?'

'I'll put my piggy in the cage if she doesn't shut up, with a couple of litres of water in her tummy, and you know what will happen then.'

She made a face but didn't reply. I was blushing slightly as I turned back to the room, but I was determined to carry the game on. Maybe I would get spanked, but it was a risk worth taking, and after the way Eliza had dealt with me in Portsmouth she would probably choose somebody new.

'Eliza, you should have the next turn, as our guest,' I suggested sweetly.

'No, no,' she replied, 'it should be Katie's turn, surely?'

'Me?' Katie queried.

'Why yes,' Eliza insisted, 'although I do think we shouldn't be allowed to take questions from our specialist subjects. What was the answer, Isabelle?'

'Eighteen-fourteen,' I told her, 'but I don't think Katie feels she could spank anyone.'

Katie nodded.

'You may delegate the task, naturally,' Eliza replied, 'but if you do so, the next go devolves to the person you choose, and not to the victim. Also, if anybody does answer a question correctly, they may either take the next go, or spank the questioner.'

'That's a clever twist,' Laura said, 'and fair to everybody. What do you all think?'

'Let's play!' Portia squeaked. 'It sounds great.'

Everybody agreed, and if Eliza had taken the game over from me, I didn't mind. They were good suggestions, and left everybody at risk, herself included, although I couldn't imagine even Laura having the nerve to spank her.

178

'I think the dominants among us should be able to decline,' Sarah suggested.

'Not at all, don't be such a coward,' Eliza said, laughing. 'Now, Katie, my dear, it is your turn.'

Sarah did not look happy at all, but she didn't answer. I'd never seen Eliza enjoying herself so much, even when she was feeding me soap in her bathroom, and I was sure it was only a matter of time before Sarah got upended.

'Er . . .' Katie began, glancing shyly around the room. 'Caroline, who wrote *Under the Greenwood Tree*?'

'That's far too easy,' Portia interjected.

'Speak for yourself,' Caroline answered her. 'I don't know, Katie, so I suppose you'd better spank me, or have Isabelle do it.'

She was pretending to pout as she stepped towards us, but plainly looking forward to her punishment.

'I think Eliza should do it,' Katie said quickly, 'she is our guest.'

There was a trace of genuine concern on Caroline's face as she turned, but she didn't protest. Eliza gave an appreciative nod to Katie and made a lap, allowing Caroline to bend over her knee. I had a fine view, with Caroline's cheeky bottom thrust high, and so tight in her sailor suit it seemed the seam would split. Katie cuddled close to me as Eliza began, easing down the taut white trousers and the bright pink thong beneath to expose the full glory of Caroline's bottom.

The spanking was given in a firm, no-nonsense manner, just as I'd been dealt with myself, hard smacks delivered full across the fat, quivering globe to make Caroline kick and squeal and toss her hair. I was stroking Katie's bottom as we watched, already quite keen to come, perhaps licked to ecstasy as I watched one of the other girls spanked, ideally Sarah.

Caroline was at last let up, and ran back to Jasmine, giggling and rubbing at her hot bottom. Like Katie she kept her trousers and panties down, so that Jasmine could rub a little ice over her hot cheeks. Eliza had done the spanking, so it was her turn to choose, and I crossed my fingers behind Katie's bottom. Sarah looked worried as Eliza glanced around the room, and I was sure she'd get the question.

'Portia,' Eliza finally announced, and I felt a little flush of disappointment, 'as you found Katie's question so easy, perhaps you would like to tell me the atomic weight of –'

'She's a chemist,' I blurted out. 'And a postgrad at that.'

'Isabelle!' Portia exclaimed. 'That's not fair!'

'No specialist subjects,' I reminded her.

'No,' she responded, 'we said the person asking the questions shouldn't use her specialist subject. It's my good luck if –'

'Portia is right, of course,' Eliza broke in, 'but Isabelle's interruption has spoilt the question, so I shall ask another. Sarah.'

To see Sarah jump was wonderful, but nothing to the expression on her face as she turned to Eliza. She'd expected Portia to be given another question, and had looked quite happy at the prospect of Eliza spanking her girlfriend. Not so when it was her own bottom at risk, and it was all due to me. I wasn't even bothering to hide my grin as Eliza considered, then spoke.

'Now you, of course, are not a chemist. Indeed, Isabelle tells me you are now head of catering at Erasmus Darwin College. Perhaps a related question then . . .'

Hope dawned in Sarah's eyes, only to fade as Eliza spoke.

'Yes. What is the atomic weight of boron?'

Sarah responded with a stare of blank horror, but Portia quickly leant forwards to whisper something.

'Eleven,' Sarah said, 'or ten point eight to be exact.'

Eliza didn't answer, merely lifting her eyebrows. Sarah's face sank again and she began to get up, very slowly, hesitant, as I hugged Katie to me in fierce delight.

'Both of you, I think,' Eliza stated. 'Cheating is not to be tolerated. Sarah, come across my lap.'

Portia made a face but didn't argue.

'Laura, perhaps if you would oblige with Portia?' Eliza asked.

'My pleasure,' Laura answered and pushed out her knees to make a lap for Portia.

I watched in open glee as the two women got into position for punishment, both reluctant, both sulky, but Sarah's emotions so much stronger, hanging back even when Portia had been placed comfortably across Laura's knee with her already naked bottom well up and her good-sized breasts dangling beneath her chest. Laura gave the chubby peach she was about to smack a couple of pats, then cocked her knee up, spreading Portia's bottom to show off neatly shaved pussy lips and a wrinkly bumhole. Still Sarah hesitated.

'Come, come,' Eliza urged, patting her lap. 'I would have hoped you would be eager, after so long.'

Sarah gave a miserable nod, her sole acknowledgement of her deeper feelings, but shot me an angry glare before getting into spanking position across Eliza's knee. It was going to happen, just as I'd hoped, and of course there was no question of Sarah being allowed to preserve her modesty. She knew it too, and I was having trouble not screaming out in delight as she lifted her hips to allow her trousers to be undone, her expression twitching between misery and bliss. The button came open, her zip was drawn swiftly down, and the emotion on her face grew stronger still as Eliza began to pull them off, slowly revealing the full pale spread of Sarah's smooth, well-fleshed bottom. She was already bare, so that once the jeans were well down a hint of dark pussy fur showed between her thighs, a sight that filled me with wicked delight.

'No knickers?' Eliza remarked. 'Really, didn't you learn anything while we were together?'

'I . . . I wet them!' Sarah wailed. 'You know I did!'

'A lady should always be well prepared,' Eliza said, beginning to gently rub Sarah's bottom. 'Didn't you bring a spare pair?'

'Only for Portia,' Sarah answered.

'And what, pray, was wrong with those?' Eliza enquired, enjoying herself hugely.

'They're frillies,' Sarah answered in the faintest of whispers.

'Don't mumble,' Eliza snapped and applied a firm smack to Sarah's gloriously naked behind.

'They're frillies,' Sarah repeated, her voice louder but no happier.

'And you're too old for frilly knickers, I suppose?' Eliza asked.

'Yes,' Sarah responded. 'And too . . . too dominant.'

'Oh ho!' Eliza said, chuckling. 'How high and mighty little Miss Sally has become! Well, we shall see who's too old, shall we? Portia, just as soon as Laura's done with you, be a dear and fetch your spare knickers, would you? I think I'll put Sarah in them for the rest of the evening, those and nothing else.'

I clenched my fists in delight, thinking of Sarah well and truly put in her place, spanked bare and made to strip, dressed up and paraded in Portia's frillies and not a stitch besides. It was glorious, perfect, and with any luck, once she was well down, I'd get to spank her myself, maybe have her lick me to ecstasy as she masturbated at my feet in wanton, grovelling submission . . .

A loud clang from outside the window broke my fantasy and I jerked round. Eliza and Laura froze, their hands raised over Sarah's and Portia's bottoms, but only for an instant before tumbling the girls off their laps. Everybody who was showing anything covered up hastily as Laura stepped towards the window.

'Who's that?' she demanded. 'Who's out there?'

Nothing happened, but only for a moment. A head appeared, and a second, then others, five in all, a row of grinning faces: Big Dave, Mo, Mike, Jack and Stan Tierney.

I was staring in dull horror, completely taken aback – by their treachery, by being peeped at, but far worse, by what might be about to happen to me. Still I was the first to find my voice, excepting Portia's squeak of alarm as she grabbed a pair of cushions to cover her nudity.

'Oh God . . .' I managed, then rallied. 'It's OK, I'll deal with this.'

'No,' Sarah spoke up, 'it is not OK, and I will deal with it.'

She made for the door, in short, angry steps, still doing her jeans up as she reached it. I followed, not sure how they'd treat her after seeing her bare, also Laura and Eliza, but by the time I got out onto the lawn Sarah was already facing up to the five of them.

'What do you people think you're doing here? Get out!'

To my amazement they went, straight away and as meek as lambs, with not so much as a sarcastic remark or a rude comment about what they'd seen. I was staring as they walked off with hang-dog expressions, plainly ashamed of what they'd done. Not even Tierney spoke up, although I knew that if it had been me he'd have been demanding all sorts of lewd acts to make them go away. I'd have been put on my knees to suck them in turn, dragged into the bushes and made into a spit-roast, sodomised and made to suck their cocks clean. Not Sarah.

'Who on earth were they?' Eliza demanded, full of disgust, as they disappeared into the darkness beyond the hedge.

'Just some awful men from the town, Cowley to be exact,' Sarah explained. 'Ask Isabelle, she seems to find them appealing.'

'I do not,' I protested.

'One moment,' Eliza stated, her voice like ice. 'Isabelle, am I to understand that you let those ghastly men know the party would be happening?'

'No, absolutely not,' I answered her. 'Just the opposite, I made them promise not to come anywhere near here.'

'How did they know we would be here at all?' she demanded.

'It's very simple,' Sarah put in with a sigh. 'They are regulars at a truly dreadful pub in Cowley, the Red Ox. Jasmine, Caroline and Isabelle strip there –'

'No I don't,' I interrupted.

'You have done,' she pointed out, 'and that is beside the point. You invited them to your birthday party last term, which was held here, and is no doubt why they turned up here tonight, hoping for more of what Isabelle gave them, the details of which I shan't distress you with, Eliza. As to how they knew, I imagine Isabelle, or one of the others, has been less than perfectly discreet.'

'Absolutely not,' I answered her.

'We certainly haven't said anything,' Jasmine added from the doorway, putting an arm around Caroline's shoulder. 'They must have followed us or something.'

'Maybe they come up here every weekend,' I suggested, 'just to check.'

'I hardly think that's likely,' Sarah answered.

'Well never mind, they've gone now,' I said, full of mock jollity.

'I do mind, I mind a great deal,' Eliza answered me. 'You assured me that there would be absolute discretion.'

'There is,' I answered, although my words sounded hollow even in my own ears and I could already feel the tears starting in my eyes.

184

The sound of a car starting came to us from a little way down the lane. I was struggling for words as the noise faded away, but the others were already trooping into the house. The mood of the party was broken, probably irrevocably, and I felt awful, but I was absolutely certain I hadn't told any of the men which night it was to be held. I was also furious with them, for betraying their promise after the snooker match, and when I'd indulged all of them in the storeroom . . .

No, not all of them. I'd refused Tierney, which probably explained their presence. He'd have persuaded the others to come up, just the sort of vindictive thing he would do. They'd gone along with it, obviously, but perhaps had felt at least some shame, which helped explain why they'd gone away with so little fuss.

I waited outside for a while, thinking black thoughts and listening for the sound of their car just in case they decided to come back. Only when Katie came out to fetch me could I face going inside, to where everyone else was sat around, now fully dressed, talking urgently. Sarah turned to me immediately.

'I really don't want to do this, Isabelle, but I really don't see we have any option but to ask you not to come in future.'

'Let's not be hasty,' Laura put in quickly. 'No real harm has been done, nothing that can't be dealt with by a court martial.'

'You're right,' Sarah answered her after a moment. 'Sorry, but I really can't bear men like that. I didn't mean you should be thrown out, Isabelle, but will you accept a court martial?'

'Why?' I demanded. 'I haven't broken any rules, at all.'

'No?' she queried.

Portia spoke up.

'Leaving aside the question of how those dreadful men knew we'd be here tonight for a moment, I thought we'd agreed that four members needed to have met a potential newcomer before she was invited?'

'Not that I mind in the least, Eliza,' Sarah added, 'but it's a matter of principle.'

'Never mind that, what about the men?' Pippa demanded.

'They've gone,' Sarah answered her, 'and yes, I think Isabelle's general conduct does need to be examined, closely.'

'Three members have approved Eliza,' I pointed out, 'and it would have been four if Katie . . .'

'Yes,' Portia said very slowly, as if talking to a particularly dim child, 'but three is not four, is it and, in any event, you met up after you, Isabelle, had invited Eliza, entirely off your own bat. Is that not true?'

I hesitated, but there was no getting out of it and I answered in a small voice.

'Yes.'

'Then there it is,' she went on, 'small points, I know, but if we are to have rules we must follow them. Is that not so?'

She glanced around the room. Sarah nodded immediately, looking very serious, angry even, although I was sure she was taking a thoroughly sadistic delight in my discomfort. Laura didn't look too happy about it, but also nodded, Pippa likewise. Katie shook her head, Caroline merely shrugged. Portia made no attempt at all to hide her delight in their response, grinning like an imp as she gave Sarah a thumbs-up signal. To my surprise Jasmine nodded, unable to meet my eye as she spoke.

'Sorry, Isabelle, but it's true. You have to follow the rules, or why should anybody else?'

Tears were welling up in my eyes as I looked up. I couldn't find words, but there was nothing to say in any case.

'It is a minor point,' Laura stated, 'but the issue with these men isn't. Are you three sure you didn't let something slip, even accidentally? Jasmine, perhaps you had to break a booking tonight or something?'

'No,' Jasmine answered, 'we were on last night. I swear we didn't say a word, and none of them mentioned it at all.'

'There's an easy way to find out,' Sarah stated. 'Do you have a number for any of them, Jasmine, Caroline?'

'Sure,' Jasmine answered, 'I've got Mike's mobile.'

'Ring it, please.'

Jasmine rang the number and Sarah took the phone from her. After a moment it was answered, and she snapped out a string of sharp, demanding questions, pausing between each. At last she broke the connection and handed the phone back to Jasmine with a long sigh.

'Mike informs me,' she said evenly, 'that some of them had apparently been spying on us last time, but only Isabelle saw. When she said she was going out for some fresh air, what she actually did was take all three of them back to their car, where she let them have her in exchange for leaving us alone.'

My cheeks felt hot enough to fry eggs on as every single person in the room turned to me. I could only manage a helpless shrug, at first, but managed to rally myself.

'I . . . I just wanted them to go away,' I explained, 'without ruining the party. They'd followed Duncan's car, and . . . and, well, actually, I think that was pretty generous of me.'

'Hardly,' Sarah replied, 'when it was only because of you they came at all.'

'Yes, but –'

'Besides,' she interrupted, now quite calm, 'it also seems that Isabelle went up to the Red Ox last Saturday to try to persuade them to leave us alone in future. Very commendable, you might think, except that in the course of the afternoon, playing strip snooker and sucking men off in the storeroom, Isabelle managed to let slip that we were meeting this weekend.'

'I did not,' I answered her. 'I swear I didn't'

Sarah merely shook her head. Everyone was looking at me, and I was blushing hotter than ever. I knew I hadn't given away any details at all, yet nobody believed me, and I could see my protests were only making me look a liar.

'Maybe . . . maybe Tierney saw my invitation card,' I said, with sudden inspiration. 'He's my scout, and he probably told Mike to say that instead of admitting he'd been going through my things. Yes, that'll be it.'

'Perhaps so,' Eliza stated, 'but if you knew this man Tierney was going to be in your room, why did you not make more effort to conceal the invitation?'

I shrugged.

'I'm sorry. I didn't think.'

'No, you didn't, did you?' Sarah said. 'But I for one don't want this to spoil the club. I suggest we give Isabel a suitable punishment and hope it's a lesson to her. Is that fair?'

Not even Katie objected, leaving me standing forlorn in the middle of the room, unwilling to try to defend myself, because if Tierney had found my invitation then it really was my fault. Laura took over.

'Very well, let us do this according to the rules. As Isabelle is the one under sentence, I will appoint the court. Does anyone object?'

Again nobody spoke up, and she went on.

'First, I would like to propose Eliza for full membership of the Rattaners.'

'I'll second that,' Pippa spoke up.

Sarah was going to speak, but changed her mind. I couldn't. Laura glanced from face to face.

'Carried unanimously,' she stated, 'and I hope you'll take a place on the court, Eliza, as I need to choose those who'll be least partisan?'

'I accept,' Eliza answered, 'and thank you, everybody. I am flattered by your confidence in me.'

'Also,' Laura went on, 'myself, and Pippa. Isabelle, do you have any objections?'

I shook my head.

'And do you accept that you have broken the rules of the Rattaners, specifically by allowing outsiders to discover when and where our party was being held?'

'Yes,' I answered to the floor, 'it looks that way, but it was an accident.'

'That will be taken into consideration. Do you wish to defend against your breach of the membership rules?'

'No,' I said and sighed.

'Guilty on both counts,' she finished. 'So what is to be done with you?'

The question wasn't addressed to me, but I shrugged anyway.

'It shouldn't be too severe,' Pippa spoke up. 'She's really just been too enthusiastic. I suggest the candle punishment, the one she gave me last time.'

I swallowed hard as I looked up, shocked out of my self-pity and wondering what she'd have suggested as a really severe punishment. Laura nodded wisely.

'That seems fair. Eliza, the punishment would be for Isabelle to be caned while holding candles in her vagina and anus. The candles are marked with stripes, and each stripe that melts away reduces some subsequent ordeal by one unit. Pippa was to drink her own pee, a glass per stripe on the candles.'

'If the candles fall out it goes straight to the ordeal,' Pippa added, 'or when Isabelle asks us to blow them out, or can't take the cane any more. When she did it she put a candle out with her cane, so I got off.'

'That detail I think we should dispense with,' Eliza suggested. 'It must be a proper punishment. It also seems a little dangerous. I suggest she be securely tied for her own safety, and that the candles be blown out immediately if the flame is too close to her skin.'

'Believe me, you know long before then,' Pippa answered. 'Also, she'll have to put the candles in herself, because the deeper she does it the easier they'll be to hold, but the fewer rings will melt. It's not easy.'

'So I imagine,' Eliza responded, for once impressed. 'Isabelle?'

'I accept,' I told her, my voice a weak croak.

'Good,' Laura answered me. 'In the playroom then and I will fetch a cane and a pair of candles.'

Katie already had my hand, and Jasmine took the other, leading me up into the carriage behind Laura, and to her large playroom. Eliza had followed and glanced around, taking in the various pieces of punishment equipment.

'Remarkable,' she stated. 'Put her on that thing like a bench, I think, girls, that way we should be able to secure her properly.'

'The trestle,' Jasmine explained, pulling me towards it.

I went, numb with shock, shaking, full of burning shame and also severe apprehension, not only for the pain, but for my own reaction to it. As they moved me gently down onto the padded top of the trestle I could barely make my body do as I wanted, and lay limp as my wrists and ankles were fastened into the restraining cuffs. Portia had followed and attached the broad leather belt around my waist, tight, to force my bottom up, bulging out beneath my skirt.

'Hang on,' Pippa's voice sounded from behind me. 'She's got to put her own candles in.'

'This is a punishment, not a game,' Eliza responded, 'but as you have the experience, perhaps you should put them in?'

'OK,' Pippa said, and I tried to crane back to see if she actually had the candles, even as one rounded end pushed to my pussy hole and up.

'This won't be easy, Isabelle,' she said, 'you're very wet. Shall I lubricate your bottom for you?'

'A . . . a little maybe,' I managed, my head swimming with humiliation as they began to make a ring around me to watch my ordeal.

Pippa began to hum gently to herself, not replying, but a moment later my beautiful black dress had been turned up onto my back, all the way, to leave my fancy underwear on show, with my bottom encased in the baggy folds of my combinations.

'These are pretty,' she said, and pulled them wide, exposing my rear view completely with one casual motion.

I knew I was spread, my bottom on full display between the open curtains of my combinations, showing everything, and Portia giggled as the rude brown star of my anus came on show.

'Have you seen her bumhole, Eliza?' she asked. 'Doesn't she look rude?'

'No ruder, I dare say, than you would in the same position,' Eliza answered, and I felt a flush of gratitude. It was bad enough to have to flaunt my bottom as I was punished without Portia's remarks.

'Mustn't spoil your lovely clothes,' Pippa said, tucking the sides of my combinations open to keep the cloth well clear of my pussy and anus. 'Don't wiggle so. I'm just going to lube you up, OK?'

Her finger touched my bumhole, cold and slippery with some sort of cream. I couldn't help but sigh as she teased me open and slid deep in, greasing my ring with her finger moving in and out until she'd decided I was open enough to take the candle.

'Keep your fanny tight,' she warned me and her finger came out with a sticky pop.

The base of the second candle replaced it, and I was grimacing as I felt my bumhole push in and spread slowly to the pressure, then the candle shaft ease in up my rectum. I had no idea how deep she'd put the candles, or even if the apparent sympathy in her voice was genuine. All I could do was squeeze my pussy and bumhole onto the candle stems as best I could, and pray I could hold on under the pain of Laura's cane. It was hard anyway, and tears of frustration had begun to squeeze from my eyes as Laura at last came in.

'Are you ready, Isabelle?' she asked, and I heard the rasp of a match behind me.

I felt the heat of the flame too, making my muscles twitch as she lit the candles. First was the one in my pussy, second the one up my bottom, the warmth of the flame moving over my flesh, then growing even with both candles burning. I closed my eyes, forcing myself to concentrate on holding the candles in and not on my raging emotions.

Laura had stepped back. I felt the thin hard line of the cane tap against my flesh, on the cheekiest part of my bottom, lift, and swish down to crack against my naked skin. I screamed, my muscles jerked, and I only just managed to catch the candle in my slippery wet pussy hole before it fell out.

'Perhaps a gag? She does scream so,' Sarah suggested.

'My bikini will do,' Jasmine said, pushing it down her legs even as I turned to protest.

'I don't need to be gagged.'

'Sure, Isabelle,' Sarah responded, and Jasmine's wadded bikini bottoms were being offered to my mouth.

'Open wide, Isabelle,' Portia said, laughing as Jasmine pushed the panty gag well into my mouth, 'and count yourself lucky they're not the ones Sarah wet.'

'Portia!' Sarah snapped, and once again Laura's cane tapped against my bottom.

I tightened my muscles and shut my eyes again, hurriedly, readying myself only an instant before the cane bit into my flesh, harder than before, enough to leave me gasping through my gag and shaking badly, but somehow the candles stayed in. Already the flame felt hotter, but I found my determination growing at the realisation that I wasn't a complete failure.

My tears had started though, trickling hot and wet down my cheeks as Laura measured up her third stroke. Again I tensed, again the cane slashed down across my bottom, this time so hard the breath was knocked from my body, to leave me with two long streamers of snot hanging from my nose and crying harder still. My three cane cuts felt like lines of fire, but no hotter than my pussy, which had begun to contract on the candle up the hole through no will of my own.

The flame felt hotter too, on the edge of pain, but I was determined to go on, to hold back until every last band had melted away. A drip of wax caught me, completely by surprise, running down the candle shaft and onto my anus. My bottom tightened, I gasped in shock, but still I held the candles, now trembling all over and dreading the touch of the next hot drop against my anal skin. I wiggled, hoping to dislodge some onto the floor, but spattered it over my own thighs and ended up jerking and squirming in my bonds.

'That's three,' Laura said. 'You're being a brave girl, Isabelle.'

I didn't feel brave, snivelling miserably as I tried to suck up the snot hanging from my nose, embarrassed by the state I was in even at that awful moment. All I succeeded in doing was making my hat fall off, so that they could all see plainly instead of through the gauze of my veil. Portia giggled and whispered to Sarah, who smiled in response, and as I looked up the next cane stroke landed across my bottom, with no aiming tap this time, and as hard as ever.

A great mass of mucus exploded from my nose, the candle shot backwards from my pussy hole and I was lost, blowing snot bubbles and wriggling in pain as I struggled for a control that no longer mattered, with my poor penetrated bottom hole in furious contraction on the candle stem. Even before I'd stopped squirming I felt somebody blow on me from the behind, the hot

193

sensation vanished and I hung my head in defeat, picturing what was about to come.

I had to drink my own pee, maybe several glasses, and if I couldn't make enough, then I was sure Sarah would be happy to oblige. Somebody's knuckles touched my burning bottom where my welts crossed my cheeks, stinging my flesh, and the candle was drawn slowly from my bottom hole, which closed with a soft fart.

'Untie her,' Laura instructed, 'we'll finish this in comfort. Is that three rings, Jasmine?'

'Four,' Jasmine answered. 'I think the one up her pussy went faster.'

'Seven in all then,' Laura confirmed. 'Not bad, Isabelle.'

If seven glasses of pee wasn't bad I didn't know what was, but I held my peace. I felt beaten, exposed too, my dignity gone. I'd been strapped down on a whipping trestle. I'd had my bottom stripped. I'd had candles put in me. I'd been gagged. I'd been caned. A little more and I knew exactly the state I'd be in, grovelling on the floor.

There wasn't a little more, there was a lot. Katie and Caroline ducked down beside me to work on my cuffs and when I was freed I stood, unsteady on my feet as I pulled Jasmine's bikini bottoms from my mouth. She was now naked but for her collar and heels, but the sight no longer brought me feelings of dominance, rather companionship. Feeling that I too should be naked, I began to undress, undoing the front of my upper dress.

Nobody commented, but stood to watch as I slowly divested myself of my armour, not because I'd been ordered to, but of my own choice. I shrugged my top free and set it aside, pulled off my gloves and kicked my boots away. Now some four inches shorter, I unfastened my skirt and let it fall, peeled down my stockings and tugged open the laces of my corset. A little work and it fell away, a little more and my combinations followed, to let me step naked from a puddle of black cloth, as if emerging from a chrysalis, once proud and dominant, now nude and submissive.

Katie took my hand once more and together we walked from the playroom and back to the extension. Caroline, eager as ever, already had a carton of orange juice open and was pouring it out into a pint glass. Portia crossed to the kitchen cupboards, no less eager as she began to take Laura's largest set of wine glasses down from the shelf. All the others sat down, making themselves comfortable to watch my repentance, seven glasses full of my own piddle, swallowed down in full view of all of them.

'There's a jug there, Portia,' Laura instructed. 'She can do it in that.'

Portia reached for the jug, a huge thing of clear glass with a wide mouth. Caroline passed me the orange juice and I took a swallow, even as Portia spoke up.

'We're not going to have to wait for you, are we, Isabelle? Look, if you can't do enough we'll just have to help you. I don't mind.'

'Well I . . .' I began, trying to save myself one final detail of humiliation, but she had already put the jug to her sex, squatting down to let her thighs apart.

She was giggling as a thick gush of pee burst from her pussy, swirling in the bottom of the jug. I knew she'd had plenty to drink, but was astonished to see the level rise, higher and higher, until she gave a little wiggle to shake off the last few drops.

'There we are,' she said happily, extending the jug to me. 'Now you hardly need to do any.'

I took the jug, looking down into the pale golden pool of what I was about to have to drink, not even my own, but Portia's, undoubtedly to her delight, and Sarah's. All seven glasses were set out, and there was possibly enough to satisfy them so I stepped toward the work-space, only for Sarah to wag a finger at me.

'Uh, uh, Portia may have helped, but you still have to do it in front of us.'

She was right. I had fought the candles, but that was a fair part of the punishment. To try to avoid any further part would be to decrease their respect for me, and for myself. I squatted down, lowering my bottom gently onto the jug, my feelings of submission and exposure rising to what seemed an impossible crescendo as I let my bladder go. My pee gushed out, gurgling into Portia's, who giggled to see me do it, the only sound in the room.

I let it all come, enjoying the sense of release despite myself, and the wanton, naughty feeling of doing something so intimate in front of so many people. By the time I'd finished I was completely lost, and fell to my knees, my head hung low, my breathing deep and even in rising submissive ecstasy. Portia came forwards, laughing in gleeful mischief as she picked up the jug and went to where the glasses stood.

'I think you need to show us all you're truly sorry,' she said.

As I looked up I realised what she meant. She'd filled a glass, the pale yellow pee for all the world like white wine, and given it to Caroline. I nodded in mute acceptance of her choice, and watched as she distributed our mingled piddle, to each woman in turn, leaving only herself before settling back against the work surface with her pretty face set in pure mischief.

'Stay on your knees,' Sarah instructed.

I didn't need to be told. Caroline was closest, and I crawled to her, the girl I'd spanked so many times, the girl I'd made kiss my boots, lick my bottom, and suck men's cocks, for her submissive pleasure and my delight in dominating her. How the tables were well and truly turned, her eyes bright with amusement, her little chin tilted up in mock hauteur as she offered me the brimming glass.

The pungent scent caught my nose, my lips touched, the rich, acrid taste filled my senses and I was drinking, gulping my own piddle down as Caroline gave a shrill, delighted peel of laughter. I took it all, every last drop, sparing myself nothing and, as I swallowed, something inside me seemed to give. Bowing my head lower still, I kissed Caroline's feet.

'She can be very sweet, if she's handled properly,' Sarah remarked.

Jasmine was next, seated beside Caroline, so I only needed to shuffle sideways. Our eyes met. Hers, normally so full of worship, now seemed full of doubt, and her hand was trembling a little as she passed me her glass, spilling pee down my cleavage. I took it, a lump in my throat as I spoke.

'Sorry, Jasmine. I tried to be your perfect Mistress.'

She gave a rueful smile and watched as I put the glass to my lips and began to drink. As the pee trickled down my throat something had changed in our relationship, as it had once before, when I'd first spanked her. Next time, we would probably be side by side.

'Now Katie,' Portia instructed.

Katie was sweeter, ruffling my hair as I came to kneel at her feet, smiling sweetly to see me take the place she usually did. I smiled back, realising that if I had lost something with Jasmine, then I had gained with Katie. Once I had gulped down her offering she would be able to give herself more completely than ever.

'Come to me, Isabelle,' Pippa said – not an order but a request.

She was curled on the floor at Laura's feet, and rose a little as I crawled up to her, kneeling as she offered me the glass. When I took it she kept holding, watching me and helping tip it up to my lips. I swallowed what I could, already feeling a little bloated, and she waited patiently until I could finish the rest. As the last acrid drop went down I was trying not to gag, and closed my eyes, but to my surprise Pippa took my head in her hands, pulling me close. She kissed me, her mouth a little open and I responded, sharing the taste until my head was swimming with it.

I could feel her excitement, and would have gone down with her, maybe head to tail on the floor, but we broke apart as Laura gave a gentle cough. She was holding her glass out to me, and I nodded, now dizzy with reaction as I took it in my fingers. They all watched as I drank, slowly now, sip by sip, with the bloated sensation in my tummy growing every heavier, and the urgent, helpless desire to touch my pussy close to irresistible.

Next came Sarah, her expression one of smug superiority as I crawled to her, naked on my knees. I didn't even feel resentment, but took the glass from her hand and began to drink, looking up into her eyes as I sipped, and rather wishing she'd mingled her own pee into the mixture, a fitting response for how I'd behaved towards her, what I'd made her do. She spoke when I'd finished maybe half the glass.

'Are you sorry, Isabelle?'

'Yes,' I answered her, 'for everything.'

'Then show it,' she answered, and her hands went to the button of her jeans.

Portia squeaked with delight.

'Yes, yes! Make her do it, Sarah, pretty please!'

'I intend to,' Sarah answered as she lifted her bottom to push her jeans down.

She was still bare beneath and, as she opened her thighs, I was presented with her warm moist pussy, into which I buried my face, licking in apology and submission. Her hand settled on my head, not hard, to stroke my hair, soothing me, now caring and gentle because I was where she felt I should be, on my knees before her.

As she moved a little forwards I knew exactly what she wanted, perhaps the deepest, most heartfelt gesture of submission one woman can give to another, to kiss her anus. I moved lower, pushing out my lips to plant a single firm kiss on her warm, soft ring. Again something inside me seemed to change, and before I really knew it I'd stuck my tongue out, licking at the wrinkly little star and pushing into the tiny central hole to taste her.

'That's my girl,' Sarah said, sighing. 'Deep in now, clean me, then back to work.'

I obeyed, pushing my tongue in as deep up her bottom as I could get before returning to lap at her pussy. Portia gave a delighted giggle for what I'd done, Eliza a cluck of approval. I closed my eyes and licked more firmly, burrowing my face into the warmth of Sarah's body. She sighed in pleasure, and again as I began to press my tongue to her clitoris. I was lost in worship as I took hold of her hips and pulled myself tighter still, working my tongue on her flesh, in up her open pussy, lapping at her bumhole again, and back to her clitoris to bring her to a long, tight climax.

I was left gasping, my pussy warm and urgent, dizzy with pleasure and with need. My belly was a tight ball, swollen out by six glasses of Portia's and my mixed piddle, and there was a seventh to come, from Eliza, the most senior among us, the one at whose feet I most wanted to be. Her expression was as cool and amused as ever as I crawled to her, very different from my wanton, grovelling nudity.

She held out the glass as I reached her, watching me as I took it, and the wicked joy in her eyes as I began to drink sent a jolt straight to my pussy. A little piddle went down my breasts, my hand shaking too much to control myself, and I began to rub it over my swollen belly and hard nipples as I finished my glass. Eliza nodded.

'Very good,' she said. 'I see you are properly contrite. Pleasant, isn't it?'

'Yes, Eliza,' I managed.

'And I suspect you'd like to come now?'

'Yes, unless . . . unless you want me to do something for you . . . anything.'

'To watch you will be sufficient, thank you, Isabelle, and when you have come, you are to tell me how much you enjoyed it.'

It was not mine to wonder what she was talking about. I bowed my head and rocked back on my heels, parting my thighs to masturbate in front of her. My hand went to my pussy, touching my swollen, sensitive flesh, only to be brought up short by Portia, her voice high-pitched in uncontrolled delight.

'Hey! What about me? Do I get left out?'

I didn't know what to say, but shook my head, puzzled. She smiled, walking towards me with a taunting sway to her hips, naked and glorious, holding the jug of our pee. I was still stroking myself, desperate to come, and my burning feelings grew stronger still as she took me firmly by the hair and pressed the jug to my lips.

'You drank it, Isabelle,' she crowed. 'You drank my pee. And on your knees, to everyone. You are such a little trollop. Come on, have some more.'

She tilted the jug, and I began to drink, swallowing down the warm, pungent liquid as my fingers began to move on my clitoris. Portia gave a fresh crow of delight as she saw what I was doing, and tilted the jug further still as she called out, 'She's playing with herself! Look, girls, Isabelle's playing with herself while she drinks my pee-pee!'

It was coming too fast. I couldn't swallow it all, my mouth filling too quickly despite my best efforts, spilling pee out at the sides and down my chest, all over my breasts and my swollen belly, onto my sex, to trickle down over my busy fingers as I brought myself up towards ecstasy. Behind me Caroline gave a little gasp of excitement, Katie a shy, urgent giggle. Portia tipped the jug higher still, full in my face, and lifted, to pour our mingled urine over my head as she screamed with joy.

I was coming, my muscles starting to tighten, my mouth wide, revelling in the warm, pungent liquid flowing down my body, all over my breasts and belly and pussy, and my bottom cheeks behind, and in the crease, to wet my anus. My hand went back, to find the little muscular knot, still slippery from my candle caning. My finger when in, deep up my rectum, two more into my pussy and I was holding myself back and front, squirming in orgasm, ecstasy made more intense still because everyone was staring at my pee-soaked body as I did it.

Everything was on plain view – my sodden hair, my wet, slippery skin, my dripping nipples, my bulging tummy, my freshly caned bottom cheeks, my penetrated bumhole and sex and, as Portia put the jug to my mouth one more time, that I was willingly, eagerly drinking down her piddle and my own. As I took the last of it down with one choking gulp I hit my peak. A scream broke from my mouth, unfettered ecstasy, and again, my whole body jerking in orgasm, my every muscle in spasm and with no control whatsoever over the state I was in.

I came again and again, oblivious to everything but pleasure, my orgasm breaking only when Portia tightened her grip in my hair and pressed my face firmly to her sex, only to rise to a final peak as she laughingly squirted out a little more piddle straight into my mouth. As my ecstasy slowly levelled off I was already licking, and still playing with my bottom and sex. She purred in delight, then called out, 'Come on, girls, form an orderly queue. Let's make her do it.'

They did, all eight of them. First Portia, Katie and Pippa, then Sarah for a second time, followed by Laura, Jasmine, Caroline and, finally Eliza, even her reserve not strong enough to resist the temptation. Some came to me, some made me crawl to them. Some stripped, some exposed only what they had to. Only Eliza failed to make an exhibition of herself, making me put my head up her skirt and coming with a gentle sigh once I'd done my job. When she'd come I was left kneeling on the floor, panting, sore, still sopping wet, but deliriously happy.

'I think you have a little clearing up to do,' she remarked, 'but first, did you enjoy your punishment?'

'Yes.'

'It was rather special, I fancy?'

'Yes.'

'And if I was to offer you the chance to experience that again, as my plaything, would you take it?'

'Yes.'

Nine

Usually, when I've been brought to a submissive high I recover my usual attitude within a few hours, or at least by morning. This time it was different. I'd not only lost myself completely, but admitted to Eliza that I wanted to be her plaything, in front of everybody.

There was no going back on it, and my only consolation was that she lived in Portsmouth, so that I wouldn't be spending half my time being given enemas, spanked and having my mouth washed out with soap. I'd have done it too, and my feelings were distinctly bittersweet on the Sunday evening when we said good-bye to her at the station.

Dr Treadle was with us too, and we had driven down from his house after offering him guest membership of the Rattaners in exchange for the use of his house for future events. He'd agreed, but I was under stern warning not to say anything to anybody about it, while Laura was going to issue the invitations with her own address on them.

It was to be immediately after the official end of term, on the Sunday of ninth week and the day before I returned to Scotland. Eliza would be there, and I had already been given my instructions what to wear: smart heels, white socks, white panties, a short tartan skirt, no top. My rather weak protest that I didn't own anything of the sort had resulted in her writing a cheque for one hundred pounds for Caroline, who was to wear the same. So were Jasmine, Katie, Portia and Pippa, to make us into six little copies of the same moppet for the others' amusement.

I should have resented it, but I didn't. I couldn't. Instead the idea turned me on, and that night Katie and I lay together on the bed, our hands down each other's panties as we masturbated together over what Eliza, Sarah and Laura might make us do, and do to us. Even as we clung together after I'd come over the image of us kneeling together in our little outfits I couldn't feel bad about it.

There were other changes to make too. I was finished with the Red Ox, once and for all. They had gone too far, not in what they'd done to me, but in betraying me. Mike especially I was disappointed by, the others only a little less so. With Tierney, it was exactly what I'd have expected him to do, although leaving him out after the snooker game had plainly been a mistake.

My feelings for Sarah were more ambivalent. Rationally, I knew she'd been in the right all along, both in terms of my lack of responsibility and my sexuality. She also fancied me, in her own way. On the Rattaners' evening she alone had made me lick her twice during my punishment, also a third time, with my face buried in her bottom as she leant negligently on the worktop, discussing how to make soft icing with Laura as my tongue worked on her anus. There was no denying that I returned her feelings either, or that everything about her filled me with an irrational annoyance.

On the Saturday of sixth week she came to see me at the Mill. Katie was with me, and we'd been lazing on the bed, fully dressed but swapping ever dirtier and more colourful fantasies, which would have inevitably led to sex. The door was still unlocked, and when it swung open the instant after an initial knock I had to jerk my hand back from teasing Katie's nipples through her jumper. Relief mixed with embarrassment as I saw it was Sarah, with Portia behind her, both wrapped up warm against the chilly autumn afternoon.

'Don't stop on my account,' Sarah said, 'but do be quick.'

'I'm fine, thank you,' I answered, trying to sound reserved and failing miserably.

'Quick?' Katie queried.

'Yes,' Sarah replied. 'I've decided to take Isabelle out for a treat, a facial, and you are to come too, Katie.'

'A facial?' I began, and then saw Portia's smirk. 'Oh . . .'

'Yes,' Sarah confirmed, smiling. 'Now come on, chop-chop girls, no time for dithering.'

'I'm not sure –' I began, only to be cut off by a now red-faced Katie addressing Sarah.

'Do . . . do you mean you're going to make her suck a man's penis?'

'And let him come in her face, exactly,' Portia added with relish.

'Hang on,' I insisted, 'maybe I don't –'

'Do it, Isabelle,' Katie cut in, 'just the way we were talking about.'

'You were talking dirty together?' Sarah queried.

'Yes,' I admitted.

'About sucking men's cocks?' Portia queried, her voice full of mock disgust.

'Sh,' I urged. 'I do have neighbours.'

'You'd better put your coat on then,' she said, 'before my remarks become really interesting.'

'OK, I'm coming,' I promised. 'If I have to.'

'You do,' Sarah insisted, 'and you needn't pretend you're being martyred either. Remember I know all about what you get up to at the Red Ox.'

'Not any more,' I assured her. 'That's not where we're going, is it?'

'I,' Sarah responded, 'would not be seen dead in the Red Ox.'

'Now come on,' Portia urged, taking down the coats from the back of my door.

I accepted mine, somewhat wistfully, although there was no denying the knot in my stomach. To be taken out and made to suck some unknown man until he came in my face was almost exactly what Katie and I had been talking about at first, before moving on to a fantasy of being held down face to face by the wives of the men we'd sucked, and spanked until we howled.

Sarah's car was in the lane, and I was told to get into the back with Portia. I obeyed, nervous but excited, also surprised, because Sarah generally shunned men and it was hard to imagine her arranging such a fate for me. Only when we'd driven through the science area and turned north up the Banbury Road did I realise where we were going – to Walter Jessop, the dirty old man who ran the antique shop in Whytleigh.

It was a bit of a disappointment, as I'd been imagining something more intense. Still, I was being taken out cock sucking by Sarah, and in front of Katie and Portia, which was enough to bring my emotions up, even if it was only old Walter. As we drove I tried to concentrate on the humiliation of it, and what the girls might do with me afterwards. The afternoon traffic had begun to pick up, and Sarah concentrated on her driving until we were past Foxson, then spoke up.

'Time to blindfold her, Portia. Katie too.'

'We've only brought one,' Portia pointed out.

'There must be something . . .'

'I've got it, don't worry. Katie, stay still.'

Portia pulled a length of dense black cloth from her handbag and wrapped it gently around Katie's head, tying it off at the back to leave her no doubt completely unable to see.

'Are you going to make me do anything?' she asked nervously.

'Not with men, sweetie,' Sarah assured her.

'That's reserved for Isabelle,' Portia said chuckling. 'Off with your knickers then.'

'My knickers?' Katie queried. 'What are you going to do?'

'I just need to borrow them.'

'I'll have to take my tights off too.'

'Then do it. Actually, I need those too.'

Katie threw me a worried look, but lifted her bottom to wriggle her tights and panties down under her skirt and off. She passed them back, beige tights and her apple-patterned panties. Portia immediately pulled the panties down over my head, fitting my face where Katie's bottom had been just a moment before, still warm. The tights she wrapped around my head and tied off behind, leaving me completely unable to see and no longer in need of working up my sense of erotic humiliation.

'She's done,' Portia said, laughing.

'I know,' Sarah answered. 'I can see her in the mirror. What a sight!'

'I think we should tie her hands as well,' Portia said, giggling. 'Come on, Isabelle, I need your tights too. Off with them.'

'May I leave my panties on?'

'Did I say anything about them, you slut? Just do as you're told.'

I nodded, feeling more chagrined than ever as I followed Katie's little strip routine, lifting my bottom and pushing down my tights, kicking my shoes off to peel them away and passing them to Portia.

'Hands behind your back,' she instructed, and I obeyed.

She took my wrists as I leant forwards, binding my tights around them to leave me feeling helpless and distinctly awkward, pushed forwards against my seat belt and swaying to every turn of the car, which I could no longer anticipate or react against. I was glad it

207

wasn't too far to Whytleigh, and hoped they had some way of getting me into the shop without being seen.

Sarah's driving changed, faster, then completely stationary and I realised we were in the traffic on the ring road, or maybe one of the bigger roads leading north. I thought of how foolish I must have looked, and how much Walter would enjoy having me brought to him tied and blindfolded. They'd make me do it on my knees, and watch, maybe while Katie licked them, but she wouldn't be allowed to see. She was blindfolded too, and could only do as she was told.

I jumped when Portia's hand touched between my thighs, but let her ease them open, knowing that the more aroused I was the easier, and better, what they were about to make me do would be. She burrowed deeper, stroking me through my panties, her knuckles pushing the already wet cotton into the groove of my sex. I sighed in pleasure, my knees slipped wider apart and I caught her giggle from beside me.

'Look who's getting excited?' she purred after a moment. 'You dirty, dirty girl, Isabelle, so wet, and over the thought of taking a load of nasty men's cocks in your mouth, and –'

'Portia!' Sarah snapped. 'Don't give anything away, or you'll be next to her.'

'Yes, Mistress,' Portia said quickly and went quiet, but still with her hand up my skirt and her knuckles working on my pussy.

I'd lost track of time, with no idea how fast we were going, and it seemed to take forever to get to Whytleigh. Portia had implied that there would be several men too, but she might have been teasing, or not. When we did stop I had no idea where we were at all, but felt as if she'd parked outside Walter's shop. Sarah got out and Portia undid my seat belt, but instead of being helped from the car I was left sitting in the back.

Nothing happened for some while, minutes, maybe a quarter of an hour, before I heard voices, Sarah, and a man speaking in a gruff undertone. My muscles tightened and I swallowed, thinking of the taste and feel of erect cock in my mouth. I heard the door open, Portia's mischievous giggle, the man's voice again as the car rocked to his weight. He slammed the door, a large, powerful hand took hold of my hair where it stuck out at the side of Katie's panties, I heard the rasp of a zip and I was pulled down. My face was rubbed against a thick rubbery cock, which I took in, sucking obediently.

'What a little tart!' Portia's voice came from the front, high with mockery and laughter.

Her words sent a stab of humiliation through me, which only made me suck the harder. The man gave a pleased grunt, tightening his grip in my hair to control me as his cock began to swell in my mouth. He wasn't Walter Jessop – too big, too coarse, and the woollen band moving against my cheek as my mouth was fucked could only be one thing, a football scarf.

Somehow they'd arranged for me to give some supporters the pleasure of my mouth after the match. I thought back to my time in the storeroom at the Red Ox, bringing my emotions higher still, but it was too late to back out, too late to say anything, with a rapidly hardening cock in my mouth and my arms tied behind my back. They'd have their way, coming in my face and leaving me in wriggling, submissive ecstasy, eager for whatever Sarah and Portia chose to do to me afterwards.

My man adjusted his grip a little, pulling my head up to make me suck on his helmet and taking his shaft in hand. He began to tug, masturbating into my mouth, already quite urgent. Portia gave a delighted giggle, Katie a little, shocked gasp, perhaps as her blindfold was pulled off, to find me sucking cock with my wrists bound and my head encased in her apple panties.

'In her face,' Sarah instructed, not in the cold voice I would have expected, but friendly and also excited.

'Turn her round a bit,' Portia demanded. 'I can't see properly.'

The man grunted in complaint, but my head was twisted around even as his cock pulled free of my mouth. Portia went into frenzied giggles as my head began to jerk up and down to the motion of his masturbation, again he grunted, and hot, wet sperm splashed into my face as he came. As soon as he'd done what they'd asked of him he popped his cock back in, making me suck as he continued to ejaculate, but now into my mouth. My nose was soiled, and my cheek, I knew Katie's panties would be too, and maybe my hair.

I was panting softly as he finally released me, but I'd barely caught my breath when the car rocked to the weight of another man. Down came his zip and out came his cock, into my mouth, to be sucked all the way. There were others too, outside the car, talking, and not paying much attention to Sarah's requests for silence. I was too busy to listen, working on the rapidly growing penis in my mouth and wishing I could play with myself while I was used.

By the time the second man pulled my head up to come in my face Katie was giggling too, and playing with Portia to excite the men. As I began on my third man somebody opened the door behind me. Rough hands took my hips. My skirt was pulled up to show my panties and I realised it was not only my mouth they'd be using. Sure enough, down came my panties, my body was manhandled into fucking position, and a long hard cock slid into my body.

Sarah had only just realised, and said something, but I wiggled on the man inside me to show I was eager for it, drawing a crow of delighted laughter from Portia. The cock in my mouth was whipped out, another substituted and they had me on a spit, my body rocking between them, bringing me so high I was fighting my bonds, not to break free, but to bring myself off while they fucked me.

'Look at her, the little slut!' Portia squealed in delight.

'Let her hand free,' Katie's voice came after, and I felt a tug at my tights.

'No, I like her tied, I love the way she squirms!' Portia called out.

'Nah, I want her to feel my balls,' a man answered, and my knot had been tugged open.

I obliged, grateful for my release as I stroked and squeezed at the bulbous scrotum protruding from the man's fly beneath his cock. He gave a pleased grunt and pulled back a little, letting me rub my face on his long slippery shaft, lick his balls, suckle them into my mouth, kiss his helmet, lost in worship for his huge ugly cock as all the while another slid in and out of me behind.

Suddenly the man behind me changed his pace, ramming himself furiously in and out, to set me gasping and clutching, no longer able to concentrate on the one in front. One last thrust, his cock was whipped free and hot sperm spattered out over my upturned bottom and thighs, into my panties too. I wiggled invitingly, hoping there was just one more, to let me come with a cock in my body from each end, and sure enough, as I once more began to lick at the stiff shaft in front of me, something firm and round pressed to my pussy.

I was purring as he slid up me, thoroughly enjoying myself, and I was just about to pop the front man's cock back in my mouth for another suck when the one behind slid himself higher, smearing the cream from my pussy between my cheeks and pressing to my anus. My protest was cut off by several inches of cock as my head was pulled down, but it would have been weak anyway, my bumhole already opening, soft and slippery with juice as the man pushed in. Portia gave a heartfelt sigh, Katie a piglike squeal as they saw I was being buggered.

'That's right,' Portia said breathlessly. 'Right up her bum, deep up.'

'Dirty animals,' Sarah remarked, but made no attempt to stop it as my bumhole spread to the pressure.

Up he went, his cock eased into my ring and deep, bit by bit, filling my rectum with a terrible, glorious bloated sensation. It was too much. My hand went back, to dab my pussy, rubbing in the sperm oozing from my hole, and further back, to touch his balls and the straining ring of my anus where his fat shaft was stretching me out. It was too good not to come over immediately, taken from my cosy room, tied up, blindfolded with my girlfriend's panties, made to suck cock after cock after cock, and take their sperm in my face. It was from men I didn't even know too, rough, crude football fans from the town, using me for their amusement, making me suck, pulling down my panties to fuck me from the rear, and last, and best, lubricating my little brown bumhole with my own pussy juice and buggering me.

My fingers were working hard on my clitoris. I was sucking eagerly, my body worked back and forth on the two cocks inside me, mouth and anus. Portia and Katie were giggling, playing with each other too. Sarah was somewhere behind, cool and aloof as she watched me used, already sodden with sperm and about to get another two loads, one up my bottom. Five men, and maybe there were more, more to grope me, and smack me and stick their lovely cocks inside me, in my mouth and in my pussy and up my bottom . . .

I began to come, my body locking in ecstasy as the orgasm hit me, my empty pussy blowing air as the balls of the man up my bottom began to slap on my fingers and my ring pulsed on his shaft. At the last instant I jerked up my jumper and bra, baring my breasts, as I wanted to show it all. With that the man in my mouth grunted and whipped his cock free, jerking it frantically into my face as my body shivered in orgasm and I struggled to lick at his balls.

'She's got to look at this,' he grunted, Katie's panties and tights had been snatched up, and I could see.

He was masturbating in my face, his big veiny cock pumping in his hand, rich yellow in the car light; the hole, frothy with white bubbles, suddenly opened, and he did it, right in my face, in my hair too, spattering everything. I was left with a long tendril of sticky white come hanging from the tip of my nose as I took him back into my mouth, wobbling as I began to suck. He gave a long, pleased sigh, pulled back, and I was left to the pleasure of a long, thorough buggering as my orgasm at last began to fade.

Katie and Portia were kneeling in the front, arms around each other, their tops pulled up to show their breasts, both with rock-hard nipples; Katie still blindfolded. Beyond was Sarah, outside the car beneath a yellow light that showed other cars, and other people: Mike, who she was talking to; Jack; Big Dave; Mo, who'd just come in my face; and, as I jerked hard around, the man who was just that moment coming to orgasm up my well-buggered bottom – Stan Tierney.

If Mo hadn't pulled my blindfold up they would have got away with it. He had, and they hadn't.

The first awful, absurd thought that hit me was that I'd wiggled my bottom to encourage Stan Tierney to take me from behind, then self-recrimination for enjoying it so much and failing to recognise their voices. Next came the flood of anger and the furious reaction, with me shouting, Tierney shouting back, Portia and the other men desperately trying to calm things down, Katie horrified, and Sarah nowhere to be seen. She'd taken one look at my face and ran.

It took me days to even begin to calm down, and the full force of Duncan's reasoning as well. His arguments were that I had been willing, that I had enjoyed much the same treatment from the same men before, and that while the blame lay squarely with Sarah and Portia, it was far better to take an appropriate revenge on them rather than throw my own dolly out of the pram, as he put it, by breaking up the Rattaners.

By Friday I admitted he was right, but I was still feeling too sensitive to take my weekly spanking. My feelings were in a muddle to say the least, the deep pleasure in submission Eliza had inspired still there, for her, but no longer general. When I finally recovered myself enough to face her, I went to see Portia and demanded an explanation. I got it and, at her request, spanked her until she cried and had her lick me to ecstasy. As I came with her kneeling naked at my feet with her hot red bottom thrust out behind I felt a touch of my old pride, really for the first time since accepting my court martial.

I made Portia tell me every detail. Sarah's behaviour had been unspeakable, even worse than mine. From the very start of term she had been determined to put me in my place, as she'd expressed it to Portia. The men from the Red Ox had not followed us to Laura's, on either occasion, and nor had Tierney seen my invitation card. On both occasions Sarah had tipped them off, knowing full well that I'd do just about anything to make them go away. I had, to her delight, first surrendering to three of them in the back of Mo's car, then having myself well and truly put through my paces at the Red Ox.

Only after the second occasion had they begun to get difficult. The whole thing had been set up, leading inevitably to my court martial, which had left me in exactly the condition Sarah wanted me – a state of utter submission, made all the stronger by my own decision to get Eliza Abbott involved. As far as Sarah was concerned, her job was done, but the men thought otherwise.

They'd gone away when told to, as agreed, but had been left high and dry, having watched the early part of the Rattaners' party but not been given a girl, as Sarah had promised. A few days later they'd given her a choice: either to let them have her, give Portia to them, or bring me to them. For Sarah there had only been one acceptable option, hence the blindfold routine, driving north out of Oxford instead of east and taking me to a piece of wasteland near the Red Ox, where they'd been able to enjoy me at leisure.

Now it was done, but I wasn't. Having got Portia to admit she'd been in the wrong, and she had seen it all as a big joke, I sent a carefully worded circular letter out to the remaining Rattaners. Every single one agreed that Sarah deserved to be given a court martial, including herself after a couple of sharp phone calls from Eliza. Soon it was agreed that her trial would be the first item of business when we met at Dr Treadle's, and that once again Eliza, Laura and Pippa would be the judges.

I would have preferred to have some input into the sentencing, as my head was full of possibilities for her punishment. Yet Eliza's carefully controlled yet distinctly wicked personality, Laura's broad knowledge of sadistic sex and Pippa's high pain threshold, guaranteed it would be done properly. The only shame was that I wanted her to know that it was me who was punishing her.

The end of term distracted me briefly with exams and parties. I did quite well, thanks to my determination to study hard when I wasn't misbehaving, and Duncan gave me a rousing spanking as a reward. With no further work to do, Katie and I slept together on the Friday night, also on Saturday, and I finally managed to come to terms with my last encounter with the boys from the Red Ox, talking over together how it had felt as we masturbated. I still felt resentment for Sarah, but told myself that once she'd been punished all would be well.

On Saturday, Katie and I went to Dr Treadle's for lunch, and were going to meet Eliza from her train after.

Katie was fascinated by his house and full of nervous excitement for what might happen there later. I was little different, excited and a little drunk, enough to pluck one of Esmond's plumes and tickle Katie until she was giggling and breathless, to Dr Treadle's delight.

We drove down to the station in excellent humour, parked and walked in together, arm in arm. The car park was almost full, the ticket hall and platforms packed with people, most of them students on their way back to their homes for the Christmas holidays. By the time we'd worked out which arrival Eliza would be on, it was already pulling in, but we went out to the platform anyway.

She was almost the first person I saw, looking more like an old-fashioned bluestocking than ever in a hat and a grey gabardine with a distinctly 60s look that was probably genuine. In front of her was somebody else I recognised, Sarah, just bending to pick up Eliza's luggage. She was dressed in a bright-red polo-neck and tight faded jeans, her full, womanly bottom pushed out, round and tempting. Drunk, full of mischief and vengeance, it was more than I could resist.

'Wet!' I barked, as loud and commanding as I could.

Sarah gave a cry of shock and dismay, but it was too late. The reflex had worked, her bladder tightening at my command, to squirt pee into her panties and jeans. I saw the tell-tale dark smudge start to spread even before she whirled around with a look of horror and fury on her face, which grew abruptly stronger as she saw who it was.

For a moment I thought she was going to slap my face, but she had other things to worry about. She was only holding her piddle by clamping her thighs as tight as she could, and the 'V' of cloth where her jeans pulled tight over her pussy was dark and wet, leaving no question that she'd soiled herself. With a brief spate of words aimed at my feet she fled for the loos, with maybe fifty people staring at the diamond-shaped patch marking where her pee had soaked in around her bottom and down her legs.

'Whoops!' I managed, unable to keep the laughter from my voice.

'Isabelle!' Katie chided, but she was laughing too, and from the expression on Eliza's face it was plain to see she was struggling not to.

Only Dr Treadle didn't seem to find it amusing, his face red and his eyes popped out in surprise and a rather different sort of pleasure.

'Hello, Eliza,' I said, leaning forwards to kiss her cheek. 'Don't worry, I'll carry your bags, and I promise I'll show a little more control.'

'You are incorrigible, Isabelle,' she answered me. 'Never in public, this is an important rule.'

It might have been true, but she was still trying not to laugh. I picked up the bags and we began to push our way through the crowds and out of the station, stopping only when we'd reached the car. Sarah's own car was there, only two rows away from Dr Treadle's, but she wasn't. It was plain to see why.

Running to the nearest loo had been an instinctive reaction, what any woman would do when she's wet herself in front of a large crowd. It had also been a mistake. No matter what she did, her jeans would still be wet, so she could go in them, in soggy panties, or bare, none of which were acceptable options.

'You must take her a skirt and clean knickers, Isabelle,' Eliza told me as she unzipped one of the bags I'd put into the boot.

'I'd rather make her walk to the car,' I admitted.

'No,' Eliza said firmly. 'You will take her this skirt . . . and these knickers, and you will apologise.'

'Apologise? She still hasn't apologised to me for –'

'Isabelle! Do not be a brat. Now do as you're told.'

Forcing back my instinctive pout at being told off, I took the knee-length skirt of blue-grey wool and folded it around the knickers. I'd do it, but Eliza wasn't going to know if I apologised or not. Just to show willing I ran back to the station, slowing only when I was in the ticket hall. The Ladies' was crowded, and there was no sign of Sarah, but all the cubicles were closed.

'Sarah?' I called softly. 'Sarah? It's Isabelle. I've brought you a skirt and some knickers.'

'Pass them over the door!' she snapped back, still with an edge of panic in her voice.

I was struggling not to giggle as her hand appeared over the top of a cubicle door. She took the clothes and I made a hasty exit, not willing to face her, or to discuss a mutual apology until she'd calmed down a little. By the time I'd reached the car she still hadn't appeared, but I said I'd given her the clothes and apologised, and that it might be an idea to leave her alone for a bit. Unfortunately Eliza wouldn't accept it, and insisted on waiting, so I was obliged to pretend Katie and I needed to get to Jasmine's for a last fitting of our outfits.

On the bus across town I was feeling both guilty and thoroughly pleased with myself, both feelings enhanced by Katie's response moving between amusement and shock at what I'd done. Caroline had no such ambivalence, openly delighted, while Jasmine, always more serious, decided it was fair as revenge.

Eliza had given Katie a bag as we left, with a parcel in it, something squishy, which we opened. Inside were four new tam-o'-hanter bonnets, in the same red tartan as the skirts we had to wear, and each with a woolly bobble on top, in Santa Claus red, holly-leaf green, royal blue and daffodil yellow. For a moment I was just staring open mouthed, trying to take in the added humiliation. As a Scot, I've always hated the romance- and tourist-industry-inspired 'national costume', finding it unbearably twee.

Near us at home there had been a shop that sold oatcakes, little plastic Loch Ness Monsters and so forth.

The girls who served there had been made to wear tartan mini-skirts and tam-o'-shanters, which I'd always felt made them look utterly ridiculous. Now I was going to look the same, and if I didn't have the frilly shirts they wore, it was only because I had to go topless.

The discovery brought me firmly down to earth, reminding me of my new status, that with Eliza in Oxford I was simply one more of the submissive girls, and would be treated no differently. Telling myself that with the whole evening focussed on Sarah's punishment I probably wouldn't suffer too much, I took the last remaining tam-o'-shanter, with the yellow bobble, and followed the others upstairs to dress.

Half-an-hour later the four of us were stood in the kitchen, looking a prize bunch of clowns. Caroline was in the worst state, her skirt so short the over-tight white knickers encasing her ample cheeks showed beneath, but she'd made it that way and was thoroughly enjoying showing off, not even bothering to put her coat on but bouncing her big naked boobs in her hands in full view of the kitchen window. Katie was at least reserved, but clearly delighted with her look, the tam-o'-shanter accentuating her blonde hair and pretty face. Jasmine was a touch self-conscious, no more, treating it in much she same way she might have done a striptease outfit.

We drove over with coats on over our costumes, arriving at Dr Treadle's in time to help with the buffet supper he'd organised. I already expected to be made to serve, but was still a little taken aback to discover that not only were we to be maids, but that Pippa had been put in charge of us. The bobble on her tam-o'-shanter was black, making it look marginally less cutesy than the rest, and she was definitely enjoying her power, dishing out orders from the moment we'd stepped through the door and smacking our bottoms to hurry us along.

Had Eliza not been there, I think I'd have turned the tables, putting Pippa across my knee for a firm, panties-down spanking that would have put her back in her place. Somehow in Eliza's presence it was impossible, and I was forced to bite down a chagrin made all the stronger by my slowly rising arousal as I served plates of cold turkey and pickles, mince pies and devils-on-horseback.

Dr Treadle had been upstairs when we arrived, but quickly came down, in immaculate black tie, as was Duncan, who had arrived early and was drinking amontillado with Eliza and Laura in the living room. Both were smartly dressed, Eliza in a black trouser suit and Laura in her uniform. Last to arrive were Sarah, in a high-necked governess dress with her hair pinned up, and Portia, looking sulky in her little tartan outfit, breasts on show and topped off with a white-bobbled tam-o'-shanter. When I went back to the kitchen to collect a fresh plate of goodies I got a chance to talk to Portia.

'You are in serious trouble, Isabelle,' she crowed.

'Am I?' I replied. 'I'd have said we were about even, wouldn't you?'

'Sarah doesn't think so.'

'She's the one who's going in front of a court martial, not me. There's no rule against making other members wet themselves in public.'

Portia giggled and picked up a mince pie, taking a dainty bite from one side. I left her to it, returning to the living room, where Sarah was now in earnest conversation with Eliza, but went quiet as soon as I entered. I offered them a devil-on-horseback, curtseying sweetly and smiling. Sarah returned a dirty look, which followed me as I moved on to the others.

We'd started early on purpose, intending to eat, then to relax for a while before starting the party proper with Sarah's court martial. She didn't seem too worried, which was a pity, but as we sat and sipped port with the light fading from the winter sky outside, she was at least a trifle nervous and certainly drinking more than she

220

would usually have done. When Eliza asked Dr Treadle to close the curtains I knew we were about to begin. Laura looked up at me.

'Isabelle?'

'I'm sorry, have I done something wrong?' I answered quickly, already with visions of being put across her knee for the first spanking of the evening in my head.

'No,' she answered, amused, 'but as president of the Rattaners, perhaps you should say a few words. After all, we won't be seeing each other again until after Christmas, most of us anyway.'

'Right ... of course,' I managed, hastily pulling myself together and resisting the urge to curtsey. 'Um ... well, thank you, everybody, for playing your part in three wonderful parties, despite er ... certain difficulties, and I'm sure you all enjoyed yourselves as much as I did, maybe more. In any case, I think we've got off to a great start, and it's wonderful to have Eliza and Dr Tr ... Isadore, as new members.

'Hopefully, next term we can continue where we left off, and I'm especially pleased to say that we'll be having no more difficulties with certain gentlemen, and I use the term extremely loosely, from the Red Ox. On which topic, I suggest we proceed with the evening, and Sarah's court martial, which should show us what happens to those who disobey the club rules.'

I sat down, feeling distinctly smug, and pulled Katie onto my lap. Sarah was already seated on a straight-backed chair directly opposite the sofa, perhaps selected as a dock, consciously or subconsciously. Eliza was on the sofa, and Laura went to sit beside her, with Pippa perched on the arm. Laura spoke. 'Sarah, I understand that you deliberately informed certain men of the location of our events, and that your intention in doing so was to get Isabelle into difficulty. Is that correct?'

'Yes and no,' Sarah answered, her voice still strong, but wavering just a little.

'Could you expand on that?' Laura asked.

'Yes,' Sarah said. 'I did tell the men, but I didn't intend to get Isabelle into difficulty. I simply wanted to make her realise her true nature, which is as ... I'll put it plainly, an irresponsible little slut. I feel I succeeded.'

'An irresponsible little slut?' Laura echoed. 'Isabelle, do you accept this description as fair?'

'No,' I protested, stung. 'What's a slut? Just a rude name for a girl who enjoys sex. If so, I admit it, and I'm proud to be a slut. As for irresponsible, I may have said one or two things when I shouldn't have done, but I tried very hard to keep the men from the Red Ox away. Sarah didn't, she led them to us, and gave me to them. I want her to know how that feels, I want her to have to satisfy both Duncan and Dr Treadle, along with another three men, big, dirty ones who don't care where they stick their cocks –'

'Let's keep this among ourselves, shall we?' Eliza cut me off. 'Calm down, Isabelle. Sarah, you have already admitted that you deserve to be punished, have you not?'

'Yes,' Sarah replied, her eyes suddenly downcast, 'but ... but Isabelle should be too, for what she did to me at the station.'

'No,' I objected. 'That was fair enough, after the way she tricked me.'

'You loved every second of it,' Portia cut in. 'You should have seen your face with old Tierney's cock up your bum, what a picture.'

'Portia!' Eliza snapped. 'Be quiet, or you'll be in that chair after your girlfriend.'

Portia went quiet. Eliza leant close to Laura and whispered something into her ear. Pippa ducked down to listen and the three of them began to talk in hushed tones. At length they pulled apart and Laura spoke up.

'This is our decision. Either, Isabelle can accept that Sarah has been punished and the slate wiped clean –'

'No!' Sarah and I exclaimed simultaneously.

'– or both of them can be punished,' Laura finished.

'She has to be fucked,' I protested.

'She should be made to wet herself,' Sarah demanded.

'We will decide what you should and should not be made to do,' Eliza responded. 'I also think that the two of you should stop bickering and make up.'

'Fine,' I responded, 'as soon as she's been properly punished I'm willing to make up.'

Sarah was still scowling, but nodded.

'It's plain that there are still issues to be resolved between you two,' Laura stated, 'and I feel that should be reflected in your punishments. Any suggestions?'

Eliza frowned, but Pippa immediately leant down again, whispering something I couldn't catch. I swallowed hard, remembering the candles and the jug of pee as Eliza leant close and they began to confer once more. Pippa could be guaranteed not to show mercy, because she enjoyed punishment herself and had no sympathy with those who wanted to dish it out but couldn't take it. When they straightened up again Laura was smiling as she turned to Sarah.

'This is our verdict,' she stated. 'Isabelle has asked that you be penetrated, but we agree that as a lesbian you cannot be asked to take a man's penis. Therefore, I'm going to fuck you.'

Her voice had been level, and completely matter of fact until the last few words, with which it changed to open satisfaction. Sarah's mouth dropped open, but she responded with a numb inclination of her head.

'Also,' Laura went on, 'in order to teach you appreciation for one another, a suggestion of Pippa's: you will be tied head to tail, and the first to make the other come becomes the other's Mistress for the evening. I'm sure you'll fit reasonably well into each other's clothes.'

I drew a deep sigh, but I knew it might have been worse. For one thing, it wasn't going to hurt.

'Oh,' Laura spoke again, 'and bare bottom spankings for the pair of you, first. Do you accept our verdict?'

I drew another sigh. Sarah spoke up. 'I accept, but I think it only fair that Isabelle be made to wet herself, if I'm to be fucked anyway.'

'Yes, but –' I began, only to break off as all three judges nodded their agreement.

'That's settled then,' Laura said happily as she stood up. 'First, their spankings. If I remember rightly, rather a promising one was interrupted last time, isn't that right, Eliza?'

'So it is, how kind of you to remind me,' Eliza answered.

Sarah was trying not to pout as she stood up and failing miserably. Just like the time before, she'd turned up looking every inch the domina, and ended up having her knickers taken down. So had I, but that in no way diluted my pleasure. I cuddled Katie to me as Eliza moved to the middle of the sofa and extended her knees, making a spanking lap. Sarah got down, her face set in consternation as she braced her fingers and toes on the carpet and lifted her bottom.

Eliza went straight to work, smiling happily as she hoisted Sarah's governess dress high, to expose a lace-trimmed petticoat. That followed, piled onto Sarah's back with her skirt, to reveal what she had on beneath, stockings tied at the knee in the old-fashioned style, and even more old-fashioned split-seam drawers. She also had a corset on and it was just the sort of outfit I might have chosen, making me wonder if she hadn't wanted to contrast her finery with my own get-up. All she'd succeeded in doing was making her own exposure all the more humiliating, and as the wings of her splitters were pulled wide to show off her soft bare cheeks she let out a heartfelt sob.

'Don't be a baby, Sarah,' Eliza chided, 'it's not as if it were the first time you've had your bare bottom attended to, is it? Oh no, I used to have to do it most nights, as I recall, and frequently with a hairbrush, so don't whine.'

I laughed as Sarah grimaced, enjoying myself immensely. However hard I got spanked myself, even if I cried, it was worth it to see Sarah get it first. Her splitters had been pulled right open and her legs knocked a little apart, leaving the plump, well-furred lips of her pussy on show, but not full view from where I was sitting. I gave Katie a nudge to get her off my lap and moved my chair.

'That's better,' I stated, replacing Katie, 'now I can see everything.'

Sarah glared at me, her face upside down and looking back from the disarranged mess of her hair, which had fallen loose. I gave her a little wave and sat back to watch the show, now with a perfect view, able to admire the expressions on her face and see right between her cheeks, even the tight star of her bumhole. It was a bad enough position for a slut in a schoolgirl skirt, never mind a domina in full rig, and in front of her girlfriend, who couldn't stop giggling.

'There we are,' Eliza said, making a final adjustment to Sarah's clothes so that she was showing full moon, with every inch of bottom flesh available for chastisement, 'and here we go.'

She began to spank, not so very hard, but it made no difference. Sarah was being spanked, and that was what mattered. Too much pain and it would have distracted from the humiliation I knew would be raging in her head, to lie bare bottom across another woman's lap, to be showing every private detail between her legs as she was given that most old fashioned of punishments, and surely the one that does more than anything else to highlight the difference in status between the one dishing it out and the one taking it.

The expressions passing across Sarah's face were something to behold, apprehension, then little winces as the smacks came down, and self-pity afterwards, mixed with the occasional glare for me, or for Portia, who was still giggling. Yet as her bottom began to warm and her fleshy cheeks to take on a rosy hue, her reaction became less pained, and she began to shake her head in a desperate effort to throw off the rising arousal all too obvious from the moist, swollen state of her pussy.

Still Eliza spanked, in no hurry at all, as Sarah's little sobs and gasps changed tone and her head subsided gradually in defeat. Her pussy was soaking, trickles of white showing among the pink folds, and wonderfully open, while her whole bottom was an even, glowing pink, well and truly spanked, well and truly shamed. Portia had come to sit by me, to get the best view of her Mistress's rising distress and rising excitement, and gave a delighted little cry as Eliza suddenly switched hands, spanking with her left as the other slipped down to cup Sarah's sex.

I had never seen a girl masturbated so clinically, or brought to orgasm so fast. A few deft touches of Eliza's thumb and Sarah was wriggling in wanton ecstasy, and grunting too, reducing me to helpless laughter even as her body shook in orgasm, spasm after spasm with her pussy and bumhole in hard contraction and her bottom still wobbling to the spanks.

As soon as Sarah was past her peak I began to clap, and so did everybody else, applauding Eliza for a well-delivered spanking. Sarah hung limp, the pussy juice trickling from her open hole, her anus still twitching faintly. Laura had been digging in her bag, and now produced a thick veiny dildo made of rubber in a particularly unpleasant pink shade. I was grinning again as she stood up, unzipped her uniform trousers and inserted the horrid thing into holding ring, Sarah watching all the while from her upside-down position with ever-increasing agitation.

I stood too, because I had to see it go in, close to them as Laura got behind Sarah. The fat dildo was pressed to Sarah's open, slippery hole, which spread to the first push, taking the full, fat, rubbery bulk in one. Laura began to fuck, holding Sarah by the hips and I clapped in sheer delight as the taut ring of pink flesh began to pull in and out on the shaft. In moments Sarah was gasping and grunting, no more dignified than I'd been with Stan Tierney up my bottom and, before Laura had finished, I was glowing with triumph.

When the dildo came out Sarah's pussy hole was left gaping and dribbling juice, while she was panting softly with little tremors running through her flesh. Eliza delivered a final, cracking smack across the still glowing cheeks and told her to get up. Sarah tried, but simply slumped to her knees, to bury her face in Eliza's chest, and suddenly she was crying, her whole body wracked with sobs as she clung to the woman who had punished her.

Everybody went quiet, even Portia, letting them have their private moment, perhaps a release of tension in Sarah that must have lasted some fifteen years. Eliza simply stroked her girlfriend's hair and, after a while, bent to kiss her, at first a peck, and then open mouthed. Nobody spoke until they finally pulled apart, Sarah remaining curled at Eliza's feet.

'Isabelle,' Laura stated.

My stomach had gone abruptly tight, but I stood up with as much dignity as I could muster, determined to take it well. I'd assumed Laura would punish me, or Eliza, but neither moved to accommodate me over their laps. I glanced around. Duncan was smiling encouragingly and seated to make it easy for me to go over, so I moved towards him, only for Portia to speak up.

'I think Sarah should do it.'

'Sarah?' I queried. 'But that's not ... I'm not sure she'd want to.'

I'd been going to say it wasn't fair, but had changed my mind, because Sarah was still curled at Eliza's feet with the tears trickling slowly down her face and her mouth set into a soft smile.

'I'll do it then,' Portia offered, but before I could reply to her Sarah had begun to rise.

'No,' she said, 'I'll do it.'

'Yes, but –' I began, only to be cut off by Eliza.

'Do at least try and take it like a lady, Isabelle.'

I threw my hands up, suddenly so close to tears myself I couldn't speak.

'I want to help,' Portia demanded. 'She was so hard on me last time, a real beast.'

I tried to answer her, to point out that she'd asked me to spank her, and said it had made her better afterwards, but the words wouldn't come. She had pulled a chair back, one of the straight-backed ones, and positioned a second as Sarah came up behind me and took me firmly by the scruff of my neck.

'Right, my girl,' she said, still trying to hide a snuffle, 'you've really had this coming.'

She pulled me down with her as she sat, opposite Portia, so that I was hauled across their laps, head well down and my bottom to the audience. With only my abbreviated school skirt to cover me my panties were already showing under the hem, and then completely as it was unceremoniously turned up. Their hands caught in the waistband, one hard jerk and my knickers were down, my bottom exposed in just seconds.

'Hold her around her waist,' Sarah instructed.

Portia did as she was told, but only with one arm, using the other to tease my dangling breasts as Sarah adjusted my knickers to half mast. I was already panting for breath, and red-faced with humiliation, not so much for the girls, nor Duncan, but for Dr Treadle, who had never seen me spanked. I knew I'd blubber and make a fuss over it, but I couldn't help it, I couldn't stop myself . . .

'Right, Isabelle,' Sarah snapped, 'you wanted to see everything, so let's see how you like to show everything.'

I cried out loud as my bottom cheeks were hauled roughly apart, not merely showing off the view between, but stretching me wide, and held, to allow the audience to make a leisurely inspection of my pussy, and worse, the wrinkled, dark-brown bud of my bottom hole.

'There?' Sarah demanded. 'How does that feel? And at least when I show behind I don't look as if I never wipe.'

Portia burst into giggles. I burst into tears, and the spanking began, my cheeks released and immediately slapped. Portia joined in, changing her grip to hold me down as she worked on one cheek while Sarah did the other. It stung like mad, on my cold skin and with two of them doing it as hard as they could. My attempt at reserve was instantly forgotten, the pain simply too intense to hold myself back as I went into a kicking, struggling tantrum.

I was bawling my eyes out and screaming blue murder, tossing my head and hammering my fists on the carpet. I was squirming and writhing and bucking my body, desperate to move my bottom away from the stinging slaps but only producing myself look more ridiculous still. I was kicking my legs in my panties and making frantic scissoring motions with my thighs, but only making a yet ruder display of my private parts.

My shoes flew off. My tam-o-shanter fell off. Even one sock came off, so hard was I kicking. Still they spanked, in perfect, merciless unison, until I'd lost all control of my body, with the tears spattering from my eyes, a blob of snot swinging from the tip of my nose, spittle running down my chin, and at last, just when I thought it couldn't possibly get any worse, I wet myself.

I felt it happen, a sudden sense of helplessness as I realised my bladder was going to burst, and then it had, a stream of hot urine squirting backwards into my lowered panties, over the floor and down Portia's leg. She gave a squeal of shock, thrust her chair back and, before I could do anything about it, I rolled off Sarah's lap, to land hard on the floor, the pee still squirting from my pussy, high in the air, all over Dr Treadle's beautiful carpet, and Dr Treadle himself.

'Sorry,' I mumbled as I finally managed to regain control of my bladder and find my voice.

He didn't answer, because he was frantically wiping my piddle from his face with a pocket handkerchief. I didn't linger, but ran from the room, clutching my hot bottom behind and my wet pussy in front, my panties flapping around one ankle. In the loo I collapsed gasping onto the seat, to let everything that was left out in one long, hot gush, and when I finally managed to raise my eyes Katie was standing into the doorway, looking concerned.

'Are you OK?' she asked.

'Fine,' I lied, snatching a piece of loo paper to wipe my nose, 'just do something about Dr Treadle's carpet, could you?'

She nodded and disappeared, leaving me to tidy myself up as best I could. By the time I got back to the living room Katie and Caroline were down on their knees, sponging the carpet, while Dr Treadle was nowhere to be seen. Sarah and Portia looked well pleased with themselves, laughing together by the window.

'There, I've wet myself, I hope you're satisfied,' I said, doing my best to put a brave face on it.

'Entirely,' Sarah answered, 'it's always a pleasure to spank you, Isabelle, because you're such a big baby, but that was truly exceptional.'

I made a face at her and went to help Katie and Caroline. Dr Treadle reappeared, now in a dressing gown of crimson watered silk, and I hastened to apologise. He lifted a hand to stop me.

'Pray don't mention it, although in future, when you are my guest, it will probably be wise to roll back the carpet.'

'I'll make it up to you,' I promised, as he was plainly hiding his irritation.

'How kind,' he replied. 'So, ah . . . what is next on the evening's programme?'

'The remainder of their punishments,' Laura answered.

Sarah nodded, determined. I responded in kind, trying to get my head around the idea of having to lick her to make her come as soon as possible, and how it would be if I succeeded. She'd be mine for the evening, to do with as I pleased. Perhaps I couldn't make her suck the men off, because as Laura had said, it wasn't fair. I could still have fun, make her go nude, or in my own ridiculous costume only without any panties, have her crawl around with a plate of nibbles balanced on her back, make her maybe wash her mouth out with soap and spank her again. Or perhaps I could have Eliza demonstrate the best way to give an enema, with Sarah as our model . . .

'Perhaps on a bed?' Dr Treadle suggested.

'That would be best,' Laura answered him. 'Do you have anything to tie them up with?'

'Garden twine?' he suggested.

He went to fetch the twine and I was led upstairs by Laura, with Sarah following behind. There were various bedrooms, and we had to wait for him to come back before choosing one, a large, square chamber with a double bed and his usual old-fashioned, masculine furnishings. I sat down, naked but for my tiny skirt.

'Shouldn't you be naked, Sarah?' I asked. 'Because when I've made you come I'm going to put you in my clothes, including my tam-o-shanter. I'll be nice though, and let you off wearing my wet panties. You can go bare instead.'

'That assumes you win,' she answered, 'but yes, this dress is a little cumbersome.'

She began to undress, taking off her dress and the petticoat beneath, her boots and stockings, even her

231

drawers, to go naked but for the rich-blue waspie corset that constricted her waist. Her bottom was still very red, and her sex swollen in arousal, but so was mine. Everybody else had packed into the room, watching as I crawled onto the bed and Sarah followed. Dr Treadle passed a large ball of green twine to Laura, who climbed onto the bed with us.

'Lie down,' she ordered, 'on your sides, head to tail.'

I obeyed, close up to Sarah, close enough to smell the musk of her pussy through her perfume.

'Put your arms around each other,' Laura ordered. 'Heads between the other's thighs.'

As I opened my legs I was wondering if Sarah found the situation as humiliating as I did, tied head to toe with me and made to lick just as well as we possibly could while our friends watched, including two men. Her thighs were also open, and I snuggled close, my face pressed to her sex as her legs came up to trap me even as her mouth pressed to my pussy.

'Good,' Laura stated. 'Now hold on tight.'

She took hold of my wrists as she spoke, and quickly had them bound tight, working with the sure skill of experience. Sarah's wrists were done next, and our waists, lashed together to keep us close and unable to separate. Further bonds secured our legs, just to be sure, and a last few to join the different ties and leave us completely and utterly helpless, enmeshed in twine with our pussies spread in each other's faces.

'You may lick when ready,' Laura said as she climbed from the bed.

I went to work, flicking my tongue onto the little pearly bud of Sarah's clitoris without worrying about warming her up, and trying hard to ignore the exquisite sensations her tongue was giving me at the other end. It was impossible, my feelings rising faster and faster, while she seemed immune. I licked harder still, my tongue already hurting, my face wet with pussy juice.

Her thighs tightened in response, the knot of her anus began to twitch and I knew she was going to come. So was I, my body in contraction despite my best efforts to think of anything but sex, yet I'd just seen her spanked, and been spanked in turn, held down across two women's legs for my little skirt to be turned up, my panties taken down, my bare bottom slapped and slapped and slapped, until I'd wet myself in my helpless pain and humiliation . . .

I came, unable to stop it, my mouth breaking from Sarah's pussy to scream out in both despair and ecstasy, but even as the orgasm burst in my head I was licking again, my tongue working frantically between her pussy lips, to bring her in turn to a long, shuddering climax. At last I slumped in my bonds, exhausted, sore, shaking and defeated, or maybe not . . .'

'A draw?' I suggested.

'Oh no,' Portia answered. 'You lost, Isabelle. Didn't she, girls?'

Not even Katie bothered to dispute Sarah's victory. I relaxed as much as possible, sweaty, hot and wondering what was in store for me.

'If you could release me, please, Laura,' Sarah asked, 'but leave Isabelle tied up.'

Laura made short work of our bonds, freeing Sarah but leaving me with my wrists and ankles tied. I rolled over onto my back as soon as we were apart, looking up at the ring of eager, smiling faces.

'What are you going to do with her?' Portia asked. 'Can I have her for a bit, pretty please?'

'Of course, darling,' Sarah answered. 'I don't wish to be greedy. In fact, anybody who wishes to amuse themselves with her may do so, for the rest of the evening. She can refuse, of course, but every refusal will cost her six of the cane at the end of the evening. First, she is to kiss and lick all the other submissive girls' bumholes, just to show us all where she really belongs, with her tongue up our bottoms. How's that, Isabelle?'

'Quite merciful, thank you,' I managed.

'Me first!' Portia sang out, and jumped on me.

I barely had time to catch my breath before she'd mounted me and jerked her knickers down to spread her full smooth bottom right over my face, and then in it.

'Lick my bumhole, Isabelle!' she crowed. 'Right in! Taste me! Oh, that's right . . . like that, you lovely, dirty little tart –'

She broke off with a sigh as my tongue burrowed deep up into her anus, and I was licking as best I could, smothered beneath her as she began to masturbate, completely shameless. Her panties were taut across my chest, her bottom wiggling and bouncing in my face as she rubbed, and she was laughing, high and happy, right up until the moment she came, with a cry of ecstasy and her bottom hole in spasm on my well-inserted tongue.

As she finished she settled a bit, smothering me completely, so that I had to twist my head away to breathe. She laughed and got up, still a little breathless from her sudden, frantic orgasm, and bounced off the bed.

'That was fun,' she said. 'Who's next?'

'I would count it a great favour to see her tickled at the same time,' Dr Treadle stated.

'I'll tickle her,' Caroline answered immediately. 'Come on, Katie.'

'No . . . hang on!' I begged as they climbed onto the bed either side of me. 'Remember what happened last time, Dr Treadle.'

'That's a risk I'm prepared to take,' he said happily, passing Caroline an ostrich feather he'd had behind his back, 'after all, this is the bed I've set aside for you and Katie to sleep in tonight.'

'Oh . . . still –'

I broke off, giggling as Caroline began to flick the feather over the skin of my tummy. My bladder tightened, but I was empty, which was just as well. Katie had joined in, both girls tickling my midriff and I was squirming on the bed, begging them to stop and giggling hysterically. They just laughed at me and tickled all the harder, Katie moving up to my armpits and Caroline applying the feather to my thighs, under my knees, the tuck of my bottom. I was really thrashing, kicking my bound legs and bucking my body, squealing and giggling, all the while with Dr Treadle staring down at me with wide-eyed joy and the others with open amusement.

'Let me help you with that, Dr Treadle,' Pippa said sweetly as I rolled over, desperate to escape.

Caroline immediately sat on my back and pulled my bottom cheeks apart, tickling my anus and laughing at my frantic jerking, which grew worse as Katie's fingers found my pussy mound, and it just happened – I came, completely unexpectedly, my whole body reacting as one as Katie's fingertips grazed my clitoris. There was a long moment of unendurable bliss, both girls in fits of laughter as they realised what had happened, and it stopped.

'Now my turn,' Caroline announced. 'Roll over, Isabelle, your tongue's going up my bottom.'

Unresisting, barely able to control my twitching muscles, I let them roll me over onto my back once more. Caroline quickly pulled off her knickers and climbed on, flipped her tiny skirt up and settled her fat bottom in my face, her bumhole to my mouth. I licked obediently, wondering if the half-erect penis I'd seen in Pippa's hand as I rolled over would shortly be introduced to my body. Sure enough, the bed rocked a little as Dr Treadle climbed on and Caroline giggled.

'May I perhaps stroke your magnificent breasts, my dear?' he said and Caroline giggled a second time.

My legs were lifted, the smooth silk of his dressing gown pressed to my thighs and calves, his cock touched my pussy and he was in, shuffling forwards to get good and deep before he began to fuck me and to play with Caroline's breasts. I'd never once stopped licking, feeling wonderfully, deliciously used, made to tongue my friend's anus as I was fucked, both of them taking out their pleasure on my bound, helpless body, just as they pleased.

Caroline came first, wriggling her fat cheeks in my face as she rubbed herself and Dr Treadle toyed with her breasts. The sight and feel was too much for him and, even as she whimpered and shook in ecstasy, his thrusts became abruptly stronger and my pussy had been filled with sperm. No time was lost, Pippa climbing onto my face as soon as Caroline had vacated it. She wiggled down, and for the third time in quick succession I was being made to lick another girl's bottom hole.

I was pushing my bound wrists down as I burrowed my tongue in as deep as it would go, tasting her, wanting to eat her. She gave a sigh of pleasure and wiggled in my face, her fingers brushing my chin as she began to masturbate. I could reach my pussy, just about, and my knees came up and open, spreading myself to the audience as I licked at Pippa's moist, open bottom hole. My sex was slick with sperm, warm and slippery over my clitoris as I rubbed.

Pippa came, wriggling herself in my face as I tongued her, and as she lifted it was to find Duncan at the end of the bed, his erect cock in his hand. I nodded, accepting it, and a moment later my vision was gone again as Jasmine sat on my face, queening me with a long sigh of pleasure as my tongue found her anus. The bed moved under me. Duncan's big powerful hands took my legs. His cock prodded at my pussy and up, deep inside me, my second fucking as Jasmine squirmed in my face, laughing as she masturbated.

It took her just moments to come and she climbed off, leaving me ready for my fifth bumhole, Katie's, my own lovely playmate, and all the more eager for having me in the place I'd put her so often. She climbed on, spreading her chubby little bottom in my face and I was doing it, licking eagerly as Duncan's thrusts grew harder and faster. He stopped, pulled out, his cock moved down, and as I realised it was going up my bum my orgasm was building in my head, immensely strong.

As my anus spread to the pressure everything came together, from being made to dress up, a little topless tart in my twee Scottish clothes, through having to serve my friends with my breasts bare and my knickers on show each time I bent, being spanked so hard I'd wet myself all over the floor, being tied to Sarah and made to lick until she came, and losing, and five girls bottoms in my face, licking them anally, Portia and Caroline and Pippa and Jasmine, and now Katie, my own lovely Katie, my tongue up her bum while my own dirty little hole was buggered by my tutor, and spunked in.

We came at the same instant, all three of us, my tongue wedged just as far as it would go up Katie's gaping, slippery bumhole, her bottom squirming in my face, my hands just as busy as could be with my pussy, Duncan's cock jammed so deep I felt it must come out of my mouth, and everybody watching. Katie had pushed right down, and I couldn't scream, or even breathe, the ecstasy of being completely smothered in her lovely bottom bringing my orgasm up high, and higher still, peak after peak, and the view of soft pink curves in front of my face went red, and dark.

I was only out for moments, but the next thing I knew Katie had climbed off, Duncan was no longer in me and Eliza was shaking my shoulder. The others were clustered around the bed, looking concerned, and I managed a wan smile.

'Are you OK?' Jasmine asked.

'I ... I'm fine,' I managed. 'That was ... that was beautiful, Katie ... Duncan ... everyone. Let me get my breath back, and I'll do anything you want.'

'In a while, perhaps,' Eliza stated as she began to work on my bonds. 'For now you're to rest, then kiss and make up.'

I nodded, completely happy for her to take over. Dr Treadle handed me a glass of brandy as soon as I was loose, which I drank down gratefully. Sarah was waiting, and when I could I got up to my knees, facing her.

'Friends?'

'I want that kiss,' she answered, turned round and presented me with her bare bottom, well flared out beneath the hem of her corset, her cheeks wide.

I didn't hesitate, but knelt lower, to plant a firm, deliberate kiss on the bud of her anus.

'Thank you,' she said, 'and now, if you're sure you're ready . . .'

Eliza coughed.

'Kiss Isabelle too, Miss Sally,' she ordered.

'Of course, sorry,' Sarah said quickly and bent to peck my lips.

Again Eliza coughed.

'I think you know what I mean, Sarah, or shall I fetch the soap?'

Sarah made a face and quickly got down on her knees. I swung myself around on the bed, pushing my bottom out, and reached back to hold my cheeks wide, offering my bottom hole to her lips. She hesitated only a moment, looking a little glum about what she had to do, before pressing her face between my open cheeks. Her lips met my anal ring in a single warm kiss, and it was done, our rivalry set aside.

'Good girls,' Eliza said as Sarah and I broke apart. 'That's what I like to see, a nice friendly kiss.'

As Sarah stood again I turned, to take her in my arms, cuddling tight. I felt genuinely sorry for my behaviour towards her, and was sure she felt the same. Yet it had been worth it, to bring Eliza into the Rattaners, and if that meant I would be spending a lot more of my time on my knees or over hers, then it was what I wanted. Besides, that would only be when she visited. The rest of the time I'd have my Katie, Caroline, Jasmine, Portia, Pippa, even Sarah, all needing their bottoms kept warm and willing to grovel to me as I would grovel to Eliza on the rare occasions she was in Oxford.

'Well, I'm glad that's sorted out,' Laura said, 'and this seems a good moment to suggest that, as we'll be meeting here, Isabelle takes full control of the society, something that clearly means a great deal to her.'

The was a chorus of agreement, and I felt a big smile start to spread across my face. Sarah spoke up. 'Fair enough, as long as she's subject to the same rules, and to discipline if necessary.'

'That's fair,' I agreed, 'but perhaps only by Eliza?'

Sarah hesitated, but at last gave a nod and a smile.

'I would be more than happy to accept that responsibility,' Eliza said. 'I also have some news. In fact, I've known for some time, but I thought I'd wait until this evening to tell you all. I've accepted a post here at Oxford. It will be such a pleasure to be back.'

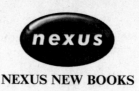

NEXUS NEW BOOKS

To be published in September 2005

SCHOOL FOR STINGERS
Yolanda Celbridge

Tomboy Caroline Letchmount enlists at Furrow Weald finishing school in Cornwall – motto 'Bare up and obey!' An institution with a military regime of merciless corporal punishment, and flagellant girl gangs – the Swanks and Stingers. When accustomed to pepper panties, bare-boxing, being bricked and canings from 'sixpence' to 'five shillings', she is ready to be auctioned as a girlslave to rich voluptuaries. Meeting her school friend Persimmon, now an adept of the naval birch, in a lust-drenched tropical island, Caroline must decide if she is truly submissive.

£6.99   ISBN 0 352 33994 2

DEPTHS OF DEPRAVATION
Ray Gordon

Belinda fears that her sixteen-year-old daughter may be falling for Tony, her handsome but cruel new neighbour, and resolves to do everything in her power to keep the two apart. She believes that by giving her body to Tony she'll be able to preserve her daughter's innocence, but she soon finds herself hooked on debased and perverted sexual acts as she plunges deeper and deeper into the pit of depravity.

£6.99   ISBN 0 352 33995 0

THE BOND
Lindsay Gordon

For some like Missy and Hank, the bond is an extraordinary passage from innocence to extreme passion. It is a need for sensual freedom and an ability to journey beyond the body. For the Preacher, the bond is a curse; responsible for a broken heart that will never heal and can only demand vengeance. Pursued by this spectre from their past, Missy and Hank flee to an uncertain future in New Orleans where the greatest mystery of all – the origin of their secret life – waits in the dark. Along the way their journey is fuelled by the hunt, seduction and domination of their lovers – the way of the bonded.

£6.99   ISBN 0 352 33996 9

If you would like more information about Nexus titles, please visit our website at www.nexus-books.co.uk, or send a stamped addressed envelope to:
Nexus, Thames Wharf Studios,
Rainville Road, London W6 9HA